HEATHER CASSIDY
AND THE
MAGNIFICENT MR HARLOW

MITCHELL TIERNEY

Heather Cassidy and the Magnificent Mr Harlow

ISBN: 9780994589781

Published by Ouroborus Book Services
www.ouroborusbooks.com

Cover by Sabrina RG Raven: www.sabrinargraven.com
Chapter background image by NovaStarX: www.novastarx.deviantart.com

CONTENTS

ADMIT ONE
COME ONE, COME ALL
THE GREATEST PERFORMANCE IN THE WORLD
PROLOGUE
No. IOIOI987

The thick, grey smoke drifted into the winking twilight of early night. The fires still blazed red across the mountains. Their flames licking the air, burning yellow and hungry for more. Where the mountains met the searing ground, hordes of soldiers had fought. The clanging of blades had sparked silver. Enchantments had been spoken with dying words, sending crimson energy across the dying fields.

There was an explosion and a cloud of bright green erupted into the air, sending a firework of cobalt and scarlet into the sky. A mother, clutching her infant son, ran barefoot across the broken and cracked clay, her heels bleeding and trailing red. Behind her, a black horse rode, its nostrils steaming with white breath. Its hide was as dark as midnight and as shiny as newly polished silver. On the enormous beast's back was a man, his limbs crooked and deformed, his eyes full of menace and determination. He yelled at his steed to fasten its pace, and it did so.

The woman dodged landing debris from the blast, taking shelter in a small, abandoned storehouse. A large, fiery ball of metal came crashing through the window and she screamed, holding her child to her chest. Towards the back of the empty house was a doorway, its frame hanging off and burning red from the fire. She crawled through the archway, holding her boy under her. On the other side were rows upon rows of shelves holding glass jars, most of them smashed and dripping their contents onto the floor. She found a dark corner and huddled tightly against the wall. Her lip and nose were bleeding, but if it concerned her, she didn't show it. Slowly, she unwrapped the small child and examined him for injury. The child giggled at his mother's touch, smiling. His lime green skin was clean, unlike hers. She smiled at his innocence. If he only knew what was happening outside these walls. Suddenly, she heard the heavy pounding of the horse as it stopped in front of the storehouse. She gasped, wrapping her child up in his blankets. He started to cry, having found the cool air comforting. She hushed him, but he would not subside. She scanned the floor for something to use. A long jagged piece of glass lay in purple liquid that bubbled and hissed gently. She wrapped her sleeve around it and hid it.

The raven-black horse grunted and stomped its hooves. Its eyes burned red, reflecting the amber ash falling around them like flaming snow. The twisted figure slipped from its back and landed like a bundle of broken sticks on the ground. It raised its head up and stared at the footprints in the ashen residue left on the ground. It looked to its left, as if beckoning, or calling to something, or someone. There was no one there, only the dead, lying in pools of their own blood. He walked forward and entered the storehouse. The brick work was crumbling; the fire had made it weak by melting the foundations used to construct it. The cloaked figure sniffed the air and went through the walkway and into the rear of the room. There was no noise, only the dead silence of death and destruction.

'I know you're here, little one.' Its voice was croaky and splintered.

The shelving was built from ancient wood, old and strong enough to hold the bottles of aged magic. They were built up into the high ceiling where the bottles were

all missing from their encasements. They were all smashed onto the floor in piles of shattered glass and fumes. A baby's cry echoed off the walls and the figure smiled, his teeth sharpened and yellow.

'Ah,' he whispered. 'I hear the voice of the young. So gentle and new...' He licked his lips and followed the path from where the cry had come.

Huddled against the wall, covered in blood, ash and tears was the mother and her child. She held him in her left hand and held the jagged chunk of glass out with the other.

'Don't come near me!' she screeched, her hands shaking.

The baby howled in fear. Its mother's eyes were relentless and locked onto the figure before her. The twisted man was wrapped in filthy scarves and cloth, all soaked in blood and burned from fire. From beneath his wraps he pulled a blade, a foot long and serrated down one side.

'You are all that is left of your kind. You don't want to be the last...do you?'

The mother didn't say a word, she pushed her back against the hot wall and held the shard of glass out before her.

'Very well, have it your way,' the man marched forward.

He swung the knife from left to right, it hit the glass and broke the tip off it. A second strike and she felt the blade cut into her, she held her child away, ignoring the pain. Blood spilled onto the floor in large droplets. She cried out, but never took her eyes off the man. The whole time, he grinned manically. She grunted, saving her energy for her attack, and drove the glass forward. It dug in under his ribs and he stumbled backwards.

'You dare cut me? I have killed your king and your queen.' He touched the place where the glass had sunk through his rags and skin, his fingers were red and gleaming. He smiled and then started to laugh.

'The Holy Mountains where you serve your greater gods now belong to us. Your statues all burnt and crumbled to dust. All your crops... gone. Your lands are now ours and you have nobody left... except your child.'

The mother lunged forward, carving the shard sideways and cutting him again and again. The twisted man laughed, sending spittle down his chin. He stepped forward, his motion like liquid and buried his blade deep within her stomach. They embraced for several seconds, the child quiet, the room dead silent. Ash flakes fell outside, onto the beast. Its skin steaming hot. The mother's last heartbeat echoed like the dying breath of her city, her race. She stumbled, momentarily blind, and fell back in to the dark recess of the room. Her eyes blinked no more.

The child, still gripped tight in his mother's arms squirmed and cried loudly. The man towered over the him, clasping the blade in his bony fingers, dripping with its mother's blood. The figure held the knife outwards.

'You are the last.' He held the knife up, his face a grimace of anger and disgust.

'Stop!'

The figure spun around. Standing in the doorway was his master. A short man with a curled moustache and slicked, jet-black hair.

'Leave him.'

'But –'

'I said leave him.'

The man looked back at the child. Its lilac diamond eyes stared up at him, forging its mother's killer into its memory.

'Come, we have much work to do.'

The figure pushed the wraps back over its small body and stepped away. The deadly, cloaked killer strolled past its master and mounted his horse once more. His heart was pounding and he had a sickly feeling in his stomach.

The master stood in the room for several moments, listening to the child cry. He stepped towards it and felt a hot iron stake sear his mind. He struggled to keep from falling.

'I fear we will meet again, young one. Perhaps I should have let him kill you?'

He turned and left the infant in the dark room. Its cries only heard by the shadows and the blood soaked walls.

COME ONE, COME ALL
THE GREATEST PERFORMANCE IN THE WORLD
CHAPTER 1
A ROTTEN TOMATO
ADMIT ONE
No. 1010101987

There was a loud *puff!* followed by a cloud of smoke. The audience gasped, then there was dead silence. Mr Harlow stood centre stage holding his top hat upside down. Smoke poured gently from its rim and faded into the bright fluorescent lighting. The crowd waited in opened-mouthed awe. A child that had been screaming and weeping throughout the entire act was now silent, its eyes wide open in trepidation.

Mr Harlow looked down at his hat; he knew something was wrong. He reached one white gloved hand into the top hat and searched around. There was supposed to be a white rabbit, but there was nothing. He slowly pulled his hand from the top hat and placed it to his side. He looked out at the audience and saw hundreds of faces now watching him, waiting, expecting. He felt nervous prickles slither up his forearms, then his fingers began to shake madly. He swallowed with difficulty and felt sweat moisten his armpits and collar. He bowed and placed the hat back on his head.

From the side of the grandstand stood Heather. Her hair was a washed out red from dye many months ago. She green eyes and long lashes. She had always imagined her mother had long lashes, but the photos she had of her were too hard to tell. Heather had a healthy sprinkle of freckles running from one cheek, over her button nose, to the other. She had been watching Mr Harlow's entire act with her fingers crossed. Inside her head she was praying for Mr Harlow, praying that his magic would work.

During the last act, which was normally his best trick, and most magical, she had closed her eyes, too scared to watch. When she didn't hear a round of applause and the hooting and cheering of a happy crowd of customers, she knew it had happened again. Mr Harlow stood dead still, looking defeated and mournful. He stood like a statue that had been left in the elements for a hundred years. He took one step back, out of the spot light and bowed again. He kept his head down for some time. The audience attendees looked at one another in confusion, one by one they began to boo and hiss.

'Get off!' someone yelled.

'I want my money back!'

'You're not a magician!' a woman called out, throwing a rotten tomato towards the stage.

Mr Harlow was hit by the rotten vegetable. It struck him on the shoulder and exploded, sending mushy red gloop down his perfectly ironed jacket and landing at his feet. One by one, more things were thrown. A box of half eaten popcorn hit his hat and knocked it to the side, but it managed to stay on. The audience members got to their feet and slowly headed for the door, yelling abuse over their shoulders. The lights in the grandstand were turned on and the spot light that was shining on Mr Harlow died slowly. In the dark, he stood and watched the people leave. They waved their hands dismissively towards him and shook their heads. He took his hat off, turned on his heels and headed for the exit.

Standing just inside the curtain was Guntha, the Belgian muscle man. He looked at Mr Harlow with sad, watery, blue eyes. Guntha was still wearing his spandex tights from his show; they displayed his enormous belly and barrelled shoulders. He placed one giant hand on the magician's shoulder.

'Never mind, Harlow,' Guntha said in his thick accent. 'There's always next time.'

Mr Harlow looked up at the giant and saw his burly, black moustache. He saw his kindness in his eyes. Whenever people saw him lift weights or flex his muscles, they would cheer and laugh and take photos, not throw rotten vegetables at him. Mr Harlow looked back down to his feet and continued walking to the rear of the tent.

Heather ran underneath the grandstand. She went past the bearded lady, the lizard man, and their son, a young boy with fleshy crab claws for hands named Bounty. They were standing just to the side and had been watching the show as well.

'Heather!' Bounty called out, waving his claws. 'Do you wanna play checkers before we pack up?'

Heather turned her head, but kept at a steady pace. 'Sorry Bounty, I gotta see Mr Harlow real quick. But I'll come back.'

Bounty watched Heather zoom past him, heading towards the back of the tent. She disappeared through the thick, velvet curtains and into the back room. Mr Harlow was walking briskly now, as if he knew Heather was trying to catch up with him.

'Mr Harlow!' she called out.

'Stop right there missy!' came a booming voice.

Heather spun around to see her father standing right beside her. She looked down.

'Stop right where you are. You leave Mr Harlow alone, he doesn't need someone like you screaming at him and following him to his carriage. Hasn't he had a bad enough night as it is?'

Heather's father was four foot, five inches tall. He wore a specially tailored suit that was wine red with huge lapels and long jacket tails that ran along the ground.

'Dad!' Heather whined.

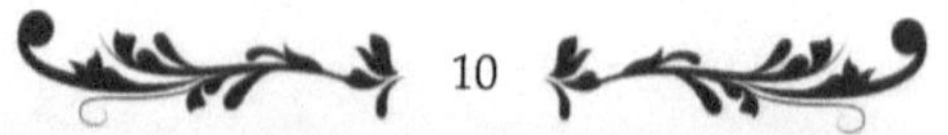

'Don't Dad me. Leave him alone… he needs his time.'

Guntha walked past carrying his weights on his shoulders; he saw Heather was worried about something and gave her a smile.

'What will happen to him, Dad?' Heather said, her shoulders slumping forward.

'I don't know, Heather,' her father said, hugging his daughter, even though his head only reached her hips. 'He's had a bad couple of months now. His performance hasn't been up to scratch. There is no magic anymore in Mr Harlow… so we best…'

Heather looked down at her father. 'Don't say it Dad. Please don't. He's been with us from the beginning. You can't let him go.'

A tear broke from her eye and travelled down her cheek. At first she didn't feel it, but she knew it was there. The hurt inside her chest was too great to ignore.

'I'm sorry, Heather. A lot of people pay to see magic and when they don't get to see any… well, it's bad for business.'

Heather nodded, understanding what her father was saying. He kissed her on the hand and turned around to instruct the drivers as they were getting ready to take the tent down and roll it up. Heather stood looking out to the rows of caravans and people wandering around, getting out of their performance uniforms and packing their personal items away for the next town. She saw Mr Harlow's caravan; a light shimmered on for a moment and then was turned off. She stood, wondering why he had lost his magic.

ADMIT ONE
COME ONE, COME ALL
THE GREATEST PERFORMANCE IN THE WORLD
CHAPTER 2
A SECRET REVEALED
No.IOIOI987

The giant truck puffed and wheezed as it pulled out of the vacant lot. It coughed blue smoke from its exhaust and creaked and groaned as it made its way from the show grounds. The circus convoy was made up of various styles of cars and lorries, from the brand new, which was owned by the ticket collector Mr Surestone, to the most wretched vehicle that was held together by tape and had to be hit with a hammer to start, which was owned by Mr Trapjaw, the trapeze artist.

Heather's father watched the vehicles slowly align themselves and head towards the main road. Heather always looked forward to going to a new city. When people in the small towns saw the tent poles, they knew the circus was in town and everybody rushed to watched them set up and beg their parents for money to see the trapeze artists fly through the air, the fire breather and the especially the magician.

Heather sat in the passenger seat with one arm cocked on the windowsill of the door. She was staring out the window.

'Come on, Larry!' her father screamed. 'Catch up to the rest. You're the only one with a map.'

Heather's father, or Ringmaster Rollo, as everyone else called him, wound his window up and slammed the ancient vehicle into first gear. The engine spluttered and puffed black smoke.

'Don't we need a map too, Dad?' Heather said, under her breath.

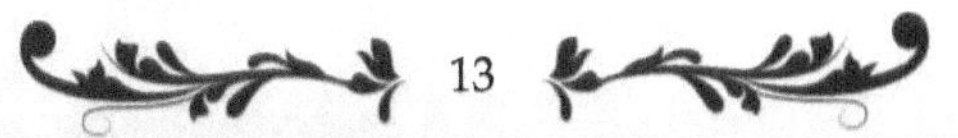

Heather's father ignored this comment and watched as the tent-truck driver and part-time clown, turned his car the right way around and slowly caught up to the lead car.

'That's better!' Rollo shouted. He couldn't help but shout, he was the Ringmaster after all. It was in his blood. In his family.

Rollo Cassidy was the seventh in line to the *Cassidy Travelling Circus and Magic Show*. His father, who was also a small person, had handed him the reigns of the circus when he was just seventeen years old. He had to learn how to control a crowd quickly, bringing on the next act if they got restless, making the audience cheer and keep them happy and wanting more. His father, before him, had been known throughout the world as the top ringmaster ever to wear the gold lapels and top hat. It was an ongoing joke among ringmasters worldwide that each Cassidy descendent, who became a ringmaster, was much shorter than the last. People say this was due to constantly ducking rotting fruit and vegetables when the show didn't go to plan, or being hit on the head with a frying pan by the clowns, but either way, Ringmaster Rollo was the shortest ringmaster known in circus history. He had hoped that one day his daughter, Heather, would take the uniform, and with some slight adjustments, be the next ringmaster. It wasn't common for a woman to be ringmaster, but times had changed and he was looking forward to showing her all the tips and tricks of the trade. Unfortunately, Heather had been more interested in the trapeze act, then being a ringmaster. Rollo felt a little disappointed, but with the crowds they got at each performance, he wouldn't be surprised if the circus stopped all together in the next few years.

Rollo pushed the clutch pedal down, which had lengths of wood tied to them so he could reach. The vehicle moaned in protest and slowly joined the convoy. It shook violently and wobbled as if a wheel was about to fall off. Eventually it stopped shaking and the drive was somewhat comfortable.

The town slowly disappeared behind them in a cloud of dust. Heather stared out the window for some time, watching the houses become less and less frequent. She looked around the filthy cabin and noticed an old programme on the floor of the truck. She picked it up and wiped the dust from the cover. She flipped through it until she found an article on Mr Harlow. It was a grand photo of him levitating off the ground while pulling two snow-white rabbits out of his top hat. There was a sparkle of purple around his fingers and his smile was from ear to ear. Her father glanced over to see what she was looking at.

'Dad, do you think Mr Harlow really did lose his magic?'

'Leave it, Heather,' he said sternly.

Heather looked at the picture again. In the far background she could see Mr Harlow's daughter, Nancy. She was a quiet girl, the same age as Heather, who didn't like talking to anyone. She always stood with her arms crossed and looked despondent. Once, after a magic show, she saw Nancy yelling at her father and pointing to her ribs. She was extremely angry and was crying. Mr Harlow just bowed his head, like he did when his magic tricks didn't work and walked away. He looked sad that day, like a piece of him was missing.

'I can't leave it, Dad. I want to know what happened. I wanna know why he can't do magic anymore.'

Suddenly the car came to a shuddering halt. A dust cloud that had been trailing behind them drifted past the vehicle. Heather turned to look at her father, thinking they had braked to miss an animal crossing the road, or to avoid a pot hole.

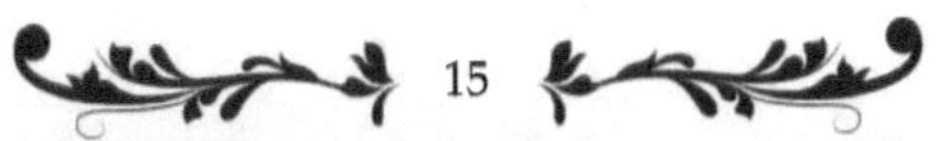

'I said leave it, Heather!'

'Buy why?' she cried out, feeling the strange burn in her stomach of not knowing.

Rollo could see the anguish in his daughter's eyes. He instantly felt bad for yelling at her.

'It's just that…'

Heather waited with bated breath. She was gripping the programme so hard the ink was rubbing off onto her hands.

'…just that I swore I wouldn't talk about it anymore.' Rollo's head looked down at his feet, as if the memory was too painful. His small shoes were laced into the driving pedals. The car burped and jolted gently and then stalled.

'I swear; I won't tell anyone else.'

Heather looked at her father and saw that he had kept a secret inside of himself for far too long and it was starting to age him. His eyes said it all, they were once cloudy blue, and they used to sparkle like reflections on a lake and now they were grey with purple bags under them. The whites were spider-webbed with red veins.

'A lot of people in the circus don't speak of this, so you can't repeat it to anyone. Understand?'

Heather nodded. He turned the key and the car started again. They drove, trying to catch up to the convoy.

'When you and Nancy were quite young, you used to be the best of friends.' Heather listened carefully, unable to remember ever being friends with Nancy.

'As you two got older, Mr Harlow started incorporating Nancy into his magical act. He would get her, at first, to bring out his hat and cape and his wand. Fairly mundane interactions, just to get her used to the spot light, then he started to get her more involved in the show. She would dress up and go into the audience and get them to pick a card while he guessed what it was, things like that.' Heather listened in amazement. She couldn't picture Nancy doing any of this.

'One night, after months of training, I allowed her to be involved in one of his more complicated tricks. She would get in a wooden box, and be spun around. Then...' Rollo stopped, as if picturing the moment in his mind, 'Mr Harlow would insert long swords through the box and out the other side. When the swords where all taken out, the box was spun around again and the participant would emerge unhurt, without a scratch on them. The way the box was designed, it appeared that there would be nowhere for the participant to hide, they had no choice but to get impaled by swords.'

Heather had a vague idea where this was heading, her skin goose-pimpled at the thought. Her spine tingled and her eyes began to water.

'I remember that night well,' Rollo said, his eyes staring off into the distance. 'Nancy had done several practice runs. She would get in the box and align her body in a specific way so the swords wouldn't touch her. There was a full house in that night and everybody was eager to see the best magician in the world. The Magnificent Mr Harlow, they used to call him.' Rollo waved his arms in the air, as if presenting him onto the stage. It was a habit that was hard to get rid of even when he was out of his ringmaster costume.

'Then it started to rain, I remember this very clearly. There was lighting and thunder. It gave the magic show a distinctive atmosphere. One of mystery and intrigue. The crowd was glued to every move Mr Harlow made. All his tricks and magic were coming out perfectly. He was getting the loudest round of applause I had ever heard in my life. Then the sword box was brought out.'

Heather watched the words spill from her father's mouth. It was as if he had told the story a thousand times,

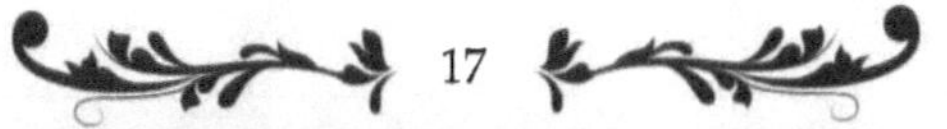

crafting every word with delicate care. But he had never told it, to anyone, ever.

'Nancy bowed to the crowd and stepped into the box. She was spun around and around and then stopped. The crowd waited anxiously. Then the first sword was slid through and out the other side. The crowd gasped. Then the second. He spun the box again to show the audience that the swords were all the way through. It also showed them that there was no place for a human to bend into to avoid the swords, but there was. That was the illusion. After the third, fourth and fifth swords, the crowd was on the edge of their seats, biting their nails. Then the sixth sword was revealed. It was thicker and longer. He dropped a piece of tissue paper on the sword and it cut it in half with no effort at all.'

Heather shivered in her seat. She was afraid of what she was about to hear.

'The sword was slid through the slits in the box and all the way to the other side. The crowd went wild! They cheered and stood up, giving him a standing ovation. Mr Harlow was so proud of himself, and his daughter. He wanted her to be a part of the applause. So, one by one he slid the swords back out. The first and second one were normal. He threw them onto the ground with careless abandon. Then,' Rollo paused for a moment, too scared to speak, 'the third one had a speck of blood on it.' He swallowed hard. 'He lifted it up to his face and studied the blood, it was only a drop. But his face went pure white. He yanked the fourth one out, no blood. The fifth had two drops of blood. He was starting to panic. The crowd was still applauding the whole time, thinking it was part of the act. Then the sixth sword was pulled out, it had the most blood on it. He ran to the wood box's door and swung it open, and there was his daughter, lying unconscious and bleeding.'

Heather choked back tears, her hands were trembling.

'But – but – but...' she stuttered, 'I've seen her, she's okay, right?'

They were catching up to the convoy; the cars and the giant truck with the tent poles were now in view. Long streams of dust clouds came from the tyres.

'We rushed her to the hospital. She was more traumatised than physically hurt. She received several stitches and stayed in overnight for observation. She fully recovered, but Mr Harlow never did. He hasn't been the same since that tragic night. I often catch him sitting in his caravan staring at the sword box. His daughter has never forgiven him for what he did to her, and he blames himself entirely. After that night his magic started to die and recently I've noticed it all but gone.'

Heather turned away from her father and spotted Mr Harlow's caravan chugging along the road in the side mirror. A mural was painted on the side – *The Magnificent Mr Harlow*. But now it was faded and almost entirely washed away by age and weather.

'What can we do, Dad?' Heather asked, her throat still tight from hearing the horrific story.

'There isn't much we can do, Heather. Either he gets his magic back, or we get a new magician.'

ADMIT ONE
COME ONE, COME ALL
THE GREATEST PERFORMANCE IN THE WORLD
CHAPTER 3
WEAVERS PEAK
No. IOIOI987

After several hours of driving, a town slowly came into view. Rollo felt relieved, as he was beginning to become tiresome of driving. His legs hurt and his calf muscles had cramped up long ago. His daughter was slumped in the passenger side seat with her headphones on, fast asleep. She had the programme still clutched in her hand. The sign for the town zoomed past, it was covered in vines and rusted around the edges, giving it a strange orange tinge. Rollo blinked to clear his eyes and read the name – *Weavers Peak*. He remembered the name on the tour schedule and was happy he had found it. Too many times they had gone the wrong way or gotten lost and had to perform in a town with only twenty people.

The lead truck slowed as it pulled off the highway and down a long dirt track that lead to the middle of the township. *The Cassidy Travelling Circus and Magic Show* always did a lap of the town first, just to show the town folk that the circus had arrived.

The town didn't appear to be very big, apart from a small clusters of buildings, a bank and a doctor's surgery. There was a lot of houses scattered around, behind the stores mostly. The streets were nearly abandoned and the people milling around looked only half awake. As the convoy grunted and slowly rolled down main street, the people became excited. They leapt from their chairs, knocking over homemade lemonade and screamed out to their children. Kids from everywhere came running to see the trucks. Blinds and curtains were shoved open and peered through by the locals as the huge tent poles and

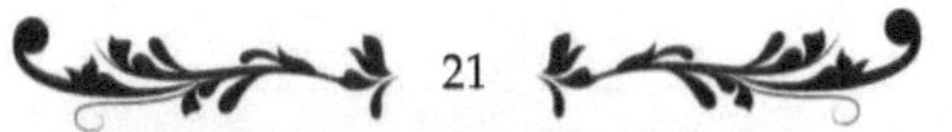

cages of animals rumbled passed them. People spilled from their houses, cheering and chanting, throwing their arms in the air and hollering loudly, barely able to contain themselves.

Rollo stopped at a gas station and looked at his daughter. For a moment, as she lay sleeping, her fiery red hair reminded him of her mother. Round bright cheeks and a button nose. He untied his pedal laces and climbed down out of the cabin. As the door shut, Heather woke in a fright, looking around without knowing exactly where she was. She shut off her music, slipped her headphones into her bag and opened the door. The gas station smelled of spilled fuel and old grease. The air hose to the right of their car hissed like an angry snake. She looked around the town, the streets were kept clean and there weren't many other cars on the road. The people who had come out to watch them drive through their town, were now standing across the street, pointing and waving.

'Are you part of the circus?' said a voice.

Heather turned to see a small boy in a wheel chair. His legs were dirty and so were his hands. There was another boy behind him with his hands on the chairs handle grips.

'Yes,' Heather replied.

The boy in the wheel chair smiled. His eyes were large as he read the signage on the side of the truck.

'When will we be able to see it?' he said, yelling with excitement.

'Tomorrow afternoon we should be all set up,' Heather replied.

'Ignore my brother,' the boy behind the chair said. His face was dirty and his clothes were ragged and torn. 'We don't get much of anything come out this way. Probably couldn't afford it any way...'

The young boy turned his brother around and started walked back towards the street. Heather watched them

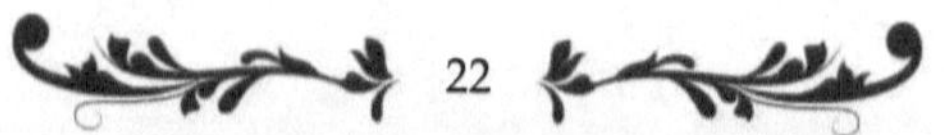

and thought of the joy she saw in the younger boy's eyes
when he found out the circus had arrived. She thought of
Mr Harlow's audience - they had the same look of
excitement. She ran back to the car and dug down into the
passenger side glove box. There was a stack of tickets still
bundled up from several months ago that were still valid.
She peeled the plastic off and tore away three tickets and
slammed the door shut, but the kids were gone. She
looked left and right, but they had disappeared. Quickly,
she ran to the road and spotted them down the street
beside an old cotton factory that was now abandoned and
dilapidated.

'Wait!' she hollered at them.

The older boy swivelled towards her, seeing her
running in their direction.

'What is it?' the boy in the wheel chair gasped, trying
to turn around.

Heather got to them in a few quick steps and started
puffing madly.

'I... have... these for you,' she said, handing them the
tickets.

'For us?'

'Yeah,' she replied. 'I want you guys to be there. For
free.'

'Wow,' the younger boy said, snatching the tickets off
his older brother.

'But you have to do me one favour.'

The brothers looked at each other, then back to
Heather.

'Anything.'

'You have to give the magician the biggest round of
applause you can give, okay? Deal?'

'There'll be a magician?' the younger one said in
astonishment.

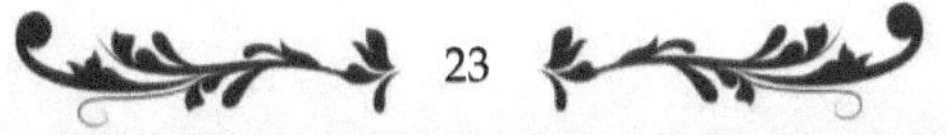

'Yes. His name is Mr Harlow and he's very good. But he needs all the applause he can get. Okay?'

'Sure!'

The two boys turned and continued their way down the street. Heather could hear them laughing and crying out in excitement. She felt a lump in her throat as she imagined them watching Mr Harlow and being mesmerised by his magic. Maybe he just needed encouragement, or for more people to believe in him, like she did. Heather turned and went back to the gas station. Her father was standing outside the passenger side window holding a map up and talking to himself.

'...It's quite easy really. All we have to do is go down Vine Street and into Miles Avenue. Then there should be a vacant lot there, where the man said we could set up. He's very lovely...' he looked up and saw that no one was in the passenger side chair.

'Dad, over here,' Heather said, running up to him.

Rollo looked to his daughter, then back to the empty carriage.

'Oh dear, I thought you were still asleep. I've been talking to myself for some time... anyway.' He folded the map and tucked it under his arm.

With a small amount of effort, he was back in the driver's seat with his pedal laces retied. Heather climbed in beside him. Waiting on the street were the rest of the trucks and vehicles, waiting for Rollo to show them were to go.

'Okay, time to find this vacant lot,' Rollo said, shifting the gearbox into first.

It spat dirty exhaust fumes and slowly peeled off onto the street.

'People here are excited about Mr Harlow,' Heather said, nonchalantly.

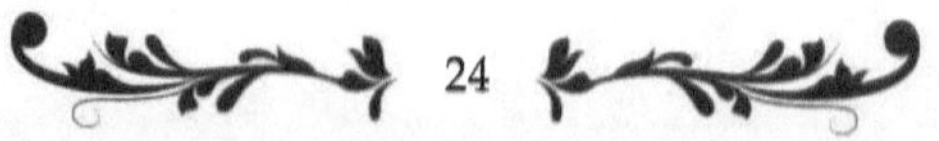

Her father farrowed his brow. 'Really? The magician with no magic?'

'Give him another chance, Dad. At least until the next town. He just needs people to want to see him, that's all.'

'Well,' Rollo said, hammering his small palm onto the horn, 'if the crowd wants him, then the crowd gets him!'

The horn honked loudly and everybody that came out to watch them cheered and clapped. Larry, the truck driver, pulled to the side of the road to let the Ringmaster through. He gave Rollo the thumbs up as he went.

'Another day!' Rollo shouted, shifting into second gear.

'Another town!' Heather finished. They both laughed as they made their way to the Vine street.

***

The day was spent putting the tent together. It was a frantic couple of hours, filled with shouting instructions to one another. Even though the men had done it a hundred times, it was still chaos to build. If one person didn't hold one pole right, the other pole wouldn't fit in the hole and the whole thing would look like it was leaning to one side. Heather and Bounty helped hammer in the large pegs at each pole while Guntha pulled the ropes tight.

The caravans were pulled up at the rear of the tent, in a long line with a grassy corridor down the middle. The squeaks of the wheels and the gentle thumping of generators filled the air and turned the overgrown lot into a small, make-shift town.

As the afternoon wore on Mr Goodwill had his hotdog stand out the front, with fresh buns cooking slowly and long, red, sausages on the grill. A red bottle for ketchup and a yellow bottle for mustard stood under the umbrella like two soldiers, waiting for an order. As the townspeople gathered to watch the sights, Mr Goodwill would sell his hotdogs and talk about how grand the circus was. People

stood and marvelled at the size of the tent, its red plastic peaks shone like a beacon. The monkeys were in their cages eating bananas and other fruit, and the performing dogs were allowed to run loose in the field while the towns children chased them and gave them pats and food.

Normally, Heather's job consisted of ticking off the sheet to make sure everyone was there and that no one got left behind or lost. After that she had to clean out the monkey cage, which she hated because they stunk and threw things at her. The circus had four monkeys, all of which were fat because they ate so much fruit and when people came past to visit they would sneak them sweets and things to eat. One of them had bitten Heather on the hand when she tried to pull away a deep fried sausage that one of the visitors had given it, and now she was over precautious when she was near them.

Rollo had been pacing back and forth all through the late afternoon, looking at the tent from different angles to make sure it was straight. Heather had brought him a cup of tea which he held until it went cold, then drunk it. She walked under the tent as the men unpacked the seating and set it up, counting as she went and ticking the sheet. Her father strolled around, yelling at the men and making them do things right. She left through the rear door and down the grassy hallway between the row of caravans and saw Bounty washing his parents' performance clothes by hands, using a tin tub with hot soapy water and a large plank of wood that had been hit so many times it was now smooth as silk to touch.

'Heather!' Bounty screamed as she walked along the side of their abode, holding her clipboard.

She looked down and ticked his name off.

'Where's your mum and dad?' Heather asked.

'Mum's inside trimming her beard and dad is lazing in the sun on top of the van.'

Heather looked up and saw a green tattooed hand dangling over the side of the roof.

'Hi Heather,' the hand said, waving.

'Hi Jeff.'

'Call me Lizard Man, darling. How many times have I told you that?' He said with a cheeky grin. Beside him was a large jug of iced tea with slices of lemon floating on the top. He was wearing sunglasses and had an open book on his chest.

Lizard Man wasn't expected to help erect the tent, as he was also a major draw card in the circus, beside Mr Harlow and Guntha of course. He got away with lazing about and reading, until he was expected to perform.

Lizard Man, or Jeff as was written on his birth certificate, grew up a very normal boy. He attended college to be an architect or draftsman, planning a career designing buildings for large cities and accommodation for single professionals with too much money. But sitting at a desk grew tiresome quickly for Jeff and he soon found love in travelling. He saw the monuments in Rome and the museums in Paris and thought for some time how he could see all these places regularly without sitting behind a computer screen. He fell in love with the Freak Show scene and soon became a regular at every circus performance. The tip of his tongue was cut in two from a car accident, which landed him in hospital for several months. Knowing now that life was too short for deadlines and ties, he tattooed his body and joined the circus and never looked back.

Heather ticked him off her list and started to walk away when Bounty stood up holding a frilly dress with flowers on it that his mother wore on her days off.

'Heather, I saw you talking with your dad about Mr Harlow and his magic.'

Heather walked closer to him so no one else could hear.

'I heard him talking to himself the other night, right before we packed up to leave.'

'What did you hear?' Heather asked, interested.

Bounty put his clawed hand on her shoulder and brought her in closer to him. They were dripping wet. His malformed hands would make a normal person blush and become curious, but Heather had been around them her whole life and was used to it.

'He was asking for forgiveness... from a box?'

Heather remembered the story her father told her in the car on the way to Weavers Peak. Her eyes darted back and forth as she tried to think of what the box could hold.

'I'm just saying...you know, that I heard it and you were interested. That's all.'

'Yes, I was. Thanks Bounty.'

She looked at her clipboard, the only names left unticked were Guntha, Mr Harlow and his daughter, Nancy. She placed the clipboard under her armpit and headed down the grassy passageway between the caravans.

'Remember, Heather,' Bounty called to her, 'you owe me a game of checkers!'

Heather was too busy in her own head to reply. She had to see this box, or at least ask about it. What if Mr Harlow blamed the box for what happened? She stopped at this sudden realisation, took a deep breath and continued on her way.

When she reached Guntha's van, she could smell an extremely strong aroma of spiced and peppered sausages. Not like Mr Goodwill's sausages either. These one's filled the air with a smell that made the dogs run in the opposite direction. She stood on Guntha's front step, eager to get him ticked off the list and get to Mr Harlow's van. She rapped on the door. There was the sound of splattering fluid and a long moan as something was dropped. Then came the noise of stirring and the gentle sucking of someone drinking something.

'Coming!' a voice boomed from somewhere in the small trailer.

Heather stepped back, and lucky she did. As Guntha the Muscle Man opened the door, a wave of odours poured out from his make-shift kitchen. It entered Heather's nostrils and made her gag instantly. She stumbled backwards and dropped her check list. Guntha stood at the door like a scientist presenting a new find.

'Miss Cassidy? Yes, come inside, taste my lucky sauerkraut.'

Guntha's smile showed all his teeth, most of them were crooked and had a slight beige colourisation. He appeared to have more teeth than the normal person should have.

'Um, no thanks, Guntha. I was just checking you were here.' Heather coughed and wiped her watering eyes. She picked up the check list from the dirt and brushed it off.

'This is the best batch I've ever made,' Guntha hollered looking up to the clouds above. 'Salty, yes! Flavoursome, more so!'

'Sorry, I really gotta go now.'

Heather walked backwards and almost tripped on his bar bells. The weights on each end were twice the size of her head. She righted herself and looked down at the last caravan. A darkness emanated from that end, something was amiss. The light never quite touched that area, as if a dark presence was watching over it. She hadn't ever really noticed it before. She walked down the grassy field slowly, taking her time to view the trailer from a distance. As she got closer she could see in through the small windows on the side. There was movement as a shadow crossed the window.

'I wouldn't bother him if I were you,' said a stern voice to Heather's right.

It made her jump and almost drop her clipboard again. Nancy stood between two caravans, under a large tree. Her body was silhouetted. Her arms were crossed and she had a bizarre demeanour about herself.

'Nancy?'

Nancy stepped out of the shadows. Her hair was black and looked like charcoaled straw as it etched down her shoulders and over her folded arms. She was wearing a black shirt with an unwashed dark blue skirt, with black shoes. She had rings around both eyes either from crying or from not sleeping enough.

'He's having one of his "days",' she said sarcastically.

Heather looked towards the van where Mr Harlow would presumably be, and back to his daughter.

'One of his days?'

Nancy looked Heather up and down with a foul eye. She ran her tongue around her lips and stared at the caravan that housed her father. She had a look of utter disgust and contempt.

'Talking to himself. Breaking his wands and cursing the box. He goes through stages of happiness, then when he has a bad show...he gets like this.'

'He curses the box?'

Nancy closed her eyes, as if to wish herself away from this conversation. She opened them again and stared at Heather with green eyes filled with malice.

'I'm sure you've heard, Heather. We were young, but not young enough to forget. It was just before your mother left, so I don't blame you for not wanting to remember.'

The mention of her mother made her heart beat faster, she felt the familiar prickles of tears behind her eyes. She forced herself to stop thinking about it before they fell from her eyes.

'I don't remember much of that day. I know you went to hospital and after that... it's a blur. I think they must have wanted to keep it a secret from everyone. They never talked about it afterwards. I guess, in a way, I thought it never really happened.'

There was a moment of silence between the pair as the words sunk in. Nancy stepped forward, closer to Heather. Her hands unfolded and she gripped her shirt and pulled it upwards. In the light of the afternoon, Heather could see three long scars running across her ribcage and abdomen. Heather stepped back in shock.

'Still think it never happened?' Nancy said with spite in her voice.

Heather was lost for words. Nancy pulled her shirt back down before anyone else could see it and stepped back into the shadows.

'I-I-I'm sorry, Nancy. I didn't know.'

'And now you do. If you want to talk to the Magnificent Magician with no magic, you'll have to come back later when he's feeling better.'

Heather nodded and walked away. As she ticked them both off the sheet her hands were shaking. She felt saddened by what Nancy had told her and drowned with mixed feelings. *Everything had been so good up until that one trick,* she thought. *Surely his magic would still work, even after the accident. It had to do with the box,* she thought. *It just had to.*

COME ONE, COME ALL
THE GREATEST PERFORMANCE IN THE WORLD
CHAPTER 4
CAN I BE OF ASSISTANCE?
ADMIT ONE
N°.IOIOI987

The next afternoon, the entire town of Weavers Peak turned out to see the spectacle of the Cassidy Circus. The line twisted around the park and down the street where kids ate fairy floss and hotdogs. They shouted and cheered and waved their arms in the air, excited to see the funfair. Mr Goodwill pushed his hotdog cart with its shiny black wheels, selling soda and hot chips; he even ran out of buns early on in the evening and had to bake more.

Eugene, one of the tent handymen, was out the front breathing fire and twirling fire sticks. Whenever a ball of fire soared into the sky, everyone would gasp in awe and clap heartedly. Eugene's chest was covered in swirling tribal tattoos. His left arm was completely covered in ink, showing different characters from the traditional circus – clowns, trapeze, muscle men and fire breathers.

Heather heard the waft of the fire breathing from back stage. There was a certain buzz in the air right before a show, like that feeling of tingles that run up your spine when you're scared. The air was electric and everyone was busy scuttling around trying to find their uniforms and getting ready for the show. Heather tied her fire-engine red hair back in a ponytail and had just finished painting her nails lime green when her father came in.

'Heather, Carol has fallen ill and I will need you to help bring the dogs out tonight.'

Heather turned to her father and marvelled at his ringleader costume. He looked so proud when he wore it, so suave and commanding.

'Yeah, Dad. Okay. I'll just change costume and be out in a minute.'

'Okay, great. Go see Carol near the pens, she'll be waiting. We go on in fifteen minutes.'

Heather nodded and turned back to her mirror. She breathed in deeply and sighed. She opened the bottom draw of her dresser and reached for her makeup bag. Her father slumped down beside her.

'What's wrong?' he asked, putting his hand on hers.

Her father always knew when something was troubling her.

'It's not Mr Harlow again is it? He'll be fine. I heard he was a banker before becoming a magician. He has that to fall back on.' Rollo's voice came out as a plea for Heather to stop worrying about him so much.

Heather turned her head slightly towards her father. She held a mascara wand in her hand, it trembled slightly.

'I just...' she put the wand down, 'I just want him to be the main spectacle of the circus again, that's all. Tonight has to go well, it just has to.'

Rollo kissed his daughter on the cheek.

'Not to worry, petal. It will. I'm sure.'

With that he stood up, straightened his sparkling red jacket and headed for the door.

'Fifteen minutes, Heather! We can't keep the adoring public waiting!'

He whipped his long coat behind him, like a superhero cape, and disappeared out the door. Heather quickly finished her makeup and slipped her shoes on. When she left the tent she could see all the circus performers warming up and trying to shake out the nerves before going out. Guntha was stretching his large arms, while eating a large ham sandwich that was dripping with mustard. Heather knew better than to disrupt them before the show, so she slipped through the throng and went around the rear of the tent where the animals were kept. She saw Carol sitting at a small wooden table, she had just pinned the last pieces of fabric together when she heard the introduction music come from inside the tent.

'Quickly, Heather! It's about to start!'

Heather stood up in front of a full length mirror and marvelled at the costume. It was navy blue with sparkling sequins down each arm. The music reached a crescendo and they could both hear the speakers hiss and crackle as her father, the ringmaster, announced the show.

'Welcome one,' he bellowed, standing in the middle of the arena. 'Welcome all! To the most spectacular spectacle in the world!'

The crowd was jam packed, not one seat was left. People were eating popcorn and corn dogs, fairy floss and candy corn. They munched on lollies and waffles dripping with cream and chocolates. Their eyes peeled open as Ringmaster Rollo introduced the clowns.

'We have a strict policy here at the Cassidy Circus and Side Show,' he yelled into the microphone. 'Absolutely no funny business!'

He stepped aside as a small car puffed its way out of the rear room and into the arena. The car was the size of a ride-on lawnmower. Smoke bellowed from the exhaust as it did a lap around the audience. Suddenly, it stopped. The crowd waited in nervous expectation. The driver's door was blown off its hinges and sent flying through the air. It landed near the small barrier that separated the audience grandstand and the performing act. The door was smoking hot. From inside the vehicle came a clown, he stumbled out, looking confused and started to blow a balloon up. Another clown appeared, this one was huge in stature, his belly hung over his stripped clown pants like a tire inner-tube. He scratched his head and smiled. His red painted lips were smeared across his face. He looked at the first clown and pulled a hair pin from his head and ran after him, trying to burst his balloon. Another clown appeared from the small vehicle, then another, and another, until there were eight clowns in all. They were all blowing up balloons and smiling and waving at the crowd. The crowd laughed at their antics, waving back and hollering at their slapstick comedy.

Heather was staring at the act through a slit in the tent. She looked at her father who was laughing hysterically. No matter how many times he saw it, he still thought it was funny.

'I thought I told you no funny business!' Rollo announced again through his booming microphone. He ran after the clowns, shaking his fist at them.

They ran in a circular motion around the rim of the stage as the audience threw popcorn at them. Then, with a loud *slam!* the clowns all ran into each other, their balloon strings getting knotted together.

'Hey!' Ringmaster Rollo shouted. 'Come back here!'

Slowly the clowns started to rise from the ground. Their legs kicking and thrashing the air. Up and up they went, the audience's mouths opening in shock and disbelief. A small flap in the tent's peak opened up and the clowns disappeared through the roof.

A lone spot light shone on Rollo. He was looking up and shaking his head. He looked down at the audience and bowed.

'Welcome to the show!'

Heather closed the slit and saw the performing dogs run with their trainers out into the spot light. The large curtain flapping shut behind them. She walked across the waiting area and down the stairs. There was a sweet smell to the air. She looked up to see large dark clouds descending over the town. There was the soft crackle of oncoming thunder and the infant sparks of lightning. A drop fell through the air, blinking like a diamond falling from the sky and landed on Heather's forehead. She wiped it away.

'Great,' she said. 'Rain.'

A flurry of voices drew her attention away from the sky and she could see Mr Harlow walking up to the ramp that led into the tent. Nancy was at his heels.

'No, Dad,' she was saying with a hard tone in her voice. 'You won't do that trick! Never, ever again!'

Mr Harlow stopped and took a deep breath. He turned to his daughter.

'You will be assisting me, Nancy. That is all, you're not getting into the box, I promise.' Mr Harlow showed deep agony in his eyes. He looked at his daughter and saw how mad she was.

'Your magic is gone, dad! So stop trying!' she screamed into his face. She turned on her heels and marched back towards their caravan.

Mr Harlow stood on the lip of the ramp. 'If I can't do it Nancy...' he said, his voice trembling, 'we're gonna have to leave.'

Heather watched as Nancy stormed off into the darkness. She could hear her gentle crying as she faded off into the night. She looked back at Mr Harlow and slowly moved towards him.

'Mr Harlow?' Heather said, gently.

He jumped a little, surprised that she was standing so close. In the gloomy light of the dying sun and dark clouds, his features looked sullen. His cheeks sunken and his lips thin and frail. He had a thin moustache that was unkempt and his hair wasn't combed.

'Heather Cassidy. I missed your check off today. I do apologise.'

'Never mind,' she replied, stepping closer to him. 'Can I be of assistance in your act?'

Mr Harlow had the look of stunned surprise. He opened his mouth to speak, then closed it again. He thought for a moment.

'You know Heather, on second thoughts, I don't really need an assistant tonight.'

Heather leapt forward. 'But, but, I know your scared to hurt someone again, but you won't! There are kids coming tonight specially to see you... I told them you were the greatest magician of all time.'

Mr Harlow stared at the young girl. His head bowed a little and he looked to his shoes.

'I'm sorry, Heather. I must go and attend to my daughter. It was good seeing you.' He turned quickly and headed back down the grassy knoll to his van.

Heather was about to run after him when she heard someone call her from the tent entrance.

'Heather Cassidy!'

She looked up and saw Carol leaning on one of the tent poles, her face was sickly white and she was sweating profusely.

'Forgetting something?' Carol said, blowing her nose.

She walked up the ramp, then noticed the sparkling light illuminating from her outfit.

'The dogs!' She had forgotten she had promised her father to help with the dog act.

She ran quickly to the curtained entrance and ran inside, hoping her father hadn't noticed.

The show continued on as normal. Rollo had noticed his daughter's absence, but was happy when she did decide to lend a hand. The monkey's rode on the backs of the ponies while they jumped through hoops, the clowns descended from the roof, with one balloon popping at a time until they fell into a giant mound of white make-up and red noses. After they had been chased out by the lizard man, the arena was left empty. The crowd had finally stopped laughing and settled down in their seats. There was a mystical, enchanting feeling in the air that made everyone hush. A soft mist twirled out onto the floor, eerie and haunting.

Heather helped get the monkey's back in the cages and ran back up to the ramp to peer through the gap in the tent. She could see Mr Harlow's magic act about to begin. To the left of her she heard someone walking up and turned to see who it was. It was Nancy. Her arms were crossed again and she had a look of disdain on her face. She took a spot near the curtains, where she could see the stage and looked on with a down-turned face. She wiped her eyes. They looked puffy from crying.

Heather looked back through the hole and spotted the brothers near the front. The boy in the wheelchair was leaning forward, his eyes gleaming and wide. His brother sat beside him, eager to see the show.

'Now, for your amusement and wonder!' boomed a voice through the speakers. He reverberated and shook the stands like thunder, 'The One. The Only. The Magnificent Mr Harlow!'

There was a flicker of lights, reds and yellows, all streaming through the mist that was pouring from machines on the side of the stage. Then, like a creature emerging from a crypt, the fog started to twist and turn, forming a large figure in the middle of the arena. All of a sudden, a top hat appeared, seemingly floating on the morbid smog coming from the ground. With a loud clap of thunder and a shower of sparks, Mr Harlow stepped forward and bowed graciously. There was a moment of stunned silence, then an uproar of the most loving and loudest ovation Heather had ever heard.

Mr. Harlow took his top hat off and placed in on the ground in front of him. He reached into his long coat and slid out a long blade. It was silver and gleamed in the lights. He lifted it up and placed the tip on his forehead, the handle was straight up in the air. The crowd gasped at the act, the sword seeming to be too big and heavy to be balanced on his nose. It should have sliced him in half. He took his hands away and the large sword was balancing, freely, on his head.

'It's not even sharp,' Nancy said, tapping her foot annoyingly.

Heather stole a glance to her, before looking back at the magician.

Mr Harlow then produced a pack of cards and walked slowly towards the audience, the sword gently wavering back and forth as he did. Carefully, the crowd backed away, scared they were going to get cut if the weapon fell. Heather watched from the side as Mr Harlow gave the cards to the boy in the wheelchair.

'Shuffle them please,' he requested.

The boy took the cards and shuffled them best he could, dropping them onto his lap several times before picking them up. He finally offered them back to the magician.

'Get your brother to shuffle them too, please,' he said, pointing to the boy beside him.

'How did you know he was my brother?' The boy in the wheelchair asked. Mr Harlow gave him a wink.

His brother shuffled them again, thoroughly, then handed them back. The whole time, Mr Harlow was staring up at the sword. The twin sharp edges looking like they could do serious damage if it went off balance and fell. The magician took the cards, fanned them out and asked the boys to take one. The older brother reached forward and slid one out of the pack and gave it to his brother. He looked at it, the ace of spades.

'Place it back, please.' He requested.

The boy did as he was instructed. The crowd watched with nervousness and admiration. Several audience members were biting their nails with excitement. Some were cowering under their coats and boyfriends, scared of the large sword looming over them.

Mr Harlow stepped back, slowly into the ring once more. The spot lights shone on him, he was not sweating or shaking with nerves. He was calm and appeared to be in control. Heather looked over to Nancy who rolled her eyes and continued to frown. She looked back just in time to see Mr Harlow finish his trick.

The magician shuffled the cards like a casino professional.

'Young boy, is this your card?'

Just as he spoke, he threw the cards into the air. They sprayed out like confetti on someone's wedding day. The cards turned in the air, many of them flying higher through the mist and lights, reds and blacks become a blur. Within the blink of an eye, Mr Harlow pushed the sword up into the air with his head, it cart-wheeled, catching the light and sparkling. He caught it, swung it around like a professional swordsman and stabbed the handle end into the dirt ground. The audience leapt backwards, seeing the blade sticking up dangerously. In the same swift motion, he snatched his top hat from the ground and placed it on his head. The cards rained down around him, until they were all scattered on the floor. The crowd looked at each other.

The boy in the wheelchair spoke, 'But...where's my card?'

Mr Harlow smiled. He took his top hat off and thrust it down the sword. With a sharp tearing sound, the hat fell down the blade, slicing through the middle of it until it hit the sword handle. Everyone gasped, even Heather. And there, nestled on top of the swords tip, was a card. Mr.

Harlow casually plucked it from the blade and looked at it. He walked over to the brothers.

'Is this the card you're after?'

They looked at it. The ace of spades. The brothers yelped in excitement.

'That's it!' they hollered.

The crowd roared with applause. Heather clapped gently to herself, still amazed at Mr Harlow's ability to impress a crowd.

'It's all an illusion,' Nancy said. She had stepped closer to Heather and had taken her eyes off her father's act.

'That's what magic is, Nancy. I don't know why you have to be so negative about it,' Heather snapped back.

'Negative?' Nancy spat, like a bad taste in her mouth. 'Maybe if your father cut you open and you had to go to hospital you would be negative too.'

'But it was an accident,' Heather pleaded. 'You have to forgive him.'

Nancy narrowed her eyes. 'Forgive him? For scarring me for life. I don't think I'll ever forgive him.'

She glared distastefully at Heather and marched back down the ramp to her caravan. The bearded lady was standing nearby and heard the entire conversation. She wandered over to Heather. She was dressed in her long red dress, waiting for her turn to go into the ring.

'You know, Heather,' she said as Mr Harlow was performing his magic just beyond the curtain, 'Mr Harlow was an incredible magician up until that night.'

Heather watched as Bounty's mother stroked her beard. It was long and dark brown in colour, with stripes of silver-grey sprinkled near her chin.

'Do you think it has something to do with her?'

They both turned and watched the sulking figure of Nancy disappear into the darkness.

'Why doesn't she leave the circus and go live with her mother?'

The bearded lady contemplated this for some time.

'Maybe she wants to punish her father for what he did?'

They both felt a strange realisation pass over them.

'Sorry, Heather,' the bearded lady said. 'I have to get my husband ready for the show, I'll talk to you later... Oh! and remember, Bounty still wants that game of checkers.'

With that she scurried off towards the Lizard Man who was covering his body in Vaseline to give it a macabre shine. Heather turned back to the magic show just in time for Mr Harlow's last act.

'And now,' he proclaimed to the audience, 'I will attempt to pull a rabbit out of my hat!'

The audience became restless with excitement. They looked at each other, and stared with their eyes peeled open as one of the acrobats brought out another top hat. Heather remembered that was Nancy's job, but she refused to be part of his act now. Mr Harlow took the hat, placed his hand inside and tipped it upside down. He walked along the edge of the ring, showing the audience that the hat was indeed empty. He stopped at the brothers and let the eldest one place his hand inside the hat.

'Well, fine sir, is there any trap doors, secret compartments, hidden messages, or animals of any species hidden within the walls of my top hat?'

'No,' the eldest brother replied, taking his hand out of the hat.

Mr Harlow walked back and slid his hand into his jacket, pulling out a wand. The tips were pearl white and the middle was charcoal black. From somewhere behind the velvet curtain came a drum roll.

'I will need quiet, please, if I am to channel the magical beings that be! From the land of another dimension, cascading with the power of the magical elders... I will summon the force to bring a live rabbit from this very hat!'

He swirled the wand around, as if spelling something in the air. Lights on either side of him flickered and strobed brilliantly. The audience looked on agog with amazement. Then, as if compelled by something spiritual, Mr Harlow stopped, tapped the wand on the side of the top hat and reached inside. The drum roll stopped suddenly. It was dead quiet. Not even a snigger, or the munching of popcorn could be heard. People were frozen, mid chew, mid sneeze, waiting to see what would happen.

'Hey Presto!' he screamed.

His hand fumbled around the hat, up the sides and along the bottom. There was nothing.

'Oh, no!' Heather cried out. She watched on in startled fear.

Mr Harlow looked down into the hat, a black void stared back at him. The brothers looked at each other, then back to the magician. Then, they started clapping, just as Heather had told them to at the gas station the day before. One by one each audience member joined in, hollering and clapping. Mr Harlow felt guilt and shame resting heavy on his chest. He held the hat outwards and tapped it with his wand.

'Hey Presto!' he screamed, twice as loud.

The audience waited, their hands frozen in mid clap. As strange atmosphere had entered the room, it felt like everyone was drained of energy and that the room was left without a soul. Mr Harlow felt it the most. He knew there wouldn't be a rabbit it his hat, but he slowly placed his hand in the top hat and felt around. It was empty. He slid the hat back onto his head and bowed.

Ringmaster Rollo shook his head and looked over to his daughter. He could see tears in her eyes. He ran quickly into the ring with his microphone, the lead had wrapped around his foot and he almost stumbled over it.

'Keep that round of applause going for the freaks!' he announced.

The lights swung to the entrance door as the Bearded Lady, Lizard Man and Crab Boy bounded through the curtains. Mr Harlow stood in the dark, looking out at the crowd as their attention was taken off him and onto the next act. Ringmaster Rollo ran forward, clasped him by his wrist and pulled him off stage.

'It happened again,' Rollo yelled, pushing him through the exit, 'I warned you Harlow... if it kept happening...'

'I can't... I can't...'

'What?' Rollo snapped, frustrated with the magician.

Mr Harlow pulled his arm away from the Ringmaster and they both stood in the darkness looking at one another.

'I can't do magic.' Mr Harlow's words spilled from his mouth and Heather could see that it was the first time he had been truly honest with himself.

Mr Harlow turned and ran down the ramp. Rollo was about to go after him, but he was needed on stage. Rollo let out a long sigh and marched back into the spot light.

Mr Harlow stood outside the tent, and looked over his shoulder at the circus. He could hear the crowds cheering the freak show. Heather saw him from her perch near the stage. She had never seen someone look so beaten and destroyed. Mr Harlow turned and walked back to his caravan, his wand and hat held tightly in his right hand. It started to rain.

COME ONE, COME ALL
THE GREATEST PERFORMANCE IN THE WORLD
ADMIT ONE
CHAPTER 5
A DREAMLESS SLEEP
No. 1010 1987

Heather finished helping with the dogs. Her job was to help feed them, groom them and clean out their cages. She didn't mind doing that job, as it helped out the trainers and she felt like she was contributing to the overall running of the circus.

She locked the cages for the night and headed back over to the tent. She walked through the main curtain and saw that everyone had collected everything from their seats and not left anything behind. Sometimes people would leave coats and mobile phones and come back to get them the next day. The crowd had piled out, their cheeks sore from smiling and laughing and their hands aching from applauding. She was about to close the front curtain when two young voices called her from across the front of the vacant lot. Heather could see two kids by a streetlight. She squinted her eyes and stepped out of the tent and into the cold night. She could see it was the two brothers. She went over to them, both their faces were beaming.

'Did you enjoy the show?' she asked the boy in the wheelchair.

'Mark loves anything with magic,' the older brother said, giving his brother a jocular slap over the head.

'Not all magic,' Mark replied. 'He didn't pull a rabbit from his hat, so I thought...maybe we weren't clapping hard enough.'

Heather felt a strange twang in her chest, as if she had just been shot with an arrow.

'It wasn't that,' she replied, pushing her red hair back behind her ears. 'It's Mr Harlow; something is wrong with his magic.'

Mark looked up at his brother.

'I told you it wasn't us, Alistair.'

The streetlight above them started to flicker. All three looked up.

'Are you two alright getting home?' Heather asked, as the eeriness of the light started to spook her.

'Mum's on her way now. We have to wait for her here.'

As if on cue, an old station wagon swung around the corner and pulled into the park.

'Well, I better be off. I have to check that the locks on the other animals' cages and make sure no one has forgotten to feed them.'

'It must be fun working at a circus,' Alistair noted, as he helped push his brother towards their mother's car.

Heather was left standing in the flickering light. 'It can be good,' she said, mostly to herself.

After all the locks had been checked and the lights switched off, Heather made her way over to the caravans. There was a soft hum of voices coming from each van, mostly the performers talking about their act – what went wrong, what went right, what they could improve on. There was smell of food being cooked for a late night snack. Heather's bones felt weary and worn. Her mind was a cloud of disappointment and confusion. She looked at her hands and they were caked in dirt and dog food. She went over to a faucet that was on the side of one of the caravans and started washing her hands when she noticed a light from one of the van's came on and the door opened gently. Heather turned the faucet off and looked at a figure coming towards her.

'Hello?' she said to the darkness.

'Heather?'

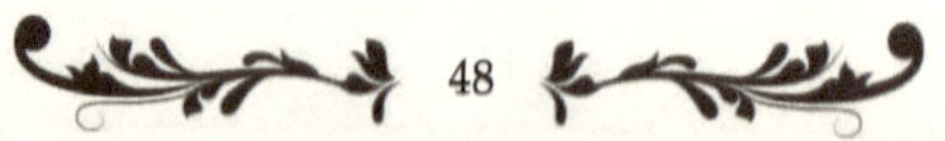

It was Bounty the Crab Boy.

'Bounty,' she said, relieved. 'You scared me half to death.'

'Sorry, Heather... but I thought you might want to see this.'

Bounty waved his fleshy, congealed hands to follow him. Heather ran behind him, quick at his heels. They bolted down the length of the make-shift homes and quickly ducked behind a large van which was occupied by Mr Surestone the ticket collector. Heather and Bounty could hear him snoring inside. It was coming through the walls like a rumbling train.

'What did you want to show me?' Heather asked, as Bounty peered around the corner.

'It's Mr Harlow... I think there's something wrong with him.'

Heather looked perplexed at Bounty. The cold air skimmed across the long grass and tickled at their heels. Heather could feel the chilly touch of a bony hand creeping up her spine. The clouds overhead moved slowly like massive boulders.

'What's he doing?'

'Come,' Bounty said, taking her hand.

Four fingers had fused together from birth, and his thumb was oddly big, with no nails or joints. He pulled her gently across the knoll, bending down so not to be seen. Heather copied. There were only a few lights on which didn't supply much glare to show where they were stepping. Her father had his light on. He would be going over the ticket sales of the night and looking at comment cards. If there was a problem, Carol would be in there and they would be arguing over new costumes or acrobatic ropes. Heather thought she only had a small amount of time to get home until he started to wonder where she was.

They ran to the next line of vans and Bounty pushed his back against the wall of the closest caravan, careful not to rock it or make a noise. He slid along the back, where the rear of the van faced the darkness of the park. Heather did the same, holding her breath the whole time. Together they shimmied along the back of the caravan. They could smell baked beans burning on a gas stove top. It was Larry's van; his sleeping quarters always smelled of burned beans. Bounty got down on his hands and knees and crawled across the ground to the last trailer.

'Get down,' he whispered to Heather. 'He'll see you.'

Heather did as instructed and crawled along the filthy, wet ground. She saw the paint on the side of the structure towering over her, it was Mr Harlow's van. Cutting through the air was the gentle hum of someone talking. Heather tried to listen carefully to who it was or what they were saying, but she couldn't make out anything through the walls. Bounty slowly got to his feet and perched his fingers on the railing of a window sill. He pointed with his hand at the window, it was open an inch. Heather didn't like the fact they were about to spy on Mr Harlow, but Bounty had been certain there was something going on. She got to her feet, her knees covered in mud and stained green from the grass and peered through the window. Mr Harlow was sitting on an upturned milk crate. He was wearing long slacks and a sagging white shirt. He sat hunkered before a large wooden, rectangular box. It stood nearly as high as the van roof and was one of the most beautiful constructions Heather had ever laid eyes on. It had a door at the front that had polished silver hinges and a beaming, chrome doorknob. The wood looked pine, clearly varnished by a professional to give it its rich dark red colour. On each end of the box were small slits, six in all.

The sword box! Heather thought. *That's the one that Nancy was in when she was hurt.*

Bounty stood on his tip toes and looked in, just as Mr Harlow shook his head wildly and moaned loudly.

'Why won't you let me do magic...' they were able to hear him say. 'You can't do this to me... you can't!'

Heather looked on as Mr Harlow stood and pounded his fists on the top of the box. His head dropped and he lay on the polished door. He sobbed openly, his long thin fingers stroking the wood.

'I want my magic... I *need* my magic...'

Bounty ducked down out of sight. Heather felt she had intruded enough. Seeing a grown man cry gave her mixed feelings. It was utterly devastating, but she felt an obligation to help him.

'He has been talking to the wooden box ever since he came off stage,' Bounty uttered softly.

'The box has something to do with his inability to do tricks,' Heather said, her brain swelling with the idea of fixing Mr Harlow's problem.

There was a clutter from inside the trailer as something was thrown.

'Dad!' came a voice, Heather recognised it as Nancy's. 'Please shut up! I'm trying to sleep!'

'I'm sorry, Nancy... I'm so sorry.'

Heather heard the sorrow in his voice and clutched Bounty by his claw and lead him back towards the massive tree. Once they were in the clearing, she could see her father in their caravan pacing back and forth, he must be getting eager to know where she is. She looked back at Bounty.

'Okay,' she started. 'The box must contain some clues as to what is stopping his magic. In his act he talks about channelling an ancient world where elders live... If we can find a way to contact them, maybe his magic will return.'

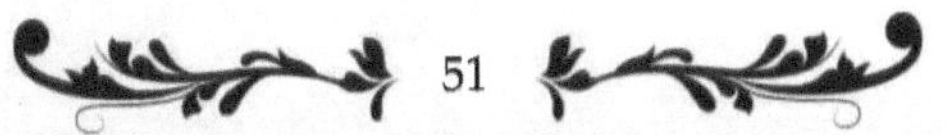

Bounty looked at her quizzically. 'An ancient world? I thought that was just talk. You really want to help Mr Harlow, don't you?'

'If we don't help him... Dad says we'll have to find a new magician.'

Bounty heard his father call him through the darkness, he was walking towards where they were standing.

'I gotta go, Heather. And so should you.' He went to run to his father, but Heather still had him by his hand.

'Tomorrow night, when Mr Harlow is doing his magic show, we'll go in and look at that sword box.'

'Break in?'

'It's not breaking in if it's part of your family.'

Bounty looked somewhat relieved at this.

'Okay, Heather. I really gotta go... Come get me tomorrow just before he goes on.' With that, Bounty ran out into the patch of grass and met with his father.

Once they had retired back to their trailer, Heather ran across the dark allotment and into her own van where her father held his glasses in one hand and a long roll of receipts in the other.

'Hey Heather. Where you been? I thought you fed the dogs an hour ago?'

'They were restless, Dad,' she lied. 'I thought I would take them for a quick walk.' She felt guilt in her stomach from lying.

'Oh?' her father replied. 'They're normally so exhausted after a show they go straight to sleep.' He shrugged and continued looking down at his list.

Carol was sitting opposite him punching numbers into a calculator. She smiled as Heather walked past, a smile that almost said I *know what you're up to* but Heather knew it was just her paranoia. She skipped quickly to her room and pulled the curtain across and sat on her bed. If she was to investigate the box tomorrow she would need all her wits about her. She dressed in her night shirt and pyjama pants and slipped under the covers, dirty knees and all. She had just started thinking about Mr Harlow and the sword box when her eyes became heavy and she fell into a dreamless sleep.

ADMIT ONE
COME ONE, COME ALL
THE GREATEST PERFORMANCE IN THE WORLD
CHAPTER 6
JUST AN ORDINARY COIN
No.IOIOI987

Breakfast for the circus family normally consisted of sitting around a rather large, make-shift table that was lop-sided and stunk slightly of wet wood. The food was cooked by Larry and Eugene and sometimes Carol helped. The Bearded Lady wasn't allowed near the gas barbeque anymore, because once her beard caught on fire and burnt it off and she couldn't perform for two months until it had grown back.

Heather had smelt the bacon and eggs cooking. She could smell the orange juice containers being opened and the coffee being percolated. Her father woke slightly before she did and had been stumbling around the trailer trying to find his pants. He had knocked over a pot and kicked the table with his big toe. Heather decided to get up too; there was no use trying to sleep when there were delicious smells outside and a ruckus inside.

'Morning, Rollo,' Carol said, dishing up a healthy serving of scrambled eggs onto a plate and passing it to him.

'Morning, Carol. The numbers looked good for last night.'

Carol nodded. 'Yes, we managed to actually make a profit. If we do it again tonight, we should be able to get those new costumes.'

She dished up two sausages and placed them carefully on his plate. Her eyes slowly crossed the banquet in front of her and met with Rollo's eyes. He knew what she was playing at, giving him an extra sausage to bribe him for new costumes.

'We'll see, Carol,' he said, turning to find a seat among the other performers and stage hands that encompassed the circus family.

Heather had found a robe, slipped it on and washed her face in the basin. She looked at her dishevelled hair, and once she came to the conclusion that she wouldn't be able to do anything with it, she just tied it back to get it off her face. Her deep green eyes looked almost hazy in the single bulb light of the bathroom. She thought about what she had planned with Bounty for this very night and quickly erased it from her mind. She had to have food first, before she thought of her plan in more detail.

She opened the door to see Bounty folding a piece of bread around a sausage covered in sauce and putting it in his mouth. He tried to talk but his words only came out mumbled and undecipherable. She looked over the table and saw her father take a seat near the end while he talked with Mr Goodwill about his hotdog sales. As she climbed down the steps and onto the grass, Mr Harlow appeared from, what seemed like nowhere, and fetched a plate for his breakfast. Heather lined up behind him.

'Where's Nancy this morning?' she asked.

Mr Harlow turned to see who was talking to him and Heather saw his eyes, they were bloodshot and sagging with purple bags. He looked like he had been awake all night.

'Nancy? Oh, she's still asleep. I tried to wake her to come for breakfast, but she said she wasn't hungry.'

Mr Harlow was served his portion and then took a seat away from the crowd. Heather thought she would sit beside him and ask more questions. Her intentions were good, but she lacked the audacity to take the seat beside him. Instead, she sat on the opposite side of the table and a few seats up, towards her father.

'Heather,' said a voice from the throng of munching mouths and slurping tongues.

Heather looked down the row of heads and saw Tina Surestone, Mr Surestone's wife. She was leaning backwards so she could see past the line of hungry performers, to look at Heather.

'I have to go to town later to put some posters up, wanna come?'

Heather nodded. 'Yeah, I'd love to. There were some kids that came to the show last night, if I can find them they might be able to help too.'

'That would be great,' Tina said, her head disappearing back into the feeding frenzy.

Heather had run her toast along the edge of her plate, soaking up all the egg yolk and gravy when she noticed that Nancy still hadn't come for breakfast.

'Mr Harlow, would you like me to take a plate of food to Nancy? She might not be well.'

Mr Harlow looked up. He still had that faint dazed look in his eyes. As if his head was swirling out of control and he couldn't get a grip on it.

'You're a good girl, Heather. I think she would like that.'

Just as Heather got to her feet, a voice from the end of the long table tapped their fork on their drinking glass and yelled. It was Larry.

'Hey, Harlow,' he bellowed over the crescendo of noise. 'Do that trick with the coin.'

Suddenly, everyone was quiet. In unison, every head at the table turned and looked at the magician sitting on his own at the other end. Larry forked a large spoonful of eggs and shoved it into his mouth. He grinned widely, knowing that Mr Harlow hadn't been performing at his best.

'Larry, no. Mr Harlow doesn't have to do magic for your entertainment, he's eating his breakfast.' Carol said, pointing her fork at him with half a strip of bacon dangling from the end.

'I just wanted to see that coin trick again, that's all.' He shovelled another spoonful of egg into his mouth without finishing what he had first.

Carol looked down at her plate, then over to Mr Harlow. Heather pushed her food around on her plate, but curiosity got the better of her, and she too looked over to him.

'The coin trick?' Mr Harlow said, a slight sparkle erupted in his eyes.

Slowly, he reached into his trouser pocket and pulled out a polished, silver, coin.

'Just an ordinary coin,' he said, handing it to the nearest person, who happened to be Bounty.

Bounty examined it closely, then bit into it.

'Seems normal to me,' he said, looking at Heather, who in turn shrugged, smiling.

He handed it back to Mr Harlow who waved it in the air with the grace of a well-trained illusionist. The coin flickered and rolled over his fingers, as if it had a mind of its own. It perched between his knuckles, on its end, and spun wildly. The gathered circus performers watched as, with a flick of his wrist, the coin suddenly disappeared.

Larry froze, a fork full of egg and sausage half way up to his mouth.

'Where did it go?' he gasped.

Heather felt a warm sensation flow over her heart. To see the Magnificent Mr Harlow perform a trick, with a grin on his face, made her happy.

Carol looked at Rollo, who had a look of confusion. *If he could do magic at the dining table, why couldn't he do it in the show?* He thought.

'Harlow,' the Bearded Lady said, 'I truly am stunned. Where on earth did the coin go?'

Larry heaved a mound of food into his mouth and bit down. Suddenly the air was cut with an ear piercing scream. Larry leapt to his feet, his hands flying to his jaw as he jumped up and down wildly. Everyone turned to him, watching as his eyes rolled back in his head and he yelped like he had been stung by a bee.

'What?' Rollo said, running to his aid, 'What is it?'

Larry lunged forward and spat the contents of his mouth out onto the table. Everyone backed away, pushing their chairs away from the mashed up food. Heather craned her neck to see what he had spat out, and there, amongst the mashed eggs and bacon was the silver coin. Her jaw was left hanging open, how could he have done that? He didn't walk over to Larry at any time, he didn't slip anything into his meal, because Larry had been eating way before Mr Harlow showed up.

The magician stood from his place at the table, bowed and took his empty plate to the wash up sink and dunked it into the steaming, soapy water. He had a grin on his face, smug and proud of himself. Larry was left rubbing his jaw.

Larry ran over to Mr Harlow, grabbing him around his shirt collar. Lizard Man and Rollo ran after him, but they were too late. Larry pulled the magician away from the washing up, flinging him over to the table. Mr Harlow sprawled across it, knocking ketchup and mustard bottles onto the ground.

'You fraud!' Larry yelled, still rubbing is jaw, 'That wasn't magic! That was... was...' Larry thought for a moment as Rollo went to help Mr Harlow up. 'That was... witchcraft!'

The entire table was left in stunned amusement for several seconds. Heather began to laugh.

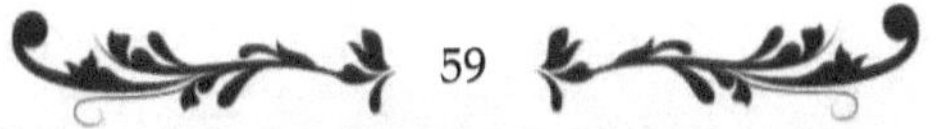

'Stop laughing, Heather. You try biting down on a silver coin,' Larry snapped.

Slowly, but surely, each person at the table started to laugh.

'Shut up!' Larry shouted. 'All of you. It's not funny.'

The bearded lady was bent forwards, her stomach in stitches. Even Mr Surestone had taken his glasses off to wipe the tears away from his eyes because he had been laughing so much.

'No one should ever ask a magician to do a trick... especially you,' Mr Harlow said, straightening his shirt.

Larry stomped his feet like an angry bull and marched away. Rollo asked Mr Harlow if he was okay. Mr Harlow nodded and patted him on the shoulder.

'It'll take more than that to annoy me. Thank you Rollo.' He snuck a quick glance to the remaining people at the table and slowly walked back towards his trailer. Rollo looked at Heather and gave her a hearty laugh.

'It's good to see Harlow still has it.'

*****

That night the crowd was lined up all the way down the street. Some people had come out a second time to see the show. They were talking about the monkeys and the performing dogs. They were telling each other about the trapeze and the magician with no magic.

Heather was standing next to Mr Surestone as he sat in his little booth selling tickets. He had started to sweat profusely. His already thinning hair was now sopping wet and stuck to his balding crown like glue. The collar of his shirt was drenched and he was guzzling water from a large bottle by his feet.

'Be a darling,' he said, without turning to Heather, 'and fetch me some more water, it's like a sauna in here.'

He ripped two tickets and gave them to the person in front of him. They slid the money under the small semi-circular hole in the glass. Mr Surestone took the money and counted it quickly, placing it in the safe box. Heather left the booth and went on the search for another bottle of water. She ran up the stairs that led to the tent and went inside. People were finding their seats and watching the empty stage area eagerly. High above them, amongst the ropes and pullies came a shout. Heather looked up to see Freddy Falconer adjusting one of the handles on the trapeze swing.

'Heather!'

It was dizzying looking up to that height, never mind actually being up there.

'Come closer!'

Heather made her way over the divider wall and onto the arena, a few young kids in the audience thought the show was starting and began to clap excitedly.

Freddy Falconer was a small man, no bigger in size than Heather. He was thin with wide shoulders and long arms. His chin looked like a cork screw with a long scar running over it and along his jaw line.

'Your Dad wants to see you!' he called out again, jumping off the thin rail he was perched on and gripping a length of free rope. He swirled around it like a kite caught in a zephyr, sliding down until he hit the ground beside Heather.

'He couldn't find you again. He thought you went with Tina to hang posters up, but she came back ages ago.'

'Oh,' Heather said, forgetting all about the posters, 'I was out the front with Mr Surestone looking for...' she stopped. She had been looking for Andy and his brother to give them more tickets for the show, but they hadn't come back.

'For?' Freddy said, looking perplexed.

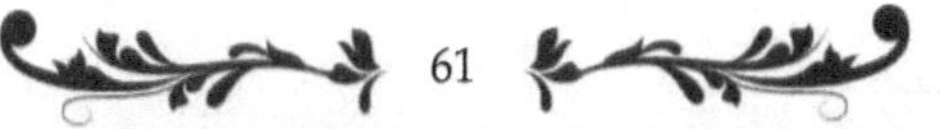

'Oh, never mind, I better go find Dad.'

With that she ran off stage and through the curtains. She had walked past all the clowns fixing their make-up and getting ready to pile in the small car when she passed the programme board. She stopped and glanced up, Mr Harlow was on at 7:00pm sharp. She checked the clock beside the board, she had one hour until she could go and investigate the sword box. Suddenly her father appeared with Carol lagging behind him trying to mend his long, shinning red, coat.

'Jumping jack-rabbits Heather! You're harder to find than the lost city of Atlantis. Now, we need you to help with the dogs again, Carol is still unwell.' Rollo glanced a look at her trailing behind him and saw her looking rather green with a bright red nose. She was balancing a needle and thread in between her lips whilst she fixed a long tear.

'Sure Dad...' she said, trying to think if she would have enough time to get to Mr Harlow's trailer without anyone seeing her.

'Get your costume on, its lying on your bed and don't be late this time.' Her father glanced up at the clock. 'Oh no, five minutes everyone!' he hollered.

All the clowns jumped up into the air, as if on cue. One of the smaller clowns had a rather large flower on his breast pocket that squirted water when he jumped. His face went red with embarrassment.

'Go, Heather,' Carol said, pinning the torn cloth together on Rollo's jacket.

Heather snapped out of her day dream and took off running down the ramp and onto the grass. All around her the performers where stretching and getting ready. Guntha was lifting weights, trying to get his muscles bigger before the show.

'Don't forget the dogs,' he yelled, heaving two hand weights over his head. His cheeks puffed out as he strained. Large veins in his arms ran like spider webs to his wrist and towards his knuckles.

Heather waved him her thanks and kept running.

'Heather! Heather!' yelled another voice.

Bounty was jogging behind her.

'I can't play checkers now, Bounty. I have to help with the dogs again!'

'No,' he puffed, stopping to catch his breath, 'Wait...'

Heather stopped just short of her trailer. Bounty looked around suspiciously.

'Are we still going to... you know...'

'Yes,' Heather said, lowering her voice. 'He's on stage at 7:00pm. As soon as the dogs come off, he'll go on. Okay? It's just before your act... so meet me outside his trailer as soon as he steps on stage. Understand?'

Bounty nodded, smiling as he normally did when about to get into mischief.

ADMIT ONE
COME ONE, COME ALL
THE GREATEST PERFORMANCE IN THE WORLD
CHAPTER 7
KEEP OUT!
No. 1010187

Ernie, the eldest dog, leapt up onto his hind legs and pushed the pram along the hard floor of the arena. Inside the pram, Lolly, the youngest puppy, was dressed in a baby's nappy and hat. The crowd bellowed with laughter. Ringmaster Rollo stepped back into the stage light and held the microphone up to his mouth.

'Let's give a big round of applause to the Cassidy Circus Performing Dog show!'

The audience stood up, cheering and hooting, spilling their popcorn and drinks. Heather ran to Ernie and helped him through the curtain and into the rear room. She glanced at the clock, it was 6:58pm. She undid his cape and rushed him over to the holding pen. The other dogs were coming through now, they all were panting, their tongues lolling from between their teeth.

'Water and food, Heather,' Carol instructed, checking the board and looking around for Mr Harlow.

Heather glanced at the clock again, *Bounty should be by Mr Harlow's van by now, waiting*, she thought. If she kept him waiting too long, he would most likely leave, or forget about his performance. Heather snatched the bowl up from the pen and filled it with water. She opened the plastic container near the left wall and lifted the heavy bag of dog food out of it. She struggled to carry it over to the empty bowls. The dogs watched with open mouths, their tongues dripping with saliva. The bag got too heavy, and as she brought it closer to the bowls, the weight became too much and food came pouring out. She didn't have time to clean it up. Plus, the dogs didn't seem to mine having a mountain of food to eat. She tied the end up and threw it back into the container, slamming the lid down hard. She turned to run down the ramp and almost crashed into poor Mr Harlow.

'Careful, Heather... Why the rush?' he said, placing his top hat on his head and pulling his white gloves on.

'Mr Harlow... oh, um, I have to help Bounty get ready for his act,' Heather lied, again.

She didn't feel good about it, in fact she made a mental note to apologise to her father and Mr Harlow after she got his magic back.

'Good luck!' she said, touching Mr Harlow's arm softly.

'Thank you, Heather. I'm going to need it.'

Towards the side of the curtains stood Nancy. She had her arms crossed. She was wearing black stockings with black shoes and a thin hooded shirt. Her eyes looked narrow and stern in the darkness.

'Don't worry, Mr Harlow,' Heather said, glancing at the clock. 'I'm sure you will find your magic soon.' Heather couldn't help but grin.

'Find my magic?' Mr Harlow said, his eyebrows furrowed.

From inside the tent came the sound of the Magnificent Magician's introduction. An orchestral score that was both hypnotic and astral.

'Oh no my dear,' Mr Harlow added, straightening his jacket and stepping up to the curtain where his daughter had been standing only moments ago, 'I believe my magic was taken from me.'

He raised his hands and disappeared through the blanket of white smog coming from the side of the stage. Heather stood watching as the curtains closed around him.

'Taken?' she whispered.

Suddenly, she remembered her pact with Bounty and turned and ran down the ramp, sprinting as fast as she could towards the magician's trailer. It was totally deserted around the caravans. The night air howled like a wolf. A chilly wind coursed around the ground and rustled the blades of grass, leaving a frostbitten mildew. Heather hugged herself for warmth, as she was only wearing her costume. She looked around frantically but couldn't see anyone hanging around. They were all up in the tent, about to watch Mr Harlow perform, even his daughter still wanted to watch him.

Heather started hiding amongst the shadows once she got closer to Larry's trailer in case there was someone still heading towards the tent for the show. She saw Mr Harlow's trailer and suddenly felt a cold shiver shoot up her spine. She looked around and couldn't see anyone.

'Bounty,' she whispered to the dark. There was no reply.

She tried it again, stepping closer to the large tree that was between Larry's caravan and Mr Harlow's.

'Bounty,' she said again, this time it came out like a hiss.

'Heather,' came a voice from the darkness. At the same time a hand clamped down hard on Heather's shoulder and she jumped with fright. Quickly she turned to see Bounty standing beside the tree.

'Don't do that,' she yelped, slapping his arm.

'There's no one around here, Heather. They're all up in the tent.'

'Come on,' she said, rolling her eyes, 'Let's go.'

Together they walked along the dark shadows of night, feeling the strangely cold breeze above them. The trees in the nearby forest shook and rustled like angry creatures. The clouds moved rapidly, covering the moon and making it harder to see. Heather went to the door and tried to turn the handle; it was unlocked.

Of course it is, she thought, *no one locks their doors here. We all know each other.* She paused for a moment.

'What's wrong?' Bounty said, standing behind her, nervousness in his voice.

We're family? So why am I breaking into Mr Harlow's house?

'I'm helping him,' she said aloud.

Bounty looked confused, he shrugged and gave her a much needed push with his claw-hand, fearing they would be caught standing in the doorway of Mr Harlow's caravan. Heather lunged through the door and into the trailer. She stood in the entrance of the trailer and looked over the magicians living quarters. There was an old Indian style rug on the floor, it was grand in design, with delicately woven patterns. To the right was a door, it was shut with a home-made sign drawn in black marker that read *Keep Out!* Obviously that was Nancy's room.

Along the far wall was a large cabinet. It looked to be an antique, the wood grain was deep and entrenched along each surface like wrinkles. The smell coming off it was rich in aromas; it smelled like a dense forest and of freshly hewn timber. Resting along the shelves of the cabinet were glass jars. One looked like it was filled with toe nail clippings, another, sand. Below were wands of all shapes and sizes. There was one that looked identical to a stick found freshly fallen from a tree, it even had a dead leaf still attached to it. The others were painted the traditional colours of Mr Harlow's wand – black in the middle with white tips at each end. Beside the antique cabinet was a hat rack, but instead of hats, a long cloak was draped over it. It looked leather and smelled like it needed a wash badly. Hunched over, and looking like a deflated balloon, were a pair of old boots. They sat at the bottom of the hat rack, almost exactly the same colour as the cloak.

Heather's eyes took in all the detail of the inside, marvelling at the pictures on the walls of Mr Harlow with famous people, newspaper articles and magazine clippings.

The Greatest Magician of them All! one read. *A True Master of Magic!* announced another newspaper headline.

Bounty stepped from behind Heather, his eyes peeling open and his jaw dropping.

'I've never been in here before. Wow, look at that!' Bounty pointed, running over to a stuffed animal on a small set of drawers.

The creature didn't look like anything he or Heather had ever seen in their lives. It looked like a rat, but with grey hair and longer ears, and about ten times bigger. It was fixed into a position of attack, its claws raised and its mouth open, showing a row of deranged teeth. Bounty copied its frozen state, waving his fused fingers in the air. He gnashed his teeth.

'Cut it out,' Heather demanded, wanting to show respect in the magician's quarters, even though they were breaking and entering. 'Look!'

In between piles of papers and books on magic, was the sword box. It lay like a slumbering beast against the back wall, almost camouflaged amongst the other antiquities. Heather went over to it, caressing the ancient wood with her hands. It felt alive, electric even. She stared at the polished silver hinges and door handle. It sparkled, like a blinking star.

'Heather,' Bounty called out from behind her. 'I think someone's coming!'

Heather turned around quickly and listened. There was the faint patter of feet running through the muddy ground outside. Both of the intruders stared wide-eyed at the front door. The footsteps stopped suddenly and Heather noticed she was holding her breath. Bounty started to shake, his eyes darting around the room feverishly. The footsteps started again, trailing off slowly into the night.

'Are they gone?' Bounty said, his clawed hands shaking.

Then came the sound of rattling keys being pulled from a pocket.

'Oh no,' Heather whispered. Her heart leapt into her throat and she suddenly found it hard to breathe.

'What do we do?' Bounty said, running in a circle.

'Hide,' Heather instructed softly.

Bounty ran to the front door, turned, panicked and ran back again. His eyes twitched and looked around, trying desperately to find a hiding place. Heather thought for an instant of standing her ground and confronting the person at the door, telling them it was all a silly idea to help Mr Harlow. She thought of how much trouble she would be in. She ran to the corner of the room, squeezing past piles of books and magazines. She reached for the sword box and opened the door. It was so small inside. Light was shining into the dark abyss through the slits for the swords on opposite walls. Heather slowly climbed in. She curled her legs up and looked over to Bounty, who was running towards the door near the statue of the rat creature. He opened it quickly, watching as Heather pulled the sword box door shut. The front door opened and Nancy stomped in. She walked into the trailer and stopped suddenly in the middle of the room. Heather could see out of one slit. She looked around the room through her curtain of black hair. Suddenly, she started going through a bundle of papers on Mr Harlow's desk. She rifled through them carelessly, tossing them onto the ground. She upturned boxes and old coats laying underneath the desk, clearly looking for something important. After several minutes she stood up and slammed her fist down hard on the desk and swore loudly. She stood for a moment, as if lost in her own thoughts. Heather could feel her body shaking with nerves. If Nancy caught them hiding in their trailer, they would be in a world of trouble.

The magician's daughter went to her bedroom and started throwing clothes around. For a moment Heather thought that Bounty had gone in there, but she would have surely seen him by now.

She waited in the sword box, staring out through the small holes and watched as Nancy picked up shoes and books and tossed them absentmindedly over her shoulder. She slid her old shoes off, they were caked in mud and threw them across the room. They smashed against the wall, almost knocking the strange taxidermy creature from its mantle. There was more shuffling and clothes being thrown.

Heather looked over to the room next to Nancy's, it must have been the one Bounty had gone into. From the layout of the trailer, it had to be Mr Harlow's private quarters. She wondered what he would see in there. Suddenly, Nancy reappeared. She was pulling on rubber boots and swearing. Her clothes were scatted all over the trailer, spilling out of her room like a flood of fabric and shoes. Where her old shoes had hit the wall, was now dripping with mud. She stood up and looked at her mud-boots. She stepped towards the front door, ignoring the mess she had caused trying to look for them and reached for the handle. All of a sudden there was a soft thump from Mr Harlow's quarters. Heather pushed back against the box, her hand covering her mouth which was open in a silent scream. Bounty must have knocked something over. She closed her eyes and prayed that Nancy hadn't heard, but she was wrong.

'Hello?' Nancy said to the room.

Heather felt a cold chill surge through her body.

Nancy stepped gingerly through the room towards the origin of the noise.

'Who's there?' she demanded to know, crossing her arms. 'You better come out...' Then her eyes caught the sword box and she froze.

Heather could see fear in her face. Maybe she had seen her? But how could she? There was a gleam in her eye and she took a step back. Her hand went straight to her ribs and she fingered her scars. She turned quickly and left the trailer, slamming the door behind her. Heather breathed a sigh of relief. As she was about to turn the handle to open the magic box's door, she saw a small silver plaque. It was bolted to the back of the door and was engraved with small circular patterns, in the middle there was something written in cursive writing. It was difficult to read because it was so dark. She leant forward, her sparkly costume reflecting the light like small violet fireworks.

'Hey Presto?' she read.

There was a loud thunder clap that ricocheted around the trailer, rattling the jars on the shelf and the window panes in their sills. A surge of light shone from the box, blinding and bright white. Bounty opened the bedroom door, then covering his ears. He saw the light dissipate back into the box, it shook violently and suddenly stopped.

'Heather! Did you hear that?'

He looked towards the box, it was still shut. There was a faint smell of something burning in the air. Bounty ran over to the magician's box and swung the door open.

'Heather!'

The box was empty.

ADMIT ONE
COME ONE, COME ALL
THE GREATEST PERFORMANCE IN THE WORLD
CHAPTER 8
GYPSY
No. IOIOI987

Mr Harlow stood in the beaming hot lights. His suit itched his skin and his bow tie felt like it was strangling him. The crowd watched in awe as his hand slipped into his top hat.

'And now,' he said, his voice stammering from nerves, 'I will say the magic word and pull a rabbit from my hat.'

The entire audience lent forward, their eyes peeled open with anticipation. All the children stopped crying and ceased throwing things to watch the single figure on stage do the impossible.

'Hey Presto!'

Mr Harlow closed his eyes and felt a deathly chill rise up through his body. His fingertips tingled and the hairs on the nape of his neck stood on end. He opened his eyes and glanced to the side of the stage. He saw his daughter there, staring at him. But it wasn't her that was giving him the peculiar wariness. Nancy sighed loudly and marched away from the side of the stage and disappeared through the curtain. Mr Harlow looked back to the crowd.

He took a deep breath and swallowed. The inside of his mouth was dry and his tongue felt like the sole of a shoe.

'And now...' he said, starting to cough, his throat restricting, 'now I will...'

He felt a pang of dark electricity cramp his stomach and he stumbled forward, almost dropping his hat.

'Boo!' someone called out, followed by another.

Mr Harlow gained his composure and stood upright once again. His hand had hit the bottom of the hat and there was nothing there but lint. His thin fingers searched manically for the rabbit, but it had not appeared. He slid his hand out, staring at his own flesh. He saw his wrinkles and his unkempt nails.

'Say the magic words again!' a child from the crowd screamed out.

'He's not a magician!' someone else hollered.

Mr Harlow stood there for a moment and pondered his empty hat. He chanced a look over to Rollo and saw that he had his head in his hands. The magician placed his top hat back on his head and headed for the exit. He pushed passed Guntha the muscle man.

'Next time Harlow,' he said in his thick accent.

Mr Harlow stopped and looked up at him with tired, worn eyes.

'I don't know if there will be a next time, Guntha.' And with his sullen words, he wandered into the darkness.

***

The thunder clap had made Heather momentarily deaf. She saw a bright, scarlet red bolt of lightning pass her eyes. Her entire body went loose and she fell against the door of the sword box. Her head spun wildly and she shook it from side to side trying to shake the feeling away. From somewhere outside the box she could hear people murmuring and hushing one another. Her first thought was that Nancy had brought the entire circus to her trailer to make sure Bounty and her were busted for breaking in. Heather felt a heavy weight on her chest and suddenly felt the unrelenting feeling of shame.

The door to the sword box suddenly opened and Heather fell out, toppling head over feet and landing on a hard, dusty, wooden floor. Sun glared down at her, she tried to look around, but the sun kept her eyes from focusing. The wood and nails were hot on her skin and she could still hear that thunder clap ringing loudly in her ears.

'Bounty,' she said, 'what happened?'

Her vision swayed and as the shapes around her gathered detail, she could see there were strange people, all dressed in eccentric gowns and robes, mulling around, staring at her. Most of them wore hoods or tunics with thick leather belts. Crude weapons poked out of sleeves and out of coats and vests. One man's belt had chains hanging low to his feet, his eyes were green and he had strange breathing holes under his ears. His skin looked like a sponge and when he knelt down to look at her it appeared to breathe. Another person, a woman, had long bleached white hair that ran down each side of her face which was striped dark orange like a tiger's pelt. Her legs were long and tattooed heavily with maps and insignias.

'Where am I?' Heather said, kicking backwards as the sponge-skinned man reached out to touch her arm.

She felt something hard hit her back and she looked around. There was a sign that was painted with what appeared to be a childish drawing of a magician. Above her it read – *Brim The Dark Mage of Hokus Pokus.*

'Hey!' said a squeaky voice that sounded like two bricks being rammed together. 'Where did you come from? That wasn't supposed to happen.'

Heather noticed the man from the badly drawn diagram, it was Brim. A hideous hat hung over his eyes and touched the tip of his nose, it looked like it had been woven from a dead animal carcass. He had several long feathers sticking out from the rope band, but they were broken and had lost all their colour. His chin was prickled with long, drain-water grey whiskers. His filthy fingers wrapped themselves around Heather's arm and he wrenched her to her feet. He had an abundance of rings on each finger. A gold ring with ruby red gems gleamed in the harsh sunlight.

'Who,' he shouted, 'are you?'

Heather stood up, her legs felt rickety and she looked out to the crowd before her. There was a small gathering of people, including a strange looking dog that had the tail of a slug, but its body was covered completely in dark, purple fur.

Brim ran behind Heather and started shuffling and banging loudly. Heather spun around and saw a wooden box, much like the sword box she had gotten into in Mr Harlow's caravan. Brim ran his fingers along the seam of the box. It was made haphazardly with twisted and bent nails poking out from each plank of wood. He stood to attention when he noticed the crowd had slowly, but surely, started to clap.

'Ah ha!' he said with much delight. 'See, I can do magic!' When he opened his mouth to smile Heather could see rows upon rows of teeth. Most were missing, or rotten.

The man with the green eyes flipped a small silver coin towards Brim who caught it in a flash.

'Thank ya, kind sir!' Brim replied with a bow.

Heather stumbled off stage, her mind reeling with confusion.

'Hey,' Brim called to her, the colourless feathers in his hat streaming backwards as he ran to her. 'Don't go anywhere, you're now my main attraction.'

Heather turned and ran. A tall woman with a snake's head hissed at her and Heather screamed, ducking away and running through the throng of nightmarish creatures. She appeared to be in some morbid, day time bazaar full of kooky and strange stalls. All the market vendors were crammed together, selling all manner of eccentric and foreign delights.

To her right a man sat behind a long table that held large jars of strange fish. The water was murky and resting on the bottom were large slabs of mud. All the fish had one eye and long, curled fins. Their scales were spotted blue and black and perched just above their top lip was a long proboscis. Heather wanted to stop and stare at the fish, but she had to get away from Brim, the mad magician.

She ran down a long alleyway and leaned against a wall to catch her breath.

'Where am I?' she asked herself, looking down each end of the filthy alley.

Wandering past the lane way were a mix of half animal, half humanoid creatures. Their clothes were strange and the languages they spoke where none that Heather had ever heard in her life. Her heart was pumping faster and she could feel tears starting to well up in her eyes.

That sword box, she thought, moving closer to the other end of the alleyway, *it had something to do with bringing me here.*

'There she is!' yelled a snarling voice from behind her. Heather turned to see Brim pointing at her. He was surrounded by large men, one had an open eye on his chest that blinked.

Heather ran as fast as she could, straight into the bustling crowd of the markets. She bumped shoulders with tall, lizard-like beings who mumbled words in different languages under their breaths. A slim woman with rows upon rows of necklaces made of bone spat down at her feet and pulled her vest open to show a long sword tucked in her belt. Heather could feel the woman's cold, hard stare and stepped quickly away.

Brim and his men were trying to fight their way through the crowd and Heather could hear them making a loud ruckus amongst the bazaar. She only had one option to get away, and that was to hide amongst the flea market goers, as she was smaller and on her own. She ducked her head down and moved quickly, trying not to walk into anyone. Her sparkling circus suit stood out amongst the earthy colours of the local garb. She popped her head up and looked around the swarm of people, desperately trying to find a way out of the foot traffic. Running along the rear of the stalls was a crude brick wall. It ran several hundred feet until it met a series of buildings. This was where the market place ended.

Heather moved quickly, dodging the people and the strange animals, she knew if she reached the wall she might be able to stay out of sight and get out of the throng and away from Brim.

She reached a stall that was selling what appeared to be small skulls of animals. The skulls where of all shapes and sizes and unlike any animal Heather had ever seen in a zoo. They had been stripped clean and shone brilliantly in the beaming sun. The man behind the stall, a rather rotund man with a long blonde beard, was fast asleep. He snored like a bad car engine and made gurgling noises. His chest lifted and fell with every struggled breath. Heather ducked down, low to his table and moved along silently until she was at the back of his stall and pressed against the back wall. She suddenly heard shouting and commotion and chanced a look through the crowd. She could see Brim barking mad orders at his accomplices. All of a sudden, they all took off running in separate directions, swords in hand. Heather waited to make sure they were out of sight before moving silently along the wall.

The smells that wafted through the market were both strange and tempting. She could smell sour meat. There was the aroma of chicken, grilling on an open flame and spices of all kind and many other bizarre aromas she had never smelt before. She walked quickly, feeling her stomach rumble. She got to a curve in the wall where there were large fissures running along the surface. In places, bricks were missing and she could feel fresh breeze passing through.

'Hey!' hollered a voice from near her.

The store holder she was currently hiding behind had spotted her. He pushed his curtain aside with long, tentacle arms. His eyes scanned the small girl.

'She's in here,' he called out.

From in front of the store Heather could see Brim's men start to head towards her. She went to run but tripped on a fallen brick and landed against the wall. She suddenly felt it give way and fell through a small hole. Bricks and mortar showered down over her head as she fell, tumbling down a steep embankment. She hit her head and felt the instant swelling as she rolled and tumbled down further. She finally got to the bottom and lay on long, soft grass and stared up at the sky. Her vision was blurry and she felt the world slowly drift away from her.

The man with the tentacle arms stared through the hole in the wall. He gnashed his teeth and made clicking noises with his tongue.

'She's dead. Go tell Brim.'

Another man behind him took off running. Within seconds Brim was pushing the crowd away from the hole. He took his hat off his head and revealed a line of small bumps, each one looked like a soft shell of flesh and veins. He lent down, carefully holding onto the side of the brickwork and looked at the girl lying unconscious. He exhaled loudly and placed his hat back on his head.

'The knoll worms can feast on her flesh,' he said, slowly fading back into the crowded flea market.

COME ONE, COME ALL
THE GREATEST PERFORMANCE IN THE WORLD
ADMIT ONE
CHAPTER 9
AM I DREAMING?
No. 1010101987

Bounty stared into the empty box. It was impossible, he thought, Heather had just been in there. Then the flash of light and the thunder clap. Now there was a strange smell. He shut the magic box's door, counted to five and reopened it. Nothing but the empty, blankness of treated wood and the aroma of hundreds of candles burning at full flame. He looked around the room. All the magical items appeared to glow for a second. Bounty felt as if all the eyes in the surrounding picture frames were staring at him, following his every movement. A ghastly shiver ran through his arms and up to the nape of his neck. He felt his bladder loosen, but held it in.

'Heather?' he said nervously. 'This isn't funny.'

There was silence. The burning smell lingered in the air, filling his lungs and making him want to vomit. He ran to the door, swinging it open and leaping onto the long, wet grass. He gagged and coughed, looking over his shoulder as the door to Mr Harlow's caravan slammed shut behind him, on its own. He stood bolt upright, forgetting he was struggling for breath, and ran. He didn't know where his legs were taking him, but they were headed in the direction of the tent, and away from the trailer.

Sweat broke out all over; on his flesh-claws, and soaking his collar and armpits. He sprinted up the ramp to the tent entrance, looking around furiously. Streaks of smoke billowed through the entrance curtains, a thin shaft of light shone onto the ground like the blade of a dagger. Bounty stood, his arms outreached, his mind a mash of panic and confusion. Then, towards the rear of the tent, lingering in the darkness, he saw Nancy. Without hesitation, he ran to her, clutched her arm with his fused hand, and pulled her away from the tent.

'Bounty, what are you doing? Let go of me!'

Nancy yanked her arm away, before he could drag her down onto the grass.

'It's Heather! Come quick!' he said, panting.

The inside of the circus tent was thick with humidity, he felt it strangle him around his neck and the warmth made his skin dry and itchy.

'I don't care what Heather is doing, I'm trying to watch my father fail yet again.' She scorned him with a look you would give a tiny ant trying to carry something far too big.

'No, no!' Bounty said, frantic and whipping his head back and forth from the tent to Nancy's trailer. 'It's serious. Quickly!'

Nancy looked at the tent. She couldn't hear the crowd cheer or gasp. There was no hooting or applauding, just as it had been in every magic show for the last year.

'Fine,' Nancy finally said. 'Show me what all this hollering is about. I don't really care, but any excuse to be away from here.'

Bounty fled down the ramp again and onto the grass. It was wet and felt slippery under his feet. The night air was crisp and fresh, and he could smell the pine trees and rich soil lingering in the wind. Nancy was walking behind him, arms crossed, with her eyes narrowed. Her hair dangled over her face in long shards, disguising her disgruntled look.

'You brought me to my own home? Well done Bounty, you idiot. I'm going back.'

'No, wait,' Bounty reached for the front door and pulled it open.

'Hey! Don't go in our house – '

Her sentence finished short as the smell wafted out the front door and across her face. A familiar stench that made her take a step back. Her eyes peeled open and her heart suddenly started to beat faster. She could feel the tips of her fingers go numb and the bones in her legs turned to jelly.

'What did you do?' she said, grabbing Bounty by his shoulders and shaking him wildly.

'I didn't do nothing! We were... we were....'

Nancy pushed past him and went inside the trailer. There was a strange tone emanating from within. A dark, electric atmosphere that made her blood feel conductive. She scanned the room between her veil of hair and caught sight of the open sword box.

'What were you trying to do, Bounty?' she said. This time her voice was monotone and calm.

'I... I... I...' he tried to talk, but he was lost for words.

Nancy looked at him with wide-eyed disbelief.

'Tell me, Bounty,' she said. 'Tell me everything.'

'She disappeared, Nancy! Heather disappeared!'

***

There was a loud *splash!* and Heather felt instantly wet. For a moment she thought she had fallen into water, but couldn't remember where she was. She woke suddenly, thrashing her feet and arms around, feeling the soft ground under her. The back of her head throbbed with pain. The long, fluorescent green grass poked up through her fingers and gently brushed her feet and knees. She was surrounded by the flora, its softness reminding her of her bed as a child.

'Bounty!' she called out. 'What happened?'

Heather tried to open her eyes but the sun was too bright. She closed them again and rubbed her eyes with her fingers.

'Another one!' someone snarled.

Heather opened her eyes, she could see the silhouette of a figure in front of her. The haziness around the figure started to become more detailed as her eyes adjusted to the sun's glare. She pushed herself up, ready to run and saw the stranger had a weapon pointed at her.

'Who are you?' Heather screamed. 'What do you want with me?'

'Get to your feet, thief!' the stranger barked, tossing the empty bucket over his shoulder.

Heather watched as several men climbed off a huge barge and wobbled towards her. They walked as if they couldn't move their knees. Their legs were wide apart and their gait seemed restricted by the shape of their bones and muscle. Heather looked up the man's body that had thrown the water over her. He was hairy, like a wolf, but with slender arms that were adorned with trinkets and strange beaded bracelets. His eyes were as black as pearls found in the deepest oceans, his nose flared and dotted with blackheads. He held a long spear with several feathers wrapped around the handle in red twine. He jabbed the point forward and it came within inches of Heather's eyes.

'Hey!' she bellowed, getting to her feet. 'Stop pointing that thing at me!'

'I am a Guardian of the Outskirts and you have trespassed on our property. You are breaking the law.' His fangs dripped with saliva and his eyes gleamed a deep charcoal.

The creature looked at her. His eyes scanned her up and down, as if he was trying to figure out what race she belonged to. Her circus suit had torn when she fell down the rocky hill and was now covered in dirt and ripped under both arms.

'Your property?' Heather said, touching the wound on the back of her head again.

She winced as her fingers rode over a bump on her head. It was swollen and sore. She pulled her hand away and looked at her fingers. There were small droplets of blood. She glanced past the guardian and saw the carriage they had obviously arrived on. It was like a prop from an old Western movie. It had large wheels that were all connected by a thick leather belt, the walls of the vehicle looked like hard tar, set by the sun and cracked to form scales. The ropes were all green and hung from the barge like vines.

There were other guardians standing by the carriage. Their faces all cork-screwed, with big upturned noses. One of the pig-men guardians on board the vessel was drinking from a metal canister while watching the proceedings, the others were all staring up at the wall behind her and looking anxious.

'Where am I?' Heather said, untangling twigs and small pebbles from her hair. She looked around at the surrounding trees and shrubbery. The terrain was sprinkled with undergrowth and long mounds of grass and weeds. Large boulders and stones were scattered across the fields and were covered in moss. Tucked away in the crevasses were the homes of small animals. She could hear the ruckus of the market far behind her, but could no longer smell the tempting aromas.

'Behind you is Hokus Pokus, to the east is Hey Presto! These lands belong to the Chamber of Magicians who hire us to protect it. You have no right on this land.'

Hey Presto? Heather thought. *That's what I had read on the back of the sword box door right before...* Her thought trailed off.

Suddenly, the skies above rumbled with an ear piercing screech. The guardians all looked up, their weapons drawn and shaking madly. Heather didn't know what was going on and stepped back, away from the guard nearest her, while he was distracted. Another noise pierced the veil of clouds and this time it was blood curdling. It was the sound of rusted metal being constantly unhinged and scraping together. The guards dropped their weapons and covered their ears as a large bat-creature emerged from the blackening clouds.

'The assassin!' a guard screamed as he caught sight of the winged beast.

Heather felt a cold shiver run up her spine and into her arms as the beast flew by with crooked and jerky motions.

'Guards!' one of them yelled. 'Stand by and protect!'

With great hesitation, they all rushed to pick their weapons up. One had barely drawn his jagged blade from its sheath when the cloud-bound creature landed next to him. The strange assassin swiped its long, haphazard wings and took the guardian's head clean off. Its neck spurted blood as it fell to the ground in a lifeless heap. The wings instantly fell to the creature's side, folding along its body with mechanical motion. Heather had never seen anything move that quickly in her life.

The creature rolled onto the ground, its wings a blur of leather fabric and clanking armour. A guard threw its spear at the bat and it caught it with ease, snapping it in half and leaping from the ground. It landed on the guard's shoulders and rammed the spear end into its throat. The guard gurgled on its own blood and fell backwards.

Heather's heart raced and her brain told her feet to run, run as fast as they could go, but her legs wouldn't move. She was frozen with utter terror. She watched as the bizarre, winged assassin bit into the dead pig-man's neck and started to drink its blood. It's head suddenly popped up and she saw bright red liquid gush from its mouth. It didn't appear to have a neck. Its small head was sitting on hunched shoulders, burnt by fire and wrapped in ancient, soiled cloth.

Two guards ran towards it. The bat kicked one, leaping again and screeching in a high-pitched squeal. It echoed off the wall of Hokus Pokus and faded away in to the grassy dunes. The beast moved so fast it left a shudder of black movement in its wake. The guard speared his knife towards it, but by the time it got to its target, the bat was gone. It stood behind him, grinning its morbid smile. It placed its hands on each side of the guard's head and snapped it to the side. The sound of its neck breaking woke Heather out of her frozen state of fear. She turned and bolted. Her flat, black shoes she used on stage were not built for the rocky landscape. Her feet fumbled and she slipped, grabbing onto the rock next to her. Her ankle throbbed with immense pain, but she kept moving. Behind her she could hear the deafening screams as the guards were killed, one by one.

The wall of Hokus Pokus slowly faded into the background as Heather sprinted for her life, away from the bloodshed. She could hear her heartbeat in her ears and her head was spinning wildly. She stopped to catch her breath and crouched down beside a boulder. Her slip-on shoes had started to shred from the jagged and misshapen rocks. The stones were cold to touch as she leaned to the side to see if the assassin was following her. She couldn't hear or see anything. She looked around and saw a line of dense trees not too far away. She looked back and saw the winged bat-creature hobbling along the ground, heading straight towards her. She spun around and ducked out of view. She could feel the paralysing horror starting to grip her once again. She looked to the forest, it was her only hope. She ran quickly, moving between the massive stones, keeping low and out of sight.

The assassin looked over the dunes that separated the two cities.

'Where are you, little one?' it said. It's voice syrupy and malevolent.

It reached into its leather vest that was adorned with rusted cogs and buckles and pulled out a small glowing red orb. The twisted creature let the ball drop to the ground and it landed with a heavy thud. Within seconds the ball levitated off the ground and hovered several feet above the luscious grass. The winged assassin eyed it with venomous interest, its tongue licking its thin, pursed lips. The ball started to glow a burning red. It shook wildly, as if it was about to explode. Then it raised higher. The leather bound killer watching it the whole time with bated breath. The sphere moved suddenly, fast and without sound. The assassin followed it, his legs creaking and moaning on bent springs and wire.

The sphere stopped after several feet and the creature paused under it.

'Show me where it went, my darling... show me,' he whispered.

The blood-red orb vibrated high above its master and started to lose all of its colour. Within a blink of an eye, it had changed to cobalt blue and was spinning faster and faster. With a gush of blue fire, a ghostly hand emerged from the ball and pointed to the forest. Then, it dropped from the sky and the assassin caught it without looking, tucking back into his coat.

***

The grass leading up to the forest was brown, and as Heather got closer she noticed some of the leaves on the trees were black. The branches were twisted and charcoal, but she couldn't smell fire. Without looking back, in fear of the assassin, she entered the woodland.

It was dark and dense. The trees around her were massive and towering higher than any building she had ever seen. Her commotion had startled the animals and they took to the air and scurried for their burrows. Huge roots intertwined through the ground like curling telephone cords. Heather climbed and scurried over the roots, moving as fast as she could. Several large, black birds squawked loudly at her as she ran under them; it left a ringing in her ears. She glanced up and saw they had four wings each, a long gnarled beak with sunken eye-sockets. Their beaks were dripping red liquid, and it hit the leaves below them it hissed violently and turned them to ash. She shrieked and suddenly tripped on an exposed root. Her hands cart-wheeled in the air, trying to find anything to stop her falling, but it was to no avail. She tumbled onto the soft, leafy ground, falling quickly down a slope. Rocks and broken tree branches rushed passed her as she slid faster and faster, cutting her costume and skin as she slid helplessly down a ravine. She couldn't help but scream. A line of stones was approaching her fast. She tried desperately to clutch anything to stop her descent. She snatched a vine, but it broke in half from her speed and weight. She hit the stones and launched into the air. The sudden drop made her stomach lurch and she felt weightless, her body finally free of the razor sharp rocks and forest debris.

The wind was kicked from her lungs as she hit the hard bottom of the ravine. A puff of dust went in to the air. It was hard packed sand, hot and exposed to the skies. She gasped loudly, sitting up. All her bones and muscles ached and throbbed. Her hands went to her mouth, trying desperately to get air back down her throat. Then it came. Her lungs filled again and she fell backwards, dizzy into a pile of rotten sticks and fallen chunks of dirt. She lay there, her head a foggy mess, trying to decipher what had just happened. If she had fallen two metres to her left, she would have landed on the pile of jagged rocks. She wiped her elbows free of sand and looked down at her costume. It was torn at the knees, elbows and around the feet. Her small slip on shoes where nothing more than shredded cloth.

After a minute, she got to her feet. She could smell water, sweet and tempting.

'Where am I?' she said looking up at the colossal canyon walls.

The only answer that came back to her was her own echo. Through the bushes and scrub where she had just slid and fallen, came an unearthly canter. Heather stared upwards, hearing the sounds of soft footsteps mingled with the gentle stroking of what sounded like a paintbrush against bark. She didn't have time to run again, or the energy. She hobbled to the canyon wall and lay in a deep crevasse. Quickly, she covered her body in the stinking wood and leaves that had fallen around the base of the canyon. She noticed her legs were shaking in fear that the winged assassin may have found her again. She held her breath and watched. The bushes were parted by a demented hand. Long fingers wiggled through ripped gloves as they pierced the plants. The fingernails on each finger were long and curved. The assassin strode out, a look of distaste on its face.

'I won't hurt you,' its voice said, scratchy and booming down into the canyon. 'If it wasn't for me, you would be in slavery camp right now with the rest of the gypsies.'

Heather had to stop herself from bursting into tears, as the very sight of the killer filled her with uncontrollable horror. She held her breath as she saw the creature climb down the ravine walls. The devilish assassin moved in awkward silence. Its leathery wings rubbed against the rocks and she now finally knew the source of the gentle brushing coming through the woods only moments ago. That eerie, spine tingling sound that made her flesh crawl and her throat clench.

The strange creature dropped the last few metres and soared gently to the floor of the gorge. It slinked close to the ground, its back hunched and its fake wings laying outwards. Its wingspan must have been several metres wide, from what Heather could see from her hiding place. It sniffed the ground again. Heather had noticed everything had gone dead quiet.

'I know you're here,' it said. 'I can smell you.'

The murky cloud had now passed over the canyon, casting everything in stormy darkness. Heather felt small creatures start to crawl up her arm and in through her spandex leggings. She closed her eyes and prayed not to scream or move. A thunder crack overhead made the creature leap into the air. The bolt from the sky hit an old, dead tree growing from the side of the ravine and it burst into fire. Flames dripped off its twisted appendages like liquid.

'Yes... I'm coming!' the creature called. He stood up straight, his body was covered in wraps of black cloth with metal rings and buckles intricately placed to help pulley his wings into position. He reached into his cloak and pulled out the sphere once again. He held it high and dropped it. It fell into the sand with a thud and didn't move. He waited, staring at the ball with contempt. Slowly he picked it up and placed it back in his tourniquet armour.

'I am Clat Rakshaw. And if I were you I would stay away from the Gates of Hey Presto! It is a dangerous place, especially those seeking... magic.'

It kicked off the sandy ground and into the sky, leaving a small cloud of sand in its wake. It soared past the flaming tree into the dark clouds above. Heather was still frozen with fear. *Magic?* she thought. *Maybe it knows about Mr Harlow's magic?*

Slowly she peeled the branches off her and got to her feet. She wiped the bugs and ants off her outfit and looked around. There was only two ways out, the left and the right. The left was dark and narrow, with no foliage or life of any sort. The right appeared to spread outwards and back into the forest. She thought she would have to get out of the ravine and find out where she was and get home before her father knew she was missing. *What if they have Mr Harlow's magic here?* she thought to herself. *Maybe I can get it back?*

As she walked to the right of the canyon the dark cloud overhead slowly edged away. Its curled, misty fingers retracted as if something from far away called it back. Its master had spoken.

***

Heather had wandered aimlessly through the jungle of brimstone trees, trying desperately to make sense of the predicament she had found herself in. Her feet started to hurt from the uneven ground. The rocks were coming through the soles of her shoes and giving her small bruises on the balls of her feet. A sour smell hung in the air and she found herself following it. Soon she was teetering on the edge of the forest, looking through a line of trees. She could see a road. It was paved with shaped stones and looked beaten and neglected by age and weather.

She stepped through the curtain of vines and debris that hung from the trees and stepped gingerly onto the paved trail. It was wide enough for a car, but extremely wonky, with sharp corners and an uneven surface. To her left she noticed a wooden plank nailed to a tree. It had two arrows, one pointing up the path, it read *Hey Presto!* The other arrow pointed back down the path to *Ta-Dah*. She remembered the sign on the back of the door when she had climbed into the sword box, Hey Presto! The strange guard that had been killed in front of her also had talked about it.

Hey Presto! might get me back home, she thought to herself, pulling a twig from her hair.

She didn't consider her options too long, as the day was getting to an end and the sun had begun its descent. She headed up the path, taking note of the strange sky above her, the reams of golden brown and tangerine lining the mountains far away. The clouds looked like rolling rapids she had once seen when they toured near a mountain range several years ago. The white tumbling clouds kept a steady speed, as if rushing away from the sun.

After several hours of tiresome walking, Heather decided to rest on a large boulder that was beside the paved road. She caught her breath as she tried to peel the now dry mud off her suit. Carol was going to be angry, the costume had tears in it everywhere; it may as well be thrown out. Suddenly, from down the path where she had just walked, came a soft humming. Heather stood up and looked down the cobbled road. A breeze rustled the tree tops. The humming continued as she watched loose leaves fall to the path like rusted sheets of paper. The soft murmuring steadily became louder. She thought it could be the guards or the assassin – Clat Rakshaw – who'd tried to kill her. She held her breath, waiting for her mind to tell her to either run and hide, or stand her ground.

The humming grew to a crescendo. From between the corridor of trees lining the path, Heather could hear a hard clacking. She dove behind the boulder as the makers of the noise came around a bend in the path. She crouched down low and peered around the side. Coming up from the winding path through the forest were a troop of bizarre humanoids. Heather had never seen anything quite like it before. Some of their outfits looked like they had come from an ancient circus. She stared, trying not to make a noise or move.

Marching up the ridge came the line of warriors, all of them walking on wooden stilts. The click-clacking became louder, as did the humming. Their boots were tied to their stilts using dark green rope. They were wrapped around and around until there was no sign of the boot left. The skin on their legs was blackened and bubbled from what looked like burns and unhealed blisters. Around their waists was a belt, thick with utility pockets and gadgets. Small lights flashed around their waists in succession, red and green, and then orange. Their hands held more elongated, wooden stilts, also wrapped in emerald green twine and ropes. The bodies of the troops were hunched over, as if their spines were made of jelly. Their heads were small, like shrunken heads in a museum. Where their eyes should be were small, dark drill holes. The blackness tunnelling through those holes made goose bumps shoot up Heather's arms. They appeared to have no neck and their mouths were sewn shut. Through their bloated, purple lips they hummed a wicked symphony. Heather was deafened as the stilts pounded the pavement, getting louder and louder as they approached. Their awkward, spidery walk gave her fearsome chills.

She watched as they climbed the peak of the road and halted, as if in some sort of telepathic understanding. One of the stilted creatures broke from the pack, clacking its long arm stilts against the uneven cobblestones. Heather could see them in their full view. Their arms were long, longer than any appendage on their eerie, gothic looking bodies. They walked on all fours in a gruesome tangle of rope and electronics. The sight was utterly horrifying, these things were not human nor animal, but they walked like a quadruped.

The creature sniffed the air, even though Heather could not see any nose holes. A thick pink tongue emerged from between its sickening lips and licked the string that was keeping its mouth shut. It let out a high pitched squeal that reverberated through the surrounding forest. Heather could feel the boulder shake gently. Suddenly, the morbid spider-creatures all reared back on their hind stilts and shook their heads wildly, as if startled. With limbs flailing and stomping, they started to run. It was a morbid gallop. Their movements staggered and jerky. The wooden poles they used to extend their arms and legs crunched against the hard stone, sending splinters and chips of wood flying.

Heather ducked down lower, afraid that they might have smelt her. She watched as the bezerker group bolted like a pack of wolves that had been startled. From behind her an arm emerged from the shadows of the forest, Heather was oblivious to the green skinned fingers heading for her mouth. She watched as the spider-creatures turned suddenly and hurled their putrid bodies towards her hiding place. Their drill hole eyes gleaming wildly, their tongues trying to push through the mesh barricade of their mouths. The hand wrapped around Heather's mouth and stopped her from screaming. She felt a hard tug and she was reefed backwards at a great speed and into the dark shadows of the forest. Whoever was holding her was extremely strong. It held her in an embrace, totally covered in darkness. Heather had tried to scream, but the hand held her mouth clamped shut. Another hand stroked her hair.

'Sshhh,' said a deep voice, calm and soothing.

Heather had a strange feeling that whatever had grabbed her was not going to hurt her. She watched through the trees and shrubs as the spider-creatures rushed to where she had been crouching only seconds before. The leader that had emerged from the pack stood on the rock and hummed again, deep and harrowing, as if the noise originated from its intestines. The others gathered around their leader and shook their heads, pounding the ground with their timber hooves. Heather froze in fear, seeing them that close had immobilised her legs. Her eyes were wide open and she had started to cry. Without warning the creatures backed away, their empty eyes looking into the forest, but past where her and her rescuer were standing. The troop merged back into their formation, the same as when Heather had seen them coming up the road. They hummed and whistled and stomped their rotten timber extensions and headed towards Hey Presto!

'You are lucky,' came the voice of the person holding her.

Heather pulled herself away, noticing the grip was gone. She spun around quickly and saw a man in loose fitting animal hide. He had long, pointed ears and blue tattoos running up both arms, all the way up his neck and onto his face. His skin was lime green and he crouched on long legs.

'You... you...' Heather struggled for words.

'I saved you, yes. They are the malevolent creation of an evil man. They are called The Meniphesto Incantana. Extremely dangerous... they would have killed you if I hadn't saved you.' The man had a long jaw line, squared off at the chin; his eyes gleamed as he looked down at the small girl.

'This can't be... I mean, I'm not... is this...' Heather's mind spun like a coin in a tumble dryer. She felt light headed and she started to sway. The green-skinned man lunged forward, but for Heather, everything went black, and she fell into unconscious. The man slid her over his shoulder. He could feel her gently breathing. At full height he was over two metres tall, muscular and moved with a subtle grace. He walked to the forest edge and looked up the path, watching the Incantana's clonk their stilts until they were far out of view.

He looked right and crossed the path to the other side where he disappeared through the thicket.

ADMIT ONE
COME ONE, COME ALL
THE GREATEST PERFORMANCE IN THE WORLD
CHAPTER 10
YOU'RE A FOOL
No. 10101987

Heather's eyes blinked open for a second and she shut them again. She could hear voices all around her, mumblings and shouting. She heard the crackle of what could only be a fire and her right side felt warm. When she tried to move she felt something heavy on her body.

'...how do you know, Kiel? She could be one of them?'

'I saw her run from the guards near Hokus Pokus. She only escaped because of Clat Rakshaw.'

'Clat Rakshaw?' someone said, as if spitting dirt from their mouth.

Heather opened one eye and could see only shadowy movement. A fiery red light crossed the woodland around her, sending long shadows of the talkers into the forest.

'Clat Rakshaw's death was nothing more than a rumour then!'

Somebody moved with great speed, toppling over a canister filled with liquid. It splashed on the fire and ignited into a shower of sparks that floated upwards to the sky. The embers drifted in the breeze, as if adding new stars to the night sky.

'Be careful, Soma Rowmoon,' an elderly voice whispered.

Heather shut her eye again. *I hope they don't try and kill me, like the others,* she thought.

'We know you're awake. You can sit up and have some food if you like?'

Heather didn't want to open her eyes, especially if she was still in this strange, dangerous place. Through the forest there came the alarming noise of snapping branches and everyone went dead quiet. The fire was extinguished immediately.

'Hush,' someone whispered by Heather's ear, she recognised the voice as the man that had pulled her away from the Meniphesto Incantana.

'A beast?'

'Shut up, Ollsop,' came a hiss.

Through the thick foliage came more snapping. Around Heather, people moved briskly. She could hear them lifting things from forest floor and slamming them into hard wood. A hand touched Heather's shoulder.

'There will be time for rest later, but for now you must follow me.'

Heather sat up and her head did another somersault. She felt woozy again, but got to her feet with the help of a young woman. Heather looked at her and noticed she had light purple skin, freckled with small yellow dots. Instead of a nose, there were two breathing holes like those of a snake. Her fingers were long and she clasped a bright silver blade. Her body was wrapped in dark rags, treated with oils that made them smell like freshly dug earth. Her hair was chocolate and caramel in colour, and flowed freely down her back. Her bright yellow eyes looked at Heather intensely.

'I am Soma. You must stay dead quiet and follow me.' She clutched her upper arm and pulled her through the dark.

Heather couldn't see much as the fire had been put out and nothing but small glowing coals were left smoking. A lantern slowly burned to life a short way in front of them and Heather could make out many wagons with strange, domed roofs. In the glimmering darkness she could see the wagons were painted, but could not see what the paintings were, or said.

'Quickly, get in. Crouch down and be quiet.'

Heather did as she was told and climbed into the carriage. The wood was soft to touch; unlike anything she had felt before. She could feel the presence of others in the wagon, but it was so dark she couldn't see. The noises came from her right and left, also above. She guessed there were at least two levels to this arcane wagon, if not three.

'Kiel,' Soma shouted near the rear door she was trying to pull shut. 'It's to the south... the smell is not of a walker.'

The person that had pulled her into the jungle and saved her from the Incantana was crouching down by a large tree; he had his fingers in the dirt and was rubbing it between his thumb and forefinger. He stood up, reacting to Soma's comment. He gripped a long spear and bolted off into the jungle, his long feet skimming across the ground as if he was running on water. They did not make a sound. His body turned to a blur of shadow and he was gone, leaving nothing but darkness and silence in his wake.

'Where are you from?' came a small voice, similar to that of a child.

Heather turned, pulling a woolly blanket over her body.

'A small town called – '

'Shush, creature,' said another voice from the dark. Two red eyes glowed from the front of the carriage.

Heather sunk down to lower herself against the floor. There was silence. For several seconds Heather thought she was the only one left in the jungle, as she could not hear breathing or murmuring of any kind. Then, a gut-wrenching howl echoed through the air. It cut through the cool breeze and rumbled the age-old tree trunks. The scream was cut short with a gurgling, followed by a loud slumping noise, like a sack of potatoes hitting muddy ground.

'Mama?'

'Hush...'

Heather closed her eyes and wished that when she opened them she would be back in Mr Harlow's trailer, hiding in the box. But when she did open them, she could see the glowing red eyes again. They were staring right at her. Suddenly, from the rear of the carriage a tall shadow appeared swinging a lamp. The light glowed dully, illuminating odd objects and wooden chests around her. Brass and silver buckles gleamed in the pale lamplight.

'It was just an animal that had lost its way. It is gone now. It's safe.'

Through the darkness came a hand, green with long, yellow fingernails. It took Heather's hand and guided her down from the wagon. The others piled out, still wrapped in blankets and rags. The darkness was suddenly filled with noise again, the clacking of wood and then the splash of something that smelled very close to car fuel. The blackness sulked away as the fire began to blaze again. All the people around her emerged from the trees and from under logs and behind wagons and carts. Now Heather could see there were several carriages, all arranged in a semi-circle around the fire. People everywhere looked at her in curious amazement. A hand landed on Heather's shoulder and it made her jump.

'I'm sorry,' Kiel spoke, his words calm and deep. 'They thought it was the Incantana's. They were scared.'

Heather looked at the tall man in front of her and had never seen anything like him before.

'I... we, saw them today. They looked horrible and disgusting,' Heather said, feeling comfortable talking to the man that had saved her life only hours earlier. 'I'm not from here,' she said, with sadness clearly evident in her voice. 'I've somehow been teleported away from my family and landed in this strange world.'

'What's your name child?'

'Heather,' she said, her eyes looking away, as if the very words softened her emotions and made her think of home.

'Come, Heather,' Kiel said, his chiselled features catching the soft light from the lantern. He waved to a quiet corner of twisted tree roots, away from the throng of people. 'Let's sit away from the rest and talk quietly, they do not need to hear.'

Heather sat and studied the trees around her, up close they were carved with small spirals, etched up the trunk and along every branch. The leaves were heavier than any she had ever touched and the colour changed when the clouds covered the sky.

'Where are you from?' Kiel asked.

'I doubt it's anywhere near here. It's called Earth, and I need to get back before my father notices I'm gone.'

'Earth? I've never heard of such a place.' Kiel's shoulders were broad and when he sat, his legs bent up high, like he was perching on a twig. 'I'm afraid there isn't anywhere here called Earth. But this is a place of magic and wonder, Heather. Anything can happen here, and sometimes... it does. You wouldn't be the first to come here unexpectedly. When magic crosses paths,' Kiel pushed his slender fingers together to form a pyramid, 'innocent people can sometimes get in the way.'

'So you mean I may have been caught in some sort of magical crossfire, and ended up here?'

Kiel's eyes reflected the far away fire, his pupils danced and his face looked stern.

'It's a possibility, Heather. Or maybe, you were just meant to be here.'

There was silence for several seconds as Heather contemplated the world around her.

'We are travelling to Hey Presto! for a performance,' Kiel said, his voice heavy in the darkness. 'There are people there that may be able to help you.'

Those words again, Heather thought. *If they got me here surely they can get me home.*

Kiel looked down. 'I saw you in the field when I had gone scouting. When we move across the land, it's important to know what lies ahead. You're very lucky you had escaped. If those guards had taken you in, you would end up in a dungeon of Ta-Dah without any food or water.'

'That strange creature, Clat Rakshaw, killed them. Like they were nothing.'

Kiel looked at her. 'He is a head hunter for an evil magician. If he had caught you, there would be no telling what he would have done.'

Heather stared at Kiel with wide eyes. The green giant picked up a long twig from the ground and cleared the forest floor around his feet.

'Here... I will explain this world in which you have found yourself in.'

Heather watched as Kiel drew a large circle with the twig. He then ran the stick straight down the middle, dividing it into two halves.

'This side,' he spoke, as the flames reflected gently across his face, 'is Abara. This side is peaceful, with lots of different creatures all living in harmony. It is a place of brilliance, of bright skies and food plantations. It is a thriving metropolis of good-will with an abundance of entertainment... that is where we are all from. But that isn't to say we haven't had our fair share of trouble and mercenaries, but all in all, we try to live in peace. And this side,' he said, pointing his stick to the other side of the circle, 'is Cadabra.'

The flames licked into the air, gnashing their fiery teeth and singeing the low hanging vines.

'Cadabra?' Heather said, staring at the dirt circle.

'It is a place of pure, unrestricted, dark magic.' Kiel crossed out the half circle with his stick, 'It is an area you best not find yourself, Earth child. Many manners of creature go there to do dark dealings and mingle with the undead and the dying. A place where magic has no rules. Peaceful people live and work there, but they become twisted soon enough...'

'And that's where the Incantana are from?'

'Yes,' Kiel said, keeping his stare at the Cadabra side. 'Two cities exist here, Hey Presto! is the capital of Abara, where we are journeying, and Ta-Dah, the largest city in Cadabra. A wicked Magician lives in the Chamber Tower watching over Ta-Dah with a maniacal ruling. If he ever finds out a being came here from another world, he would want you as his own.'

'What good am I to him?' Heather asked, worried.

'You may not know it, Earth child, but you smell of magic. Strong, yet...' Kiel paused, 'dying.'

'Dying? You can smell magic on me?' Heather said, her eyebrows furrowing.

'I smell a little on you. Residual, but extremely strong. Either you have it in your blood, or you have been in close proximities to someone that has.'

Heather looked away from Kiel and thought of Mr Harlow.

I thought magic was all showmanship and sleight of hand. I didn't think there was real magic, Heather thought.

'You look worried, Heather. If you stay with us, no harm will come to you.'

'Stay? I need to get home before my father finds out I'm missing.'

Kiel looked to his right. The fire danced across his hands, licks of colour illuminated his slender fingers and large knuckles. His eyes glowed like twin orbs.

'Tell me everything that happened, Heather. If we can piece it together, we may be able to help you get back.'

Heather thought for a moment. 'Me and my friend Bounty were trying to help a magician called Mr Harlow. We went into his quarters and tried to find clues as to why he couldn't perform magic.'

'Couldn't perform magic? Sounds like the workings of a greater magician,' Kiel said, not taking his eyes off the fire.

'I stepped into a box. It was just an empty, wooden sword box that he never used. I read the words Hey Presto! and here I am.'

Kiel looked at her. 'Did you land in the field where you were attacked?'

'No, I came out of another box...'

'Another box?' Kiel said with strain in his voice. 'Amateur magicians who try to dabble in teleportation are extremely dangerous, if they know what they're doing. The Dark Emperor will have his minions scouring the lands for that person and his magical item... especially now that they've brought someone back from another realm.'

A minute passed where neither of them spoke. Heather could feel the strange tightness in her chest – the feeling of being completely helpless and stranded. She felt relief in the fact that these people had helped her, and didn't appear to be a threat. Looking at Kiel with desperation in her eyes, she opened her mouth to speak, but closed it again, unsure what to say, or ask.

'There are men in Hey Presto! who have dealt with such things,' Kiel said, taking his eyes off the fire and looking at Heather. 'They do not like to do business in the area of such dark magic, but they owe us a favour. I will take you to them once we get into the gates of Hey Presto!'

Heather felt a sigh of relief wash over her.

There was the soft breaking of twigs as someone stood from the camp fire and strolled over to where they were sitting. It was a woman holding two bowls of broth. The steam rose in great big plumes before disappearing into the silent night air.

'Kiel,' she said, handing him the first bowl, 'I hope you are holding your tongue.' She gave him a stern look.

She was the same species as him, but her build was slenderer, with curvy hips and long legs. She wasn't as tall and her skin didn't shine like his did. She turned to Heather and studied her for a second before handing her the soup. It smelt divine, yet unlike anything she had ever smelt in her life. Heather picked up the crude, sculpted spoon and sipped the broth. Her senses came alive and it filled her body with warmth and calmness.

'This is Soma Rowmoon, daughter of Angusto Rowmoon,' Kiel said before lifting the bowl up to his mouth and drinking.

'We met before the scare,' she said with a flat tone of voice. 'He announces my father like you would know or respect him, but you are not from here, are you?'

Kiel handed the empty bowl back. 'She is from somewhere called Earth. I told her we would take her to Hey Presto! to meet with William and Scarper.'

Soma gave him a scornful look and snatched the bowl from his fingers.

'You're a fool, Kiel,' she spat. 'Using our lifeline for someone we don't even know!' She looked at Heather who was still eating. She then turned and left them, heading towards the encampment.

Heather looked at Kiel for a reason for Soma's rudeness. She drank her soup, trying not to let Soma's anger get the better of her.

'Ignore her,' he said. 'She hasn't been the same since... well, never mind. Tomorrow we travel. It will be a long day, so it's best if we get some sleep.'

'I...' Heather said, looking down into the misty soup. 'I don't want to use a favour or lifeline for those people you know. I just want to get home.'

Kiel stood up and placed his large hand on Heather's shoulder.

'As I said, Heather. Ignore her. She's stubborn and there's no changing that. Plus, William owes me the favour, not her. So I can use it any way I please. Now, good night.'

Kiel walked her over to the carriage Heather had been hiding in when the commotion erupted and retrieved two blankets. The fire crackled softly, keeping the surrounding area heated and barely lit. He left one with her and then strode off into the wilderness, either to stand guard or sleep himself, Heather did not know. Her eyes were heavy, but her mind was awake. She kept thinking of the situation she had found herself in - this strange world, with strange people. She would have given anything to be home, in her own bed. She wrapped the blanket around herself and fell asleep.

ADMIT ONE
COME ONE, COME ALL
THE GREATEST PERFORMANCE IN THE WORLD
CHAPTER II
YOU WANT ME TO FIGHT?
Nº IOIOI987

When Heather woke she felt she was moving. The wooden flooring underneath her was rocking and swaying. She opened her eyes and peered out the thick red curtain that hung at the rear. She could see another wagon behind her, covered in a dust cloud. There was a greatly worn road without cobblestones trailing behind her. The trees on either side took on new life in the daylight. Their leaves were strange shapes - diamonded and oblique. The trunks of the massive trees all had carved patterns, like strange maps of forbidden realms. She wondered how she got in the back of the wagon and could only guess Kiel and lifted her up in during the night without waking her.

She wiped the sleep from her eyes and moved through the cabin, trying not to fall on other sleeping people, and got to the front. She climbed through a small door that had been locked with a pin and entered into a small area with cooking utensils on one side and folded blankets on the other. Through another door she could see the sky. A long seat rested on springs. Heather climbed through and up the small set of stairs. Sitting on the driver's seat was an elderly man. He was wearing a long shawl of dark red - the colour of rich earth. His beard was long and white and there were small scars around his lips. His nose pointed out towards the front, like the tip of a spear. Under folds of old skin and bushy, snow white, eyebrows hid small eyes. They gleamed like black pearls.

'Come up here and sit with me young one.' His voice was old, yet calming.

Heather hesitated at first but felt warmth radiating from him. She climbed onto the long bench seat and sat down. In front of her was a small foot rest, and along the floor were weapons of all sorts - long spears, short swords, shields and an arrangement of twisted walking canes.

The old man had hold of two leathery straps that were attached to two creatures that Heather had never seen in any zoo or any animal book she had ever read. They had six legs each, four at the rear of their scaly body and two at the front. They had large fins on their backs that were as thick as the bench they were sitting on. Along their necks where the straps where the old man was able to steer them. Their heads were thin and long, like an anteater, with round, silver-coin eyes and a single horn protruding from their forehead. Heather sat and looked from the creatures to the old man.

'They're called the Gazzoo. Excellent stock beasts with strong hides. They only need to eat every three days and barely ever get tired.'

'I've never seen such an animal before.'

The old man turned to her, taking his eyes off the road. In front of them were two more wagons, the one at the front was shorter and further ahead. There were several men holding their weapons on the wagon's roof, staring off into the distance.

'So, it's true. You really are not from Abara or Cadabra?'

'No, I'm not from anywhere really. I travel in a circus. We're always,' Heather looked down at the road under her, 'moving.'

'A traveller,' the old man said, curling the words around his tongue as if they tasted of sugar water. 'You truly are lucky. Kiel was right, you have come to the right place.'

'I don't understand?' Heather said.

'We are the Festival of the Soul – The travelling performers from Pickacard. We travel from town to town, entertaining the crowds. From peasants to great kings, we have made them all applaud.'

'Kiel said you are headed to Hey Presto! Is it for a performance?'

'It is,' the old man said looking away, as if something deep inside him didn't want to admit it.

There was movement from the rear of the cabin and a small child poked their head through the door.

'I smell them grandpa Ollsop... I can smell them close.'

The child had long, dreadlocked hair that ran down the side of its ears and down along it's jaw line and onto its chin, like a great Lion's mane. The small child's lips were bloated and purple, with matching eyes.

'Thank you, Sonjay.'

From under his seat Ollsop pulled a small mirror. He looked around the heavily wooded area, his eyes dark balls of oil, gleaming and retaining great knowledge.

'Is that your grandson?' Heather asked, trying to see what Ollsop was looking for.

Suddenly one of the Gazzoo gave a loud chortle through its nostrils. Ollsop caught the sun light with his mirror and motioned it back and forth to the lead carriage. A man sitting on the rear rail, who looked like he was napping, was momentarily blinded by the reflection and instantly woke, leaping to his feet and waving his long bow around wildly. The carriage driven by Ollsop came to a sudden halt.

'Get in the back, child. We are about to be attacked!'

Heather got to her feet, feeling the wagon rock back and forth on uneven ground. She ran down the steps into the rear of the carriage and to the back where she peered through the curtains. Through the thick bars of tree trunks came black figures, running on all fours. Their hair wavered behind them as they ran. From a distance Heather thought they looked like wolves. They stomped the ground with great speed and weight until they reached the clearing where the road had been built. Once they were in sight of the wagons, they started to walk on their two hind legs. The wolves grunted and howled, motioning to one another. There was a howl of pain, followed by two of the wolves dropping to the ground dead with arrows protruding from their chest and throat. The Gazzoo reared up on its hind quarters, knocking the wagon backwards. Heather fell, gripped the edge of the rail and toppled over onto the ground. The fall was several feet and knocked the wind clean out of her chest. The second Gazzoo was struck by a wolf and had its neck broken instantly. It fell with a heavy thud onto the dirt road forcing the wagon to spin sideways. The children in the back of the wagon screamed and started to wail with fear.

Heather sat up, her throat was clenched shut and her lungs cried out for air. She choked and grabbed at her neck. The wagon now far behind her. The wolf-man who had begun eating the Gazzoo saw her writhing on the ground and grinned through blooded fangs.

Heather saw his eyes and suddenly felt oxygen rush into her chest. She got to her feet and started to run, but her ankle buckled under her weight and she hit the ground again, hard. She looked down in a frantic panic and saw her ankle start to swell and turn purple. Her eyes darted from her foot, to the black blur leaping through the air. She closed her eyes and waited for the impact. She was sure she would feel the wolves curled talons tear her flesh, feel its ravenous fangs open up her rib cage and feast on her innards. As the creature came down upon her it was swept up in a rush of blue and green and tossed to the side. There was a screech of horror, followed by the splatter of blood across the dusty ground. Standing over the corpse of one of the wolves was Kiel. His spear dripping with red liquid.

'Are you alright?' he said.

Heather tried to stand again. Her ankle gave, but she managed to switch her weight to her other foot.

'I'm fine...watch out!'

Two more wolves came from behind the carriage, leaping at Kiel. He moved with elegance, like liquid across silk. He ducked low to the ground, swept his spear upwards and impaled one as it flew over him.

'Heather!' Ollsop called out from the rear of the wagon.

She looked over to see him holding a long sword. Its blade was chipped and it looked blunt. She ran to him as the howls pierced the air all around her.

'Take this!'

'You want me to fight?' Heather yelped, taking the battered sword from his elderly fingers.

'We must all fight if we are to survive.'

Ollsop dropped from the cabin and landed on the ground like a starving predator eager for the hunt. From below the driver's deck he pulled a long bō staff. He swung it around in a windmill, swirling it through the air and bashing it down on the hard ground. A wave of warped light rippled across the ground, knocking several wolves off their feet. From the throng of falling bodies came Soma. She held a short sword in each hand and sliced them in giant X marks in front of her stride. A large wolf, with gnashing teeth, got to its feet just in time to be sliced across its abdomen. Various organs spilled from the injury and the wolf dropped to the ground, lifeless. Heather looked at the other carriages. They had all pulled down armoured plates over the open areas of the wagons. All of the defensive surfaces were battle scarred and burnt.

'We have to find the pack leader; it's the only way to be rid of them!' someone cried out over the gnashing of teeth and the guttural cries of revenge.

Soma and Ollsop ran around the cabin where the frightened children were whimpering inside. Heather followed, her heart was pounding through her chest. She could feel her palms begin to sweat madly; it loosened her grip on her sword. A wolf, that had been hiding in a large tree, leapt through the shrubbery and landed between her and Ollsop. Soma turned around quickly, raising her swords, but the wolf was too fast. With its spring-loaded arms, it knocked her back several feet with one giant swipe of its claws. Her weapons flew through the air and disappeared into the foliage and jagged rocks. Heather stepped back from the beast, watching its thick, long, black coat hide its body mass. It looked like the embodiment of nightmares, terrifying and horrific. Ollsop started speaking words that Heather could not understand, he raised his staff.

'You're a foolish magician, Ollsop!' the wolf growled. Its voice was gravelly and deep.

Before Ollsop could cast his spell, the wolf sliced him across his chest, blood splattered along the ground, deep, velvety red and thick like treacle. Heather screamed until she was deaf. Every limb on her body froze in fear as the wolf turned to her. Its canary-yellow eyes fixing upon her fragile frame.

'You...' it spoke. 'You are not from here... you smell of...' it sniffed the air.

Heather could see a long grey streak on its chest, it stood out from the others. It was also taller and appeared to be the only one that could speak.

'Otherworld!' it howled in morbid excitement.

Heather felt death grip her shoulder with its cold fingers. She would die away from her father and her circus family, she would die away from her home. She pulled her sword up high and held it in front of her body.

'Don't come any closer!' she begged the beast.

The wolf smiled and bared its viscous fangs. It hunched its back and started crawling towards her, mocking her with the easiness of the kill. Its thick tail whipped the air, kicking up dust from the ground. Heather hadn't been one to sit back and let something happen before her eyes, it's what had gotten her into this mess in the first place. Her father always had said she was pig-headed and stubborn, just like her mother. Heather charged forward, swinging her sword in an arch. It clipped the wolves arm, shaving hair and skin from the bone. Blood poured onto the ground, mixing with Ollsop's blood.

'You'll pay for that, child,' the wolf barked, holding its arm. It had a surprised look on its face as blood spilled from between its claws.

The wolf rushed towards her, pushing the sword to one side. It quickly grabbed Heather, wrapping its massive hands around her torso and rolling her onto the ground. She felt the power behind its body, it was unlike anything she had ever felt before. She was helpless. She still gripped the blade. Without hesitation, she swung it to the side, pushing the sword down and felt it cut through the thick fur and into its abdomen. The wolf tossed her across the ground like a rag doll and howled its deathly call. Heather fell on sharp rocks and twigs. They tore at her skin, drawing blood. She was flat on her back as the beast jumped on top of her, pinning her down. She was almost nose to nose with the wolf. She could feel it's stinking breath, rancid and metallic. It's gleaming eyes burning a hole into her soul.

'Prepare for death, child!'

The wolf opened its maw. Saliva hung from its molars, slithering over its red tongue and down its spiral throat. Heather watched as its teeth headed towards her face. Everything went black and silent, then, through the darkness was a scream, followed by the sound of rotten fruit being torn asunder. Heather watched in slow motion as the wolf's head lifted from its body, detaching from its neck and soared through the air, over her. It landed with a sickening squelch. Through the rain of blood, she could see Kiel standing with one of Soma's swords. He was cut all over his chest and shoulder, bleeding profusely. Heather felt her heart stop for an instant. The ringing in her ears made her momentarily deaf. Kiel held his hand out and Heather took it, getting to her feet.

'That was close,' he told her.

Heather was too shocked to talk.

'Look!' Soma said, staggering over to them. 'That must have been the leader, they're retreating.'

Like blurs of shadow, the remaining wolves bolted into the forest. The trees shook, letting a thick curtain of leaves fall to the ground. Then everything was quiet again, all they could hear were the wind whispering.

Soma and Kiel ran over to Ollsop. He had already preformed magic on his wounds and they had closed, but not healed.

'We must check the others,' he said, his voice raspy.

Kiel stood with Heather, who looked shaken.

'That is the risk we take on this road. A short cut to Hey Presto!'

'A short cut?' Heather asked, watching as Soma aided the fallen.

'We are limited for time, Heather. It is of the essence.'

'But why? Surely it isn't worth the extra danger to be on this road.'

Soma watched from a distance. Kiel noticed and pulled Heather close to him.

'I cannot reveal all, Earth Child. But there is more going on than meets the eye.'

Heather looked up at his square jaw and glittering eyes. He held deep worry, she could see it.

'All will be explained in time,' he said, then left to help wrap the dead for burial.

Heather stood near the pooling blood of the wolf. She thought of what it had said right before it died – *Otherworld*. She knew they could smell something about her, something different, but how did they know where she came from? When she didn't even know how she got here herself? Something struck her as strange.

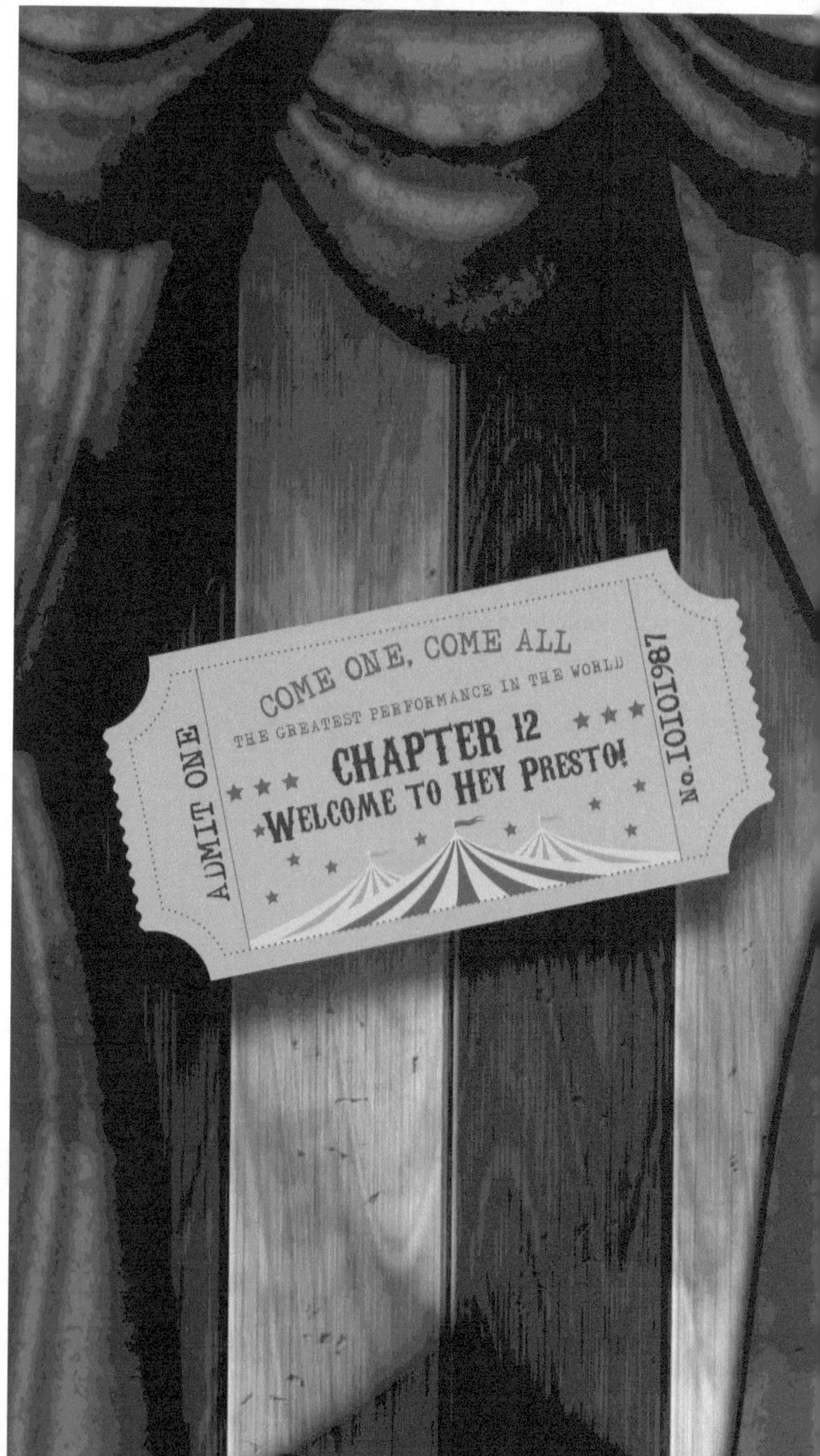
COME ONE, COME ALL
THE GREATEST PERFORMANCE IN THE WORLD
CHAPTER 12
WELCOME TO HEY PRESTO!
ADMIT ONE
No.1010I987

They had been travelling for what Heather estimated to be close to four hours. The roads were bumpy and at places, running water was flowing over a small catchment and across the path. The wagon's wheels splashed it up and Heather could feel the streams coolness from inside the carriage. Strange birds crossed the sky, some with long legs, dangling from their bodies like branches. Others had beaks that curled up into themselves and she wondered how they ate or breathed. Every now and then the ground would thump loudly and a loud howl would shake the trees. Ollsop told her they were mountain giants waking from a long and harsh winter, soon they would be ready to eat and this place would be even more dangerous.

Hey Presto! came into view over a small range of hills on the horizon. She had glanced it at a distance when she had arrived, but nothing could prepare her for seeing it up close. At first glance it looked like the bizarre dream of an ill architect. The buildings were all leaning and crooked, twisted and deformed. They defied gravity in every sense of the word. Tall, cathedral like, structures with tiering peaks hatched across the skyline. The closer the carriages got to the city, the more Heather could see steam rising from the rooftops and smoke from the chimneys. There was a radiance glowing from the town, of celebration. She had felt that sort of buzz before, from people in small towns when her circus arrived. Her father called it the carnival spirit.

Their old rickety wagon, with the dead rolled in cloth piled in the back, took the winding road to the entrance of

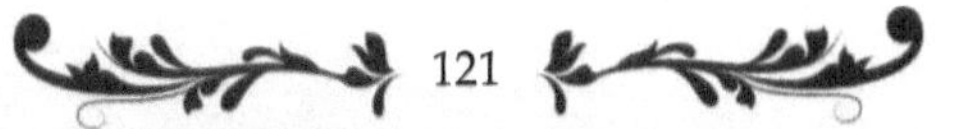

Hey Presto! where guards stood out the front with long spears and chain mail armour. The gates were poorly built and looked like they had seen war in their life. Kiel climbed in the back well before they came into view of the guards and hid under old rags and blankets. Ollsop had his arm in a sling and sat beside Heather. In front of them was the largest wagon carrying all the equipment for their show, and in front of that was Soma's wagon with the guards resting on top. She spoke to the guards quickly and waved her hands around, obviously arguing with the tallest guard about their appointment to put on a show.

'Is there something wrong?' Heather asked Ollsop.

'No, they are just weary of smugglers and warrants for people. Hey Presto! is a great city with clean magic, and they like to keep it that way.'

'What if they... smell me?' Heather asked, suddenly becoming worried.

'Guards can't smell magic. They can barely get through a day without taking a nap or forgetting what they're doing.'

Suddenly the wagon's started to roll forward. They rocked and rolled through the gates and under a great big sign that was written in a language that Heather had never seen before.

'It reads – *For Light. For Dark. We can live as One*,' Ollsop said, seeing that Heather was staring at the jumble of symbols. 'It is Old language, not spoken anymore.'

'What does that mean?' Heather asked.

Ollsop stroked his injured hand and saw blood rising to the surface of the wraps, 'It simply means this city will house either dark or light magic, as long as we all live in peace, together. But lately,' Ollsop said, lifting his head up to meet Heather's eyes, his white eyebrows furrowing together, 'there's been a ripple amongst the dark magic users; it's too early to tell what is happening.'

'A ripple?'

'A disturbance, Heather. Something will change soon.'

Heather thought of the name of the city. The exact word that she had muttered that bought her here. *It can't be a coincidence*, she considered.

The guards they passed on the ground stared at Heather as their wagon slowly moved forward, now only being pulled by one Gazzoo. Once inside the gates Heather could see the bustling metropolis. Market stalls selling food and magical equipment. Bars and shops with bubbling liquid in long glasses and strange creatures drinking them. People and beasts alike, rummaging through the crowds, pushing and shoving, making their way down the long dusty corridors of the city. The buildings overshadowed the stalls along the ground. There appeared to be large roads for carts and wagons, and smaller corridors for the foot traffic. From behind them Kiel appeared. He had wrapped his body in a veil and had a hood over his head. He now wore long black gloves and boots.

'First, we bury our dead. Then we find the arena where we are to set up for our performance. Then Heather, we can search for the William and Scarper Emporium.'

Heather had momentarily forgotten about finding a way home as she was far too mesmerised by the city of Hey Presto!

A small boy ran up to the carriage and held up a handful of fruit and spoke in a tongue that Heather didn't understand. Ollsop beckoned him over and pulled out a monetary note from his belt and brought the entire handful of fruit. The boy smiled, stepped back away from the wagon and bowed. He stared at Ollsop and saw the scars on his lips and suddenly got very scared. He ran back into the hubbub of the busy morning commerce. Ollsop took a bite out of the first bulbous piece of fruit. It looked like a curled banana, but was purple on the outside and dark pink on the insides. He munched it between his old teeth and swallowed, he then appeared to be waiting for something. After a second he nodded and handed the rest back to the children sleeping in the back. He gave one to Heather and Kiel. Heather looked at it. Her piece of fruit was a cross between a pear and a strawberry, but tasted nothing like either. It reminded her of the beach, with its coolness and freshness. It had a nut in the centre that resembled an eye.

The wagon took a detour away from the busy city centre and soon was on a dusty, almost vacant road, running down the large wall of Hey Presto! Stretching out among acres of land were shanty shacks made of wood and metal. Tents were strung up as houses, looking old and cumbersome. Heather saw the people cooking outside their houses. They looked happy and even waved when they caught her eye. She saw a man performing magic for a group of children. They watched the elderly magician with pop-eyed amazement as he levitated and made cobalt blue sparks shimmer out of his finger nails. It made her think of Mr Harlow and why she was in this mess to begin with. The old man clapped his hands loudly and a black dove appeared from nowhere. It flew into the blazing sunlight, casting its wings wide and flying off into the distance. All the children clapped and cheered. Heather smiled and tried not to let a tear fall from the corner of her eye as the fresh memories made her homesick again.

'There it is,' Kiel said, still keeping out of view from the villagers.

Ollsop looked ahead and saw a large field that had been freshly cut. A rather obese man in a bizarre looking vest and baggy trousers was standing on the field with a parchment of paper and a pen. He wore a had that looked like he had made it from a potato sack. His arms were leathery from the sun and he had food stains down his undershirt. He looked up, hearing the noise from the carts and saluted the oncoming wagons.

'Hear ye! Hear ye!' he hollered.

Kiel motioned Heather into the back. She thought it was strange, as she wanted to stay up the front with Ollsop and examine this new world.

'It is very important Heather that no one knows you aren't from here, understand?'

'Yes, I guess,' Heather thought. 'But if more people know, maybe they can help me find a way back?'

'It's not that easy. To bring someone from another world takes a very dark magic that is illegal in Hey Presto! or even Abara, I should say. It's only in Cadabra where you would find such darkness. For now, keep your head covered.' He handed her a similar veil to what he was wearing. 'And keep your eyes diverted. If they look into your eyes, they might be able to see where you are from.'

Heather slipped the veil over her head and wondered why Kiel was being so secretive. The wagon halted and the Gazzoo let out a thirsty chortle.

'Unk Blacksoup!' Ollsop cried out to the pudgy man with the parchment.

'Ollsop Grimwore!' Unk called back, waddling over to where the convoy had stopped, just short of the grassy knoll.

Ollsop climbed down from the wagon and gave the plump man a hearty handshake. Unk patted him on the back and they both smiled widely.

'Is this room big enough?' he asked.

'I'd say it is,' Ollsop said, scanning the grassy area.

Unk looked past him and noticed the wagons, one after the other. He saw the first one with fresh scratch marks, then the one with all the equipment, then the one with the performers and the last at the rear. The wagons stood like old battle horses, worn from age and war. They had travelled thousands of miles and visited countless cities and towns. They had their own aura about them that demanded respect, but also laughter.

'That rapscallion Kiel isn't among you... is he?' Unk said, spitting to his own feet and glancing behind Ollsop shoulder.

Ollsop turned to the wagons, as if looking for him.

'Kiel? Didn't he die at the hands of Clat Rakshaw, the Dark Emperor's assassin?'

Unk looked back at Ollsop. 'That's what I heard, but no body has turned up for burial.'

'Too bad,' Ollsop said. 'He was a great performer.'

Unk nodded.

'We will leave two of the wagons here to set up. The journey here has not been without its battles. We encountered flesh hounds not far back. They killed several of our set-up crew and they need to be buried before sun down.'

Unk unrolled the parchment and inspected the scribbling. He glanced up once, then twice at the wagons. He looked over to Ollsop who was remaining calm. Unk signed the bottom and handed it to him.

'Two days... tops. Then you'll need another permit from the king. Do we have an understanding?'

Ollsop nodded slowly. 'Yes, thank you friend. And for also waiving the fee, it is much appreciated.'

Unk said nothing, instead, he wandered past the wagons, inspecting them slowly with every hobbled step. The guards atop of the first wagon watched him go, their spears and swords still gleaming fresh with blood. Unk soon disappeared into the bustling city of Hey Presto!

Ollsop walked over to Soma Rowmoon. 'He didn't seem overly convinced.'

Ollsop didn't look up at her. 'Without Kiel, this would never had happened.'

Soma glanced over her shoulder at the wagon behind her, she could see Heather talking with Kiel.

'We should have never brought the child with us; it is already too risky.'

'I agree, but she seems harmless. As long as she keeps out of sight, she won't be a threat.' Ollsop looked at the parchment and slid it into his long jacket.

'It is time to wake the ring leader,' Soma said to herself.

Ollsop walked to the second carriage and climbed aboard. The Gazzoo bucked and shook its scaly hide like an animal just emerging out of the water.

'What do we do now?' Heather asked, looking at some of the occupants of Hey Presto! as they emerged from their dwellings to watch them set up.

'We erect the tent... then we head to the cemetery,' Soma replied, half ignoring her.

Heather climbed up beside Ollsop. He grabbed the reigns and clicked with his tongue. The Gazzoo followed his instructions and pulled the wagon around the first wagon and onto the grassy arena. Heather moved across, making room for Kiel but he stuck to the back of the carriage, wrapped in scarves and rags.

It was hard to imagine that this strange world had a circus. Heather couldn't help but think, *Just like the one I've been a part of all my life.* She knew the way the circus people operated, she knew they were all family and watched out for one another, but this circus was different. There were no animals and they had to fight to get from one town to the next. Growing up, she'd never had a stable home, not one that was made of bricks and steel, with windows that didn't rattle, but instead she had a travelling home, with wheels. She often wondered what it was like to live in one place for more than a week.

She watched as Soma leapt off her wagon and onto the grass. She stood for a moment and smelled the air. Quickly the others followed, all helping to pull the tent poles out and lay down the foundation for the floor. Heather was suddenly excited to see what kind of circus they had. From the corner of her eye she saw Kiel, in disguise, slip from the rear of the wagon and make his way into the city. She turned back to the grass and Soma was standing right in front of her.

'Whatever you think of this world, Earth Child, you can forget it. This place isn't like the place you are from, or are used to. If we do not put on a good show, there could be danger. Now, instead of standing there gawking with your mouth open, why don't you go over and help LaFare with the ropes?' Soma's long fingers brushed Heather's arm and it sent a shiver up her spine.

Heather nodded and went straight to work, understanding the need to set up quickly. Soma watched her from afar. Ollsop caught her staring and went over to her.

'She won't get in the way... if that's what you're thinking.'

Soma shook her head, 'It's not her I'm worried about. It's Kiel.'

ADMIT ONE
COME ONE, COME ALL
THE GREATEST PERFORMANCE IN THE WORLD
CHAPTER 13
THE RING LEADER HAS ARRIVED
No IOIOI987

When the tent was erected, Heather stood back and marvelled at the construction. The fabric was bright orange and would have stood out from miles away. People would have seen it peeking out from the fence that surrounded the city. There were intricate patterns weaved all over it, in strange cross hatchings and circles. It looked more like a fortune teller's booth, than a circus. The children who had been sleeping in the back of the wagon were now fully awake and dressed in their outfits. They were juggling balls and walking on the tight rope. Heather felt like she was at home and it filled her heart with joy and warmth. The familiarity of the circus put her nerves at ease.

'You handle the ropes like you've done this before,' LaFare said, taking several lengths of dark red rope from her shoulder.

LaFare had large, strong arms and a small waist that had a thick black belt running around it. His eyes were small and green and glittered every time they caught the sun.

'I used to... I mean, I work in a circus, like this one. But we have animals and a magician and...' Heather had noticed LaFare's face become sullen and heavy.

'You have a magician in a circus?' he said, his tone of voice was low so no one else could hear.

'The audience love him; his name is Mr...'

LaFare stepped closer to Heather. 'He performs in front of an audience? I would not go around telling people that, especially if it's dark magic.'

'Dark magic?' Heather thought for a moment, 'I don't think Mr Har...'

She was cut off again by an oncoming wagon. It was smaller than the rest and polished till it was shining black. Its wheels were massive, with gleaming silver bolts and clips. The creature that pulled it was equally black, with three narrow eyes running down a rather horse-like snout. Its feet were thin and covered with a luscious black hair. Its rear legs were longer than its front, but it still walked with flawless motion.

'Ah!' LaFare yelped, stepping around Heather. 'The Ringleader has arrived!'

Heather turned to the black wagon and noticed several people emerging from their camp sites and make-shift houses. A thin man in a rather expensive looking suit stepped down from the sleek carriage and bowed towards the tent. Everyone around him dropped to one knee and bowed also. Heather noticed she was the only one left standing, so she quickly copied the others. Looking up through the corners of her eyes, she watched the new arrival stare with still, hollow eyes at the performing tent. Once the suited man had scanned the area, he wandered to the back of the glossy black transportation and started unlocking large silver latches that were keeping, what looked like, a coffin lid in place. As he did this, LaFare looked over to Heather, his head still placed beside his raised knee.

'We must pay our respects to the Ringleader or else he will not control the performance. It is a tradition that goes back many hundreds of years.'

Heather looked from LaFare to the black wagon. The suited man had now unlocked every latch along the rectangular box. He stood back, slipping gloves onto his hands and mumbling something under his breath. Small sparks of orange appeared around his mouth. They circled one another, like glow bugs and slowly floated towards the carriage. The man then walked over and lifted the lid. It hardly creaked at all, in fact, it seemed to open almost by itself. Heather couldn't see what was inside. The glowing balls of light paused in air, suspended for several seconds and then shot towards the open casket. There was a moment of silence, when everyone around them waited in silence. Then, as if taking breath for the first time, the Ringleader gasped and sat up. His face was skeletal, with greying skin and long white hair that ran over his face and shoulders. The tangerine spheres of energy attached themselves to the Ringleader's decaying flesh and sunk through his rotten skin and into his bones like hot, melted butter. The Ringleader corpse was dressed in a fine red coat with large silver buttons stitched down one side. They were covered in dust and worms. They squirmed and popped off him, shaking themselves from the cabin and onto the ground.

'Hey Presto! has its own Ringleader that we must hire, as ours had died in battle nearly two years ago,' LaFare said, trying not to look at the reanimated Ringleader.

Heather could barely believe her eyes. The Ringleader stood up and looked around, as if he was a new born animal. Its eyes were hollowed sockets with tiny pin pricks of light. They glowed with dull life.

'Rise,' the Ringleader said, his voice scratchy and soft.

Everyone got back up on their feet and applauded wildly. Heather watched as the black suited man helped the Ringleader down from his coffin and onto the ground. He took several steps and almost fell, he was caught by the man, who stabilised him again. He took another step, watching his feet the entire time. After seven steps, he could walk almost like normal. He looked up at the tent and his mouth opened. All his teeth were rotten or had fallen out. Some lay on his suit, decayed with age and fused into the cloth. His eyes became fiery and filled the sunken sockets with beaming light.

Suddenly there was someone beside Heather and it almost made her jump in fright. It was Kiel. He eyed the Ringleader with intense scrutiny, as if he didn't like the idea of having him in his circus.

'You're back,' Heather said, taking her eyes off the Ringleader.

'You must come with me, the cemetery has been arranged and we need to get there and bury our fallen before the night's show begins.'

The Ringleader kneeled down and scooped up a handful of dirt. He raised it high above his head. The skin covering his skull was rancid and peeling. He smiled as he watched the hazy sun shine through the dirt as it fell onto his face. The suited man at the wagon bowed to the Ringleader, who paid him no attention. He remounted his ride and turned the coffin-wagon around.

'You want me to help bury the dead?' Heather asked, feeling a cold shiver run up her spine. 'I've never done anything like that before?'

Kiel turned and looked at her. 'You won't be burying them. You'll be escorting me.'

Kiel began walking towards the busy city centre. Heather followed at his heels.

***

The streets of Hey Presto! were filled with the smells of cooking food. Heather sniffed loudly and felt her saliva glands clench. It was delicious beyond what words could describe but she couldn't identify any of the foods she was smelling. Kiel walked ahead of her with his face guarded by a long brown piece of cloth. His glimmering yellow eyes kept peering back at her, making sure she wasn't getting lost in the fray.

They passed a long market stall that sold silver jewellery, all glittering and sparkling brilliantly in the dying sun. Heather couldn't help but stop and glance at the magnificent items.

'You like?' said a man behind the stall.

Heather looked up and was met by a man that had an eye patch over one eye. His head was balding and he only had one arm. Where the other arm should have been was an empty shirt sleeve. He waved at the jewellery with his left hand and the diamonds and rubies lit up like fairy lights. Heather's eyes peeled open. She felt a heavy hand on her shoulder and turned to see Kiel leaning over her.

'As with all good salesmen, there is always a catch,' Kiel said, clicking his fingers together.

Suddenly, all the sparkle and glitter disappeared from the items and what was left was nothing but rusted pieces of jewellery that looked like it had been scavenged from the bottom of the ocean. The one-armed man looked at Kiel. Heather stood back, blinked, rubbed her eyes and looked again. *Where's all the beautiful jewellery gone?* she asked herself.

'Dark magic...' the salesman whispered, taking a step backwards.

Kiel leaned over the ginger, corroded bracelets and necklaces. 'If you don't tell, then I won't.'

The one-armed man stood stock still. Kiel took Heather's hand in his and shuffled her through the busy streets. The salesman kept his one eye on them until they were out of sight.

'What was that?' Heather asked.

'A spell. Nothing too strong; it's just to trick your eyes. If you had the currency of Hey Presto! you may have bought the whole lot and when you got home you would have nothing but worthless, rusted junk.'

'Home,' Heather said, sighing loudly.

Kiel looked at her and then back to the path ahead. They wandered up a paved road crowded with people. Heather saw a man with long, spiked horns coming out of his neck. He licked his lips as he brought a strange broth from an elderly woman. His tongue was scarlet red, and forked.

The chatter of the city folk grew quieter as Kiel led the way out of the busy centre and down several side streets. A large animal with tufts of golden fur sloshed madly in a puddle of murky water. It waddled past Heather and grunted annoyingly. As the market stalls began thinning out, the alleyways becoming more and more darkened. A large tower leered over them. As Heather walked under it, she felt a hundred eyes watching her. A cold shiver ran up her spine and Kiel felt it also, in his fingers.

'Don't worry, Heather,' he said in a low tone. 'It's the Chamber of Magicians. They're watching out for Dark Magic that might enter the walls of Hey Presto!'

'What about that guy back there? With the fake jewellery?'

'It's not Dark, just a trick. They wouldn't care to fry such a small fish.'

Heather shook off the eerie feeling and soaked in the marvel of the city. The walls were made of red mud bricks and littered with posters for magic shows and theatre plays. The streetlights were lit by a man on large stilts, very similar to the Incantana's morbid leg extensions. He held a lit lamp in one hand and a long stick in the other that had a green flame dancing on the end of it. The air started to chill as they got more and more out of the city.

'There,' Kiel said, stopping.

Heather looked over a small plateau of fruit trees and could see a large grassy field full of headstones and grave plots. In the far back corner were people standing around in a circle. Heather thought their cemeteries looked very

similar to the ones where she was from, but this one didn't have a sadness associated with it. Instead, it emanated a feeling of calmness and peace.

'Good,' Kiel added, heading towards the winding road that lead up to the rear of the sepulchre, 'they've arrived.'

Along the side of the path were blackened stones. Splattered on each one was a hand print. Some had three fingers, some of the prints were tentacles and others were undistinguishable.

'Who's arrived?' Heather asked, looking up at the circle of people.

'The Conjuring Priests of Takeabow.'

Heather looked up at the priests and saw them covered in hoods, chanting and bowing in rapid succession. They made their way through the first gate, it was old and rusted with age, but still intricately designed and beautiful. There was a second gate, not far from the first that was made of simple wood and wire. Heather thought it strange, but dismissed it. As they passed under the gate, her skin was caressed by a slight tingle.

'It's to guard against magic,' Kiel said, not turning to her. 'Some dark magicians must use bones in order to cast their wicked spells, this keeps them out.'

Heather looked around at the gate surrounding the graveyard as they wandered up the path. Etched into the gate were words, similar to those that Ollsop had translated for her when they first arrived in Hey Presto! The trees growing along the boundaries were thick with luscious coloured leaves. There texture looked like sandpaper. The smell that came from the foliage made Heather close her eyes to savour the aroma. It reminded her of lollies and vanilla. She looked ahead and saw Kiel moving quicker now.

The winding path that took them up into the hillside was paved with ancient cobblestones. They were polished by time and use, by weather and magical elements. Heather looked down and the stones reflected her image back up to her. Her borrowed clothing and unwashed hair made her think she was looking at someone else. Underneath her veil and vest she could feel her uniform start to itch and become uncomfortable, but it was the only thing she had from her own home. Kiel stopped suddenly and looked around the mass grave site.

'What is it?' Heather asked.

'The Priests of Takeabow... They are without their Shaman.' He bent low to the ground and scooped up some dirt and sniffed it.

Heather looked over to several, freshly dug graves. A small transporting wagon was nearby filled with the bodies wrapped up in cloth. Two men, who Heather assumed worked for the city, were lifting them up, and carrying them to the holes and gently lowering them in. They paid the utmost respect to the bodies. They bowed low to the ground and muttered a prayer. Heather felt sombre, sadness and disillusionment. She could feel a knot of home-sickness clench in her throat and she had to try her best to shake it out of her body, but it wasn't much help.

'Something's wrong,' Kiel said, the dirt tumbling from his fingertips.

Just as he spoke, the three priests tossed their robes aside. One, Heather recognised straight away as Clat Rakshaw. His make-shift wings expanded with terrifying creaks. Sparks flew from his metallic joints. His eyes scanned the graveyard, but he hardly took any notice of Heather. His dead-eyed gaze was on Kiel. He sprinted forward as Kiel got back up to his feet. The deadly assassin reached into his right sleeve and threw his hand forward, the motion was so fast it looked like a blur. A length of chain shot out from his cuff. Kiel ducked quickly and the chain soared over his head and it wrapped itself around the magic-guard fence. Blue and orange sparks spat from the thin wire. Smoke bellowed from the wood and the etchings began to glow menacingly, as if setting off some alarm.

'Heather!' Kiel turned to her. '*Run!*'

Coming from beside the graves was a creature that had two black holes where its nose should have been and his entire body was covered in thick red hair. Its ears were elongated and ran backwards from the sides of his head like antennas. Heather saw it and shrieked. Its mouth was clenched into a snarl. She stumbled on the grass and started to run. There were headstones all around and she managed to dodge between them not knowing the whole time if the red haired beast was at her heels. She started to run out of breath. Her heart was beating so fast she thought it would leap into her throat. She took refuge behind a large gravestone pillar, her lungs crying out for breath. Holding her back to the structure, she snuck a peek around, trying to find Kiel. He was fighting with Clat Rakshaw, but now his robe and hood had been torn away exposing him to everyone around. The other priests where attacking him from all sides.

'I have to do something,' Heather said, her mind shouting it and her mouth making the words.

A hand gripped her shoulder and she felt her heart sink into her stomach. She turned slowly to see Soma Rowmoon behind her.

'What are you doing down here?'

'Sshhh,' Soma said, hiding against the pillar. 'Just shut up Earth-child, unless you want to be captured also.'

'But why aren't we helping him?'

'Look for yourself,' Soma exclaimed.

Heather looked again and saw Clat Rakshaw hit Kiel hard against his jaw with his long, mechanical wing. Kiel spun around in a half circle and dropped to the ground unconscious. Heather covered her mouth with her hand.

'If we go to his aid, we will not be captured Heather. They will kill us. They're powerful rivals with the strength of the Dark Emperor behind them. At least this way we know who has him... then we can follow them.' Soma showed a rare sign of compassion and held Heather's hand for a moment.

Kiel was wrapped in chains. He barely moved the whole time they were cuffing him.

'Pick him up, Sas-Lotch! The Dark Emperor will be very pleased.'

The red haired beast picked Kiel up as if he was as light as a feather and they marched towards the carriage. Clat tossed out the remaining bodies onto the grass and climbed aboard. Quickly, they rode off over the other side of the hill and out of sight.

'They must have someone on the inside of the graveyard to be able to get in like this,' Soma said. She looked at Heather and saw deep sorrow on her face.

'There was no use in us going to him. You can see what they are capable of, Heather.' Soma looked her in the eyes. 'You must choose your fights Heather; we will get him back. Now come, first we must finish this funeral.'

Soma lead the way with Heather dragging her feet behind her. Tears were streaming down her face. She could no longer control her emotions. They crossed the tombstones and reached the open graves where Kiel had been kidnapped only moments earlier. Soma took no time to reminisce, instead she dragged one of the wrapped bodies over to the grave and gently lay them down.

'Heather. The quicker we do this, the faster we can find their trail and get Kiel back.'

Heather looked at the humanoid shaped mummy lying only meters away from her. Never in her life would she

have thought she would be doing this. She walked over to the body and picked it up by its ankles, Soma grabbed its shoulders and they carried it over to the hole. She felt strange the whole time, a little bit sickened in her stomach and most of all she felt sadness. She positioned the body so it lay straight and climbed out of the hole. Soma threw a shovel over to her.

'This will take a while, then we have a show to put on.'

Heather caught the shovel, having completely forgotten about the performance tonight. Slowly, she shovelled dirt into the holes. The soil was rich and dark red, filled with worms and other unearthly creatures. The sun above them slowly died down over the mountain ranges until a morose orange hue was left in the sky.

Heather's hands were thick with blisters and one finger tip on her right hand was bleeding from the shovel handle. They patted down the last mound of soil over the burial ground. Soma stood and said a few words in a language Heather did not know and together they walked back through the city, on the way to the circus tent. The whole time Heather was anxious about telling the others that Kiel had been taken. She felt horrible for not trying to fight off the attackers, but Soma had seemed to know better. She picked her feet up and held her head high as they walked through the darkened backstreets of Hey Presto!

COME ONE, COME ALL
THE GREATEST PERFORMANCE IN THE WORLD
ADMIT ONE
CHAPTER 14
THE WILLIAM AND SCARPER EMPORIUM
No. 10101987

The streets of Hey Presto! was dimly lit by candle light. The bazaars that were opened earlier in the day were now shut and a whole new range of stores were open. Even though this was a city of peace and true magic, some of its occupants were dark and hid behind sinister glances and sold black market goods. Men in red trench coats wandered the streets in pairs. Their hands gripped long wands and their faces were covered. Soma explained to Heather that these were mages employed by local businesses to keep the peace. They had stopped raids on store fronts in the past years, but every now and then one would be found face down in a puddle of his own blood with a dagger protruding from his back. But this was a rare occasion and red trench mages were not to be talked to or dealt with in any way.

Heather wrapped her scarf around her chest and pulled it up to cover her mouth. As cold as the night was, she still was fearful that someone would know she was not from this world.

The smells coming from a nearby stand were rancid and rotten. The small animal carcasses hanging from the metal beams were old and dried out. A man behind the stall, who had no ears, just small holes the size of a coin, was motioning people with his hand over to his grotesque meat. The street lights flickered as Heather and Soma rushed past him. The store vendor held Heather's gaze and returned to his dealings. Soma noticed, and hurried.

At first, Heather thought she was heading back to the circus for the night's performance. She was even excited to see how this circus differs from the one she was from. Soma took Heather's arm and tugged gently towards a dark alleyway.

'What's going on?' she said.

'Shush,' Soma snapped. 'Do you want everyone to know our business?'

Soma took a few steps in front of Heather and started heading down the long, dark alley. Heather paused momentarily at the mouth of the passageway. She looked left and right. She didn't entirely trust Soma yet; she didn't even think she liked her. Although she had shown some compassion earlier, she may have caught her in the moment. Soma stopped suddenly, her body was cast in the dark shadows of the adjacent buildings.

'Come, Heather. If you want to get back to your realm, I suggest you stop staring at everything and walk with some speed.' She turned and continued through the shadows.

Heather watched her march into the darkness. Washing lines were strung up over head with no clothes on them, only wooden pegs that gleamed like stars in the moon light. She swallowed and found her throat was dry and clenched, it felt like a brick was in her throat. She stepped forward into the stinking alleyway. The walls were seeping brown water and it smelled like rotten vegetables and sewerage. A shadow passed in a nearby window and Heather jumped with fear. She hurried along the stone path, her feet feeling the cold from the stones as it raced up her legs and into her stomach. She got to a T section at the end of the alleyway and looked down both sides, Soma was nowhere to be found. Suddenly she heard a noise. To her right there was a door, painted dark red with a single lantern above it. Soma was holding it open.

'In here, Heather.' Then she went inside. The door shut behind her.

Heather walked over to the door and looked up at the sign. In gold script were the words: *William and Scarper Emporium,* below in small letters: *General Magik and Historical Artefacts.* There was a large window to the right of the door, oily and almost impossible to see through. Heather looked through the window, the glare from the lamp gave just enough light in order to see through it. A wooden shelf was constructed on the other side of the glass. It looked poorly made and rotten to its core. Along the shelf were blood-red candles and metal buckles which were constructed with such precision that Heather could not believe a hand, made of flesh, had made them. There were several lengths of chain wound up along the next shelf, it gleamed softly from the light inside. Heather looked down and almost shrieked when she saw a skull. It wasn't human but of some animal with large incisors and a heavy-set bottom jaw.

Howls from the end of the alleyway echoed off the old walls, bouncing from brick to brick. It made Heather shiver with unease. She went to the door and pushed it open carefully. A small metal bell chimed and the door shut behind her. Inside was warm and cosy, the smell was of roses and vanilla. It was dark inside and incense burned softly in the corner, the aromatic smoke curling in great plumes and made Heather's skin feel soft and comfortable. The emporium was cluttered with tools of magic, some looked practical like wands and hats and jewellery. Others looked as if they had been created by some torturous magician. Soma was standing at the counter talking to a very tall man in a grey suit. They both stopped talking as Heather walked in and turned to look at her, neither had a pleasant look on their faces. To Heather's right was a large glass tube with an animal carcass floating in it; it's leg moved.

'Come forth, Earth Child. Let Mr Scarper look at you.' Soma waved her over.

Heather walked gingerly over to the enormously tall man. His suit was made with fine stitching and several different shades of grey cloth. His cuff links were gold and gleamed in the dull candle light. Heather walked to the bench and saw a large book that was open in front of Mr Scarper. It was open to a page that showed planets and an oddly drawn car and house. The bottom of the page had the start of a signature, but it had been torn off.

'Look up at me, child,' Mr Scarper snapped.

Heather looked up at him and saw his eye flicker golden yellow for a moment.

'Tell me your story.'

Heather hesitated for a moment. She heard shuffling behind a velvet curtain to the rear of the store, followed by footsteps.

'Well?' Mr Scarper spoke, crossing his arms over his chest. 'Mrs Rowmoon here is paying me by the minute, so it's her money you're wasting.'

Heather took a deep breath and tried not to look at Soma.

'I am part of a circus. My father runs it. He is the ringleader,' Heather said, finally getting her voice.

Mr Scarper looked at Soma with wide eyed amusement. 'A Ring Leader?' he repeated with slight astonishment.

'I broke into the magician's caravan and hopped into his sword box. When I uttered words I saw on the back of the door, I woke up in another box... here.'

'A magician?' Mr Scarper spat, he stepped around the counter and hobbled awkwardly over to the small girl. 'A real magician? In another world? Who?' he shouted.

Heather took a step back at his sudden outburst.

'Mr Harlow,' she said softly.

Mr Scarper looked to his left, as if pondering the name in his mind. As if chewing it over and over like a piece of gum.

'And what were these magical words you spoke that brought you here?'

Soma watched on, her face unchanged the whole time. She neither showed emotion nor surprise.

'Hey Presto!' Heather shouted.

The candles flickered and the creature in the tube kicked wildly. A short man appeared from behind the velvet curtain, he wore odd glasses that were perched on top of his head. They were long, tube like spectacles with a green and yellow lens.

'Did you feel that?' the small man spat.

Mr Scarper, who had been hunched over to speak to Heather, now brought his body up, as tall as it could be. Strange amulets and chimes hung from the ceiling, brushing against his soft, white hair. He stepped back, as if now cautious of Heather's words, and went back behind the bench. Soma watched the two men have a hurried discussion. Finally, Mr Scarper broke from the conversation and placed his hand on the small man.

'Mr William here and I have concurred,' he announced, as if Heather or Soma didn't see this happen. 'And we believe a link has been set up to transport magic into another realm.'

Soma looked down at the floor, as if disappointed. Heather looked from one person to the next, as if waiting for someone to add to the announcement.

'What does that mean? H-h-how do I get back?' she stuttered.

The small rotund man with the long lensed glasses walked over to her and slipped his glasses down onto his eyes. His cork-screw chin curled up as he concentrated on her facial features. Heather looked perplexed. He looked her up and down with his goggles, nodding and humming as he did so.

'So, you want to get back?' Mr William announced, brushing some dirt off Heather's chin.

'Of course I do! My father will miss me; he'll be sick with grief that I've been gone this long.'

'Time is different between realms,' Mr William said, finally taking his eyes off Heather and focusing on Soma. 'If you've come from another dimension, then time may be slowed... or fastened.'

'If?' Heather said.

Soma pulled her jacket to the side and flashed a knife handle in her belt. Mr William quickly pulled his lenses off and turned back to Heather. Soma knew the two men were apprehensive about speaking about the realms and transportation. She eyed the two men, letting them know she was in no mood for games.

'Time, it doesn't stand still for anyone, nor does it move at the same rate.'

Mr Scarper took a glass bottle from under the counter and sniffed it loudly. His eyes gleamed yellow again and he wiped his nose with his long fingers and snorted abruptly.

'A link between worlds has two doorways, obviously you have found the other. Unfortunately, there is only one place where the other door can be without detection.'

Heather looked up at the tall man, his eyes reminiscent of a lizard's.

'Where?'

'Cadabra.'

Soma looked at Heather, and for the first time, Heather saw true horror on her face.

'There must be a way to build a doorway, here, in this city where it is safe?' Soma tried to bargain.

'Mr Scarper is right, Heather,' Mr William intervened. 'The doorway could only be contained in the Dark Emperor's tower. It is the only place with enough concentrated dark magic to maintain such a link.'

'Dark magic?' Heather said, 'What about the gateway... door, box thing I woke up in? Surely that's still there? It was run by someone called Brim something.'

Mr Scarper looked at Mr William and together they shook their heads.

'If you've come through it, the Dark Master would have sensed it. The magician you called Brim would have been killed for trying to make that link, but by all means... please try and find him. Unless you can get up into the Emperor's tower, it may be your only hope of getting home.'

'Come on, Heather,' Soma said, slamming several coins down on the counter top that rattled the glass jars lined up on the shelf. 'We can find another doorway. Let's get out of here, it's getting late.'

They made it to the door and Soma flung it open.

'I'm afraid not Mrs Rowmoon,' the deep voice of Mr Scarper said. 'If a doorway was created outside of Cadabra, the Dark Emperor would know. He is the only one that could create another. It is common knowledge that he houses one. Look for a box, Miss Cassidy, small and wooden. Inside you'll find your doorway.'

Soma tried to push Heather out of the store and onto the dark alleyway, but Heather shoved backwards.

'If I find the doorway... the box, how do I get home?'

'Utter the word, just as you did before and you'll be home.'

Heather took several steps backwards, and felt Soma's hand on her shoulder. Together they left the store, Heather's mind feeling numb to the obstacle that lay ahead of her.

'What am I going to do?' Heather asked, as they walked down the alleyway and out into the night markets.

'We'll get you as far as Cadabra, but the rest will have to be up to you,' Soma replied.

'You'll take me there?'

'Our last performance is there, the grand finale. It's in two nights' time, everyone will be there, especially the Emperor.' She stole a look at the young girl. 'It'll be your only chance.'

They walked quickly through the throng of people and creatures. Pops and sparks of magic flew into the air, like the fireworks Heather had seen as a child. But these were different, these had colours Heather had not seen before, they lasted a lot longer in the sky and danced and spun wildly.

'What about Kiel?' Heather asked as they approached the road that led to the tent.

Without turning back to her, Soma said, 'Tonight... we find him and free him.'

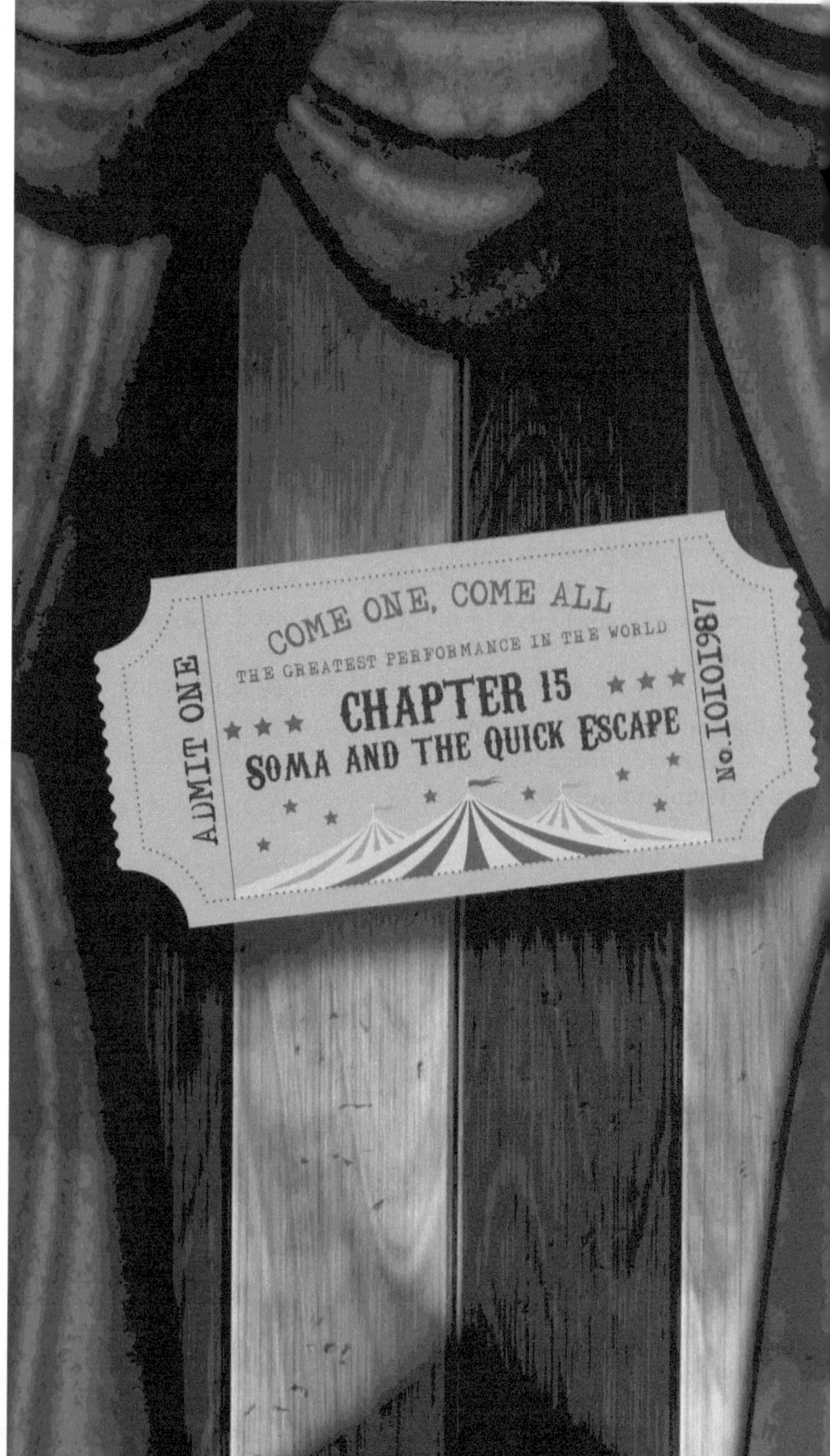

ADMIT ONE
COME ONE, COME ALL
THE GREATEST PERFORMANCE IN THE WORLD
CHAPTER 15
SOMA AND THE QUICK ESCAPE
No. 10101987

The Ring Leader stood in the middle of the tent. His red jacket was now dust and worm free, and his silver buttons had been polished and gleamed brilliantly. A crowd had gathered outside the tent and were eager to see the performance inside. Heather stood behind the curtain and watched as the residents of Hey Presto! made their way in and sat at their allocated seats.

It was exactly like the circus that Heather knew and loved. She expected to see the trapeze artists standing at the wings, warming up and practising their flips. She could almost see Guntha doing some arm curls with heavy weights and oiling up his biceps. She looked to the darkest corner and for a moment, her mind imagined Mr Harlow. He would stand there, as if he wasn't nervous at all, and wait for his turn. His top hat would be resting gently on his head. His hands would be either behind his back or criss-crossed in front of him. It was reassuring seeing someone so calm right before the big event.

Heather watched as the jugglers juggled knifes and stakes on fire, tossing them between each other and into the air. They threw them so high that they brushed the tent ceiling and sent a shower of small embers floating down onto the arena floor. The crowd gasped in excitement and ate strange fruit that Heather had seen in the markets for sale.

After the jugglers was a thin woman Heather had seen on the night they fought the wolves. She was carried out by LaFare and placed on a wooden seat. LaFare then went back behind the curtain and carried out a glass box the size of two shoe boxes on top of one another. He placed it in front of her and walked back out of sight. Heather wasn't sure what was about to happen. She looked on with trepid curiosity. The woman, who announced herself as Yemin, started to dance. Her legs were long and slender, her arms equally so. She waved her fingers around like she was underwater, and the crowd looked on, as if hypnotised.

Slowly, Yemin started to contort her body, wrapping her limbs around her torso. She stood in the glass box and folded her legs down. Her ankles bent at odd angles and her toes curled into themselves. Heather stared with open mouthed amusement. The entire audience were silent. Then, Yemin slid downwards into the glass container, her spine curling around the edge, the whole time hypnotic music hummed gently in the background, eerie and dark. Finally, her head slid into the corner and her arms folded over the top. LaFare came out from the shadows one last time with a glass slate. He placed it on top. Yemin had fit her entire body into the small glass box. The crowd applauded loudly, standing up and cheering.

For a moment, Heather thought she was home, watching the crowd react to Mr Harlow. From behind her Soma walked over and stood to her right, she was close enough that Heather could hear her breathing. She didn't say anything. Heather turned to Soma, her eyes clearly full of tears.

'Do you perform in your circus?' Soma asked, seeing her clearly upset.

'No. Well, sometimes I help. I don't really do anything. I just help with the dogs,' Heather said, watching LaFare pick up Yemin in her glass container and walk back to the rear of the tent and through the curtain.

'Dogs?' Soma said quizzically.

Heather forgot momentarily that they were not in her world. Suddenly, there was a great sound of drums beating and the lights around the tent began to flash and flicker in time to the beat. Then they stopped dead and the audience looked on as another sound filled the small arena. The clip-clop of wood against wood. Heather stepped backwards in fear, she had heard that noise before. Then, from between the curtains came Ollsop. His face painted white with a red zigzag running over his lips. Attached to his arms and legs where long wooden planks.

'The Meniphesto Incantana,' Heather whispered. She had seen them when she was at the crossroads that led to Hey Presto! and Ta-Dah, when Kiel had rescued her.

'Very good, Heather. You're starting to learn the workings of Abara and Cadabra,' Soma said, moving so she was slightly behind Heather.

Ollsop moved awkwardly to centre stage and stood like a demented spider, staring out at the audience. The entire crowd was too scared to move. The Meniphesto Incantana were widely feared. They had kidnapped children and women for the Dark Emperor. They had ruined crops and set entire villages on fire. One elderly resident stood up, his knees shaking wildly and started heading for the exit. Then, Ollsop moved quickly and fell, his legs sprawling upwards. He kicked wildly, like a turtle on its back and yelped like a helpless animal. The crowd laughed loudly. Ollsop managed to get on his wooden legs once more, before slipping again, sending him spread-eagled on the ground, his pant leg ripping on one side. The elderly man sat back down, laughing so hard a tear fell from his eye.

Heather looked at Soma, 'Ollsop is a... clown?'

'Yes, one of the greatest in the lands.'

'He teases the Incantanas?' she said, surprised.

'Of course, he used to be one.'

Heather was in shock. She remembered seeing scars on his lips from where the stitches were placed. It all made sense now. She turned back to see the audience laughing and chortling hysterically. Soma turned her head, and sniffed loudly. Heather looked over to her.

'What is it?' Heather asked.

Soma didn't answer. She sniffed again.

'Come on, we have to go,' Soma said, running for the stairs.

'What is it?' Heather repeated. 'Where are we going?'

Soma glanced at her over her shoulder, her eyes were canary yellow.

'I've just found Kiel.'

***

Soma and Heather had left the compounds of the performance tent and run through the quiet streets of Hey Presto! heading towards the front gates. Heather struggled to keep up, but knew time must be of the essence if they had to leave immediately without warning the others.

'Heather,' Soma croaked over her shoulder. 'If you fall too far behind, I'll leave you. We must hurry.'

They passed a pen full of what Heather could only describe as a cross between a pig and a rabbit. They were small animals, fat and appeared to have no neck. They had long ears that dragged across the ground. Their hide had filthy short white fur and they were snoring loudly. A sign on the pen read: *Perblans – 3 for 80 Quas*. She looked up and noticed Soma was way ahead of her, so she ran to catch up. They reached the gate, only to see the large irons doors shut and guards standing to attention every few meters. Soma hid alongside a brick wall and looked around. Heather finally caught up to her and noticed she wasn't struggling for breath or even appeared to have sweated in the slightest. Heather was bent over, trying to breathe as fast as she could. Her head was light and she thought she was going to faint.

'Damn,' Soma said, stepping backwards as one of the guards broke from his station and followed a noise that had come from the right of the gate.

'Won't they let us out?' Heather said, finally catching her breathe.

'Not without good reason. It's too dangerous to be out in the forestry at this time of night. They don't like risking their people's lives, even the visitors. Hey Presto! has a duty of care to all civilians inside their walls.'

'Even the dark magic users?'

Soma turned her head slightly and glared at Heather. '*Most* of the civilians... not all.'

Heather watched as the lone guard spotted two drunks that had stumbled out of a tavern and were mock fighting near a closed market stall. The guard shooed them away and told them not to come back. As he wandered back to his position at the gate he stopped and marvelled at the archway that Heather had seen on the way in. He read it out loud, as if enormously proud of the saying and straightened his belt and returned to the gate.

'We need a distraction,' Heather said.

Soma turned, surprised at her. 'Yes, that's it. But how?'

Heather looked over to the worn dirt path where they had come from and remembered the animals she saw.

'Stay here,' she ordered Soma, who didn't like to be told what to do at the best of times.

Heather ran, following the shadows back up the path from where they had come. She looked over the pen at the Perblans. Their stuck-up snout and messy fur was grotesque and odd. One of them looked at her and lunged forward, snapping its jowls.

'Just like in the circus,' Heather told herself, climbing over the pen. 'Just like handling the dogs in the circus...'

She avoided their menacing sniffs and bites and unlatched the pen. The door swung open with a creaking, rusted squeak. Suddenly, as if the Perblans had been waiting their whole life to be free, they bolted out the gate. Heather was nearly knocked over by one as it zoomed past her, brushing its filthy mane against her leg. She almost vomited, the smell was absolutely putrid. The Perblans ran in every direction, running into stalls and knocking the make-shift gazebo's over and sending giant tubs of yellow and red powder spilling out onto the ground.

The guards all turned to see what the commotion was and ran towards the creatures. Heather snuck along the side of the pen and crept through the darkness. From there, she could see Soma looking for a break in the mayhem to make a run for the gate. One guard was ordered to stay at his post and stood holding his weapon with trembling hands. Soma ran, fast through the haze of darkness, oblivious to the guards around her shouting at the Perblans. Heather saw her chance and ran too. She bolted through the darkness, the stones under her feet pushing through the soles of her shoes. Sweat ran down her neck and she could feel her heart beating faster and faster. She knew if she got caught they would take her away, maybe lock her up in some prison. For a second she thought maybe Kiel or Soma wouldn't come for her. She saw the gate ahead and slowed her speed, sticking to the shadows. They both reached the gate at the same time.

'Quickly, Heather,' Soma whispered, watching the remaining guard laughing at the beasts as they bit his fellow guardsmen. 'Unlock the gate, I'll keep watch.'

Heather looked down and saw the gate had several latches and chains. She pushed and heaved giant metal handles, it made a scraping noise that made the remaining guard look over, his hapless grin soon turned to a grimace.

'Hey!' he screamed. He was holding a blunt looking sword in his hand, which he started flailing wildly.

'Quick!' Soma cried out, watching Heather fumble the last latch. She pushed her hands out of the way and slammed it upwards, then across.

The lock fell loose onto the ground and the gate moaned open. Soma knew the guard would be only a few paces away, she grabbed Heather by her shoulder and shoved her through the gate. Heather stumbled and managed to gain her footing as she stood on the opposite side of the gates of Hey Presto! The guard came running up to Soma, swinging his sword back and forth. It sliced through the air, making whistling noises as it passed her ears.

'No leaving through the night!' he called out, which now made all the other guards turn and see that the Perblans had all just been a distraction.

Soma leaned towards the oncoming sword and her eyes glowed yellow. She curled her lips away from her teeth and snarled viciously. The guard suddenly stopped, his sword fell from his hands and he turned on his heels and ran in the opposite direction. Soma slipped through the gate and onto the other side, pulling the gate shut behind her. Heather stood rubbing her sore shoulder, looking at Soma's back as she slowly moved away from the gate.

'That was close,' Heather said, watching as Soma avoided eye contact. 'How do you know where Kiel is?'

Soma looked at the ground, then up at Heather. Heather yelped in surprise, her hand rushed to her mouth and she stared at Soma with wide eyed fear.

Soma's nose had gone black, and resembled a small button. Her ears had grown upwards, to a point. Her forearms were now covered in a hide of thick, black hair. Her eyes illuminated the cold darkness.

'I never wanted you to see me like this, Heather,' she said, looking at her. 'But it is too late. I'm turning, Heather. Long ago I was bitten by a caged wolf, it had the ability to communicate telepathically, it used me as a puppet to do wrong and one day when I refused to help it any more, it bit me. I ran away from that time and joined the Festival of the Soul.' Soma sniffed the air and her head shot east.

'This way Heather,' she growled, getting down on all fours. 'Get on my back, we don't have much time.'

Heather looked at her as Soma's legs grew longer and thicker. Her shoes busted open and elongated, gnarled, silver claws appeared where her nails used to be, tearing at the dirt like hooks into butter. Her nose became elongated and it formed a snout. She blinked and howled up towards the moon. She had transformed into a wolf in front of Heather's eyes. Soma kicked at the dirt and shook her wild, soil coloured mane. She crouched lower and arched her back so Heather could climb upon her. Heather did, with much trepidation. Her hair was thick and exquisite. She held on tight as Soma leaped into the air, soared for several meters and landed on a path on the other side of the clearing. She sniffed the ground and started galloping into the dark.

ADMIT ONE
COME ONE, COME ALL
THE GREATEST PERFORMANCE IN THE WORLD
CHAPTER 16
FOR THE CAUSE
No.IOIOI987

The wind that caressed Heather's face was sweet, and held a hint of a faraway fire. The darkness around her became a blur as they rushed through woodlands and bounded over fallen trees and small streams. The sky above would blink through heavily leaved canopies. The moon, dim through the clouds, watched as the small Earth-child rode the back of a beast that she had only read about in fairy-tales or seen in horror movies.

The forestry was dangerous at night, and only those brave enough would dare venture into its gullet. Morbid beasts of all shapes and hunger would merge to feast on weary travellers. The stories from this part of the world were plentiful and often used to keep children indoors at night. Heather hadn't heard any of these wistful stories, but she knew very well that it was not a place she would like to be on her own.

As they forged their way through the thicket, she could hear large animals scatter out of their way, or take refuge. Heather hoped in silence that the transformed Soma *was* the fierce creature in the forest tonight, or else they would be in a lot of trouble.

The walls faded away from Hey Presto! and they travelled east through the night. Soma suddenly stopped, Heather could feel her heart through her legs which saddled either side of her. It was pumping fast, a rhythmic pounding that could only be comparable to a drum roll. When Soma breathed out, large plumes of great white smoke bellowed into the night air. She sniffed and growled.

'We're close,' she said in a voice that was not hers.

The were-beast moved with extreme stealth through the thorny shrubbery. They stopped by a large mound of branches and foliage while Soma tried to calm her body. A little in the distance, Heather could hear the squeaks of rickety springs. Its rusted sound reminded her of the Festival wagons they rode to Hey Presto! in. Soma lay on the ground, her large black claws dug into the dirt.

'Get off, child. They will cross this path shortly and we must be ready.'

Heather slid off Soma's back and down onto her knees amongst wicked looking thorns and the coldness of the ground. The dirt was strangely spongy and if pressed too hard, water came up through small earthly pores. Heather could feel fear seeping through her blood; her hands shook wildly and her eyes would not stay focused on anything. The large beast beside her huffed and clawed at the ground, like a rodent digging at the entrance to its burrow.

From the darkness came a grotesque singing. It was a combination of whistling and humming. Words were spoken in a fluid trance, but none that Heather recognised. A dull light appeared over the peak of the roadway and bounced from side to side. Heather could see a gnarly silhouette leading a procession. It was the ravenous creature Heather had seen before - Clat Rakshaw. Its morose wings draped outwards like an injured bird, dragging across the loose soil path. Its head was hung down, as if it wasn't looking where it was going. The hinges of its wings squeaked and grinded on rusted cogs and hinges. The faux bird looked up momentarily and its wicked eyes gleamed. Heather ducked her head down further, and was unnoticed by the deadly assassin. Heather turned to Soma, but she was not moving; her body was deathly still, her breathing almost stopped completely.

Behind Clat Rakshaw came another creature, he was the one from the cemetery, dressed in robes. His arms and shoulders were comparatively larger than the rest of his body and covered in a thick hide of crimson red hair, he was pulling a cage. His body was leaning forward and his mouth was a grimace. The chains he held in his hands had rubbed the fur from them, down to his skin. The clunky, thick chains ran over his shoulder, digging into his fur deeply. Blood trickled from his shoulder and back from the friction. He heaved and groaned, gnashing his fangs. The cage was dome-shaped and constructed from pieces of rusted wire and metal. Heather had a glimmering thought that it looked like a bird cage, but fifty times bigger. It had four small wheels that rolled and wobbled as the beastly-man, Heather remember Clat calling him Sas-Lotch, pulled it along. Laying inside was Kiel. His nose was bleeding profusely and he appeared to be either asleep or dead. Behind the cage was another creature. He was dressed in long robes and held both hands together, his fingers knotted in a ball, held chest high and swaying.

'Anything, Amol?' Clat shrieked.

'Small creatures... nothing large enough to be a threat,' Amol answered, humming and murmuring in birdsong.

Soma turned slowly towards Heather. She saw the full were-beast, teeth as sharp as rail road spikes, hair was coarse as a horse's tail, and she almost screamed in fear.

'When I give the word, you run to Kiel and unlock that cage, understand?'

Heather nodded, her heart pounded, not only at the sight of what Soma had become, but at the task she had now been given. The rickety cage bumped and squeaked over the rough terrain. Heather watched with baited breath as Clat skulked past her, his arcane wings tracing the ground and giving off a scratching thump with every step. Soma moved silently and deadly to the rear of a large fallen boulder and hugged it with her long, chiselled arms. Her claws dug under the boulder and it started to pull it from the wet soil like a rotten tooth. The cracking and snapping roots that held the rock made little noise, but just enough to be heard by the preacher they called Amol. His head snapped upwards, gleaming, smoky white eyes looked to their position.

'Now,' Soma growled and lifted the massive stone up, over her thick shoulders and threw it.

Heather felt every instinct hesitate but she gathered her strength and courage, and bolted towards the cage. The boulder soared over her head; she felt the wind brush her long hair, pieces of dirt and foliage fell onto her back. The boulder struck Amol, crushing him against the ground and pinning him to a tree trunk. He let out a dying hum. Clat kicked the ground hard and took to the air, his apocalyptic wings flapped like the broken rotor blades of a windmill. Sas-Lotch dropped the chain he was pulling and crouched down on all fours, he opened his mouth wide and howled from the pit of his stomach. Inside Heather's mind there was a curtain of white that she used to try to block out the danger that was before her. Her ears were ringing with the commotion, but she held her gaze directly at the cage, and nothing else. Her feet pounded the ground as she tried to move as quickly as she could. When she reached the cage, she yanked at the lock, but it was triple bolted, with no way to open it.

Soma dove towards the Sas-Lotch, swinging her arms wildly. Connecting with the crimson beast's bottom jaw and sending blood spilling onto the well-worn path. The Sas-Lotch fell backwards, his massive hands holding his face, cupping the blood. Heather saw a large shadow pass over the lantern at the front of the cage, but dared not look. If the winged assassin was going to take her then she would rather not see him coming.

As of right now, Heather had control of her fear. She pulled and yanked at the locks, thumping them with her hand and using all her strength to open the door, but it was no use. The lock was jammed. She glanced inside the cage and saw Kiel lying deadly still. A shadow flew over again and she looked left, just in time to see Soma being struck by nothing but a blur of movement. Soma let out a shriek of pain, as she was launched into the air and tossed back several feet. Clat landed on the path, near the boulder and looked at Amol's legs sticking out from underneath.

'You'll pay for that, travelling scum,' Clat growled. He then looked over his shoulder at Heather. 'Then you're next.'

The white curtain dividing fear from courage suddenly became a little smaller in Heather's mind. She turned back to where they had been hiding and searched for a rock. She found one big enough to carry on her own and tore it from the ground. She lifted it up over her shoulder with all the strength she could muster and carried it back to the cage. She stood in front of the cage with trembling legs and slammed it down hard on the locks. The first of three locks broke loose and crumbled to dust when it hit the ground. She lifted it again, and struck it harder. Her wrists burned with fiery pain.

Soma woke to find she was looking up at the stars. A wide grinning moon stared down at her. For a moment she didn't know exactly where she was, that was until she saw the evil Clat Rakshaw fly over her. Like a whirling torpedo, the assassin dove, claws out, towards Soma. The sounds of its mechanical wings whistling in the cold night air made her body shiver. Soma moved, quickly rolling onto her side as the dark figure struck the dirt where she had just been laying seconds ago. Dust and rocks exploded into the air in a puff of brown soot. Soma was already on her feet, her eyes narrow and deathly staring.

Clat emerged from the cloud of earth and looked at his claws, they were bent and bleeding. Soma lunged forward, grasping Clat around his neck. She felt his leathery wings beat against her skin, the rusted bolts and screws scratching at her back and shoulders, drawing blood and tearing flesh. They wrestled viciously, knocking down trees and crumbling boulders to dust. They fell backwards, with Clat on top of Soma. His menacing face was relentless.

Heather could hear the commotion near her, but knew if she didn't get Kiel out of the cage there would be no chance of escaping. She lifted the stone again and pounded the lock. It gave a little, splitting down the middle. Again, she hit it, this time the stone bounced back and crushed her finger against the third bolt. She let out a howl of agony. A small cut had opened up and had now started to bleed. The curtain was finally drawn back to reveal all the fear Heather knew was waiting at the edge. Her heart pounded faster and faster. She saw her bleeding hand and started to cry. She tried to pick up the stone, but could not.

'Please...' she whispered, a lost word to nobody.

Clat struck Soma's face again and again, tearing thick clumps of hair off her cheeks and neck. Soma lifted her knee up and crushed the assassin's spine. She felt a relieving crunch as something metal snapped in two. Clat roared with pain, spitting droplets of saliva down upon Soma's face. Another kick and Clat was tossed head over heels onto the ground behind Soma. She rose to her feet quickly and swiftly pummelled the assassin with several harsh blows of her ham-sized fists. Clat struggled to his feet and kicked off the ground, his body hovered for a second, jerked in a bizarre twitch and fell to the ground.

'You broke my spine...' he yelped, Soma seeing true anguish in his face. 'You broke my spine!'

He kicked off again, this time gaining flight, but struggling to gain any height. Soma pounced at him, trying desperately to clutch his feet. Clat flapped his make-shift wings, his body jerking and seizing in mid-air. He fell a few feet, and then gained flight again and soared off through the trees crashing into branches and vines. Soma went after him.

Heather looked down at the lock, one was intact, one nearly broken. Her right hand was red with blood, and her other was filthy dirty and scratched. A hand emerged through the darkness of the cage, equally bloody and dirty. It lay on her wounded hand and Heather felt the pain drift away. She looked up, her eyes red from crying and marked with trails of tears down her face. Kiel was looking at her. His eyes bruised and puffy.

'Keep going Heather... you can... do it,' he said, barely keeping himself conscious.

Heather nodded, smiled and picked up the stone. She lifted it and smashed the second lock off. Then tried for the third. From behind her she heard an animalistic grunt. Kiel's eyes widened.

'Heather, ignore the lock, just run!'

Heather turned around to see Sas-Lotch hunched behind her. Its bottom jaw hung loosely and dripped with red fluid. The beast tried to speak, but its teeth and tongue wouldn't connect with a broken jaw.

'Heather, run! Ignore the lock, just go!' Kiel screamed at her.

Heather felt the ground move as the Sas-Lotch bolted for her. She didn't turn around, she lifted the stone up high again, shut her eyes and drove it down as hard as she could. The cage shook wildly. The beast behind her snatched her up in its massive arms and spun her around. She was looking up into the eyes of the Sas-Lotch. Thin slits for pupils stared at her, an evil Heather had only seen once before, in the thinly masked sockets of Clat Rakshaw.

'Death will welcome you with open arms!' the Sas-Lotch managed to growl, lifting one almighty hand up behind its head, its long claw-nails sliced through the air, its target – Heather's throat.

Heather closed her eyes and thought of her father. She thought of Bounty the crab boy and Mr Harlow. She thought of her life in the circus and how she loved every minute of every day. She could see pictures of her extended circus family, all sitting around eating breakfast and talking about the previous night's show. She missed them badly and would miss them even more now that she knew she would never get home.

The strange chill of death Heather expected to feel never came, she opened her eyes when she heard a fleshy tear and saw the Sas-Lotch claws a mere inch from her throat. She looked into the eyes of the beast and saw its pupils widened, blood trickling from its nose. A piece of barbed metal protruding from its own throat, travelling over Heather's head and originating from deep within the cage. Heather turned around to see Kiel holding a twisted piece of metal. He had pulled it free from the cage wall and impaled the Sas-Lotch. He let it go and the beast fell back to the ground, its lungs empty of air, its throat gurgling with blood.

Heather helped Kiel from the cage and he hugged her. His skin was warm and sticky with blood, but she didn't care.

Something large moved from behind them. From the thicket Soma emerged, not as a were-beast, but as herself. Her skin was torn and bleeding and one of her eyes was barely visible through swollen skin.

'He got away,' she said.

Kiel walked to her and placed a hand on her shoulder.

'I can never thank you two enough,' Kiel said. 'They were taking me to the Dark Emperor for my warrant. There would be no escaping once he put me in one of his magical prisons... I owe you my life.'

Soma hugged him and Heather could hear her whisper, 'For the cause.' But did not ask what she meant.

'Come,' Soma said, limping. 'We must move hastily towards Hey Presto! and sneak back in before dawn. We will have to pack and move before the Dark Emperor hears of this and sends out more assassins.'

'But...' Heather started to say, then chose to just be silent. She wanted to ask about getting home and why there was a warrant on Kiel's head, but decided it wasn't the right time. There would be time for questions later.

COME ONE, COME ALL
THE GREATEST PERFORMANCE IN THE WORLD
ADMIT ONE
CHAPTER 17
THE ALLIANCE
No. 1010 1987

They slept beside the wall of Hey Presto! until the sun rose. Canary yellow beams of light split through the surrounding trees and birdsong echoed along the empty trails leading into the city. Heather had trouble sleeping on the ground as it wasn't entirely flat, and they weren't sleeping on a mattress or blanket. When she had awoken during the night, her neck and back were aching, she had spent most of her life sleeping in a small, cramped room of a caravan and thought she would never miss it. Now she would give anything to be in her own bed.

When she opened her eyes she could see the stars gently fading as red splashes of sun etched across the sky. She turned to look at Kiel, but he was gone. She sat up and looked around. He was standing by the road looking down towards the main entrance. His coat was fastened tightly around his waist, a hooded scarf was wrapped around his head, so his face was hidden, but his long fingers were bare. Bronze and silver rings gleamed off each finger. Heather stood up and stretched. A few feet away Soma rose and felt the swollen bumps on her face. She winced when she got to her bruised eyes.

Kiel turned and casually walked back towards the wall.

'The gates are open and the market people are going in. Now's our chance.'

Together they strolled down the path that led to the entrance. The guards from the night before were still on duty, their uniforms filthy from chasing the Perblans. One guard was leaning on his staff, half asleep, ignoring everyone that wandered through the gates. Kiel, Soma and Heather strode through calmly and headed towards the performance tent. Soma was ahead of the others, she was keen to pack up and leave before the guards had a chance to come around questioning them about the late night escape.

LaFare saw Soma marching towards them, her head was down and dried blood still caked her shirt and neck.

'What happened?' LaFare said, dropping the rope he was tying.

Soma went into his arms and they embraced. Heather thought she saw Soma shed a tear and felt an emotional side to her that she had never seen before. LaFare looked up as Kiel and Heather joined them.

'It's good to see you return,' he said to Kiel, his tone of voice not quite convincing.

'How is the packing?' Kiel said, almost as an instruction.

'Stage is packed, the poles are away, just the ropes and to fold the tent... then we can go.'

'Very good,' Kiel said. He turned and headed towards one of the wagons.

Soma and LaFare spoke to one another, softly and privately. Heather stood back and watched the city as it woke from the long, cold night and reopened their stores, digging out their fresh food and merchandise. She looked back at Kiel and saw him standing by the wagon. She felt the questions float around in her mind, the ones she had wanted to ask him after they rescued him from the assassins. She strode over to him, watching as the huge tent collapsed down on itself and the acrobats and performers scurried to fold it and roll it into a long tube for travelling. She strolled around the wagon to see Kiel looking down toward the cabin floor.

'Kiel, something's been playing on my mind... I wanted to ask...'

Kiel was holding a trap door open and looking down at hundreds of small cylinders. Printed on yellow and red paper, strapped to each one, was a stamp. Some had bleed out, while others were smudged. It was of a golden skull. Coming out of each tube, like a tail of a rodent, was a wick. They were packed into small crates with words scrawled across the lid in a language Heather could not read. Kiel slammed the make-shift door down and grabbed Heather by the shoulder moving her quickly away from the carriages.

'What was that?' Heather said, pulling away from his grasp. 'Are they... explosives?' Terror entered Heather's already fragile mind.

Kiel looked her in the eyes for a moment and then over her shoulder at the others. No one had seen their altercation.

'Heather, listen to me...' He looked back at her and could see her deep worry. 'I know you have many questions, but we are not what you think.'

Heather started to shake. Kiel tried to speak, but he was lost for words. He took her hand and led her to the wagon and helped her up into the seat. Ollsop was watching them from far away, helping to secure the tent to the second wagon. He looked down at his feet, knowing what was about to be revealed to Heather. He felt a strange electricity emanate through his scars. He rubbed them with his fingers and felt a sinking feeling in his stomach.

Heather and Kiel sat in silence for a moment, until Kiel took her hand and felt her shaking.

'Why are we going to perform for the Dark Emperor in Cadabra when the assassins were after you? And why do you hide your face all the time?'

Kiel nodded. 'Heather, I'm about to reveal to you all answers. Some you won't like, or maybe won't understand, but this has been planned for a very long time.' A soft breeze stroked the grassy knoll where the tent had been. It pushed against Kiel's coat gently. 'What you saw in the back of the wagon, you should have never have seen. We were going to help you get home, then...' he paused, 'we were going to kill the Dark Emperor.'

Heather looked into Kiel's eyes and saw a deep pain she had never seen before. She saw his sorrow and conviction in what he was saying.

'Why?'

Kiel smiled, 'It goes back many years, Heather. Possibly before you were born in your world. The Dark Emperor has taken on many names in his lifetime, he has killed many of our people, not only mine but many of those that make up the Festival of the Soul you see here. I, myself, am but one of a handful of HazzahKiel's left. We were rounded up by the Dark Emperor and slaughtered for our land and what our mountains held. The Dark One is only interested in land and control, no matter what the cost. His dark magic use has warped his mind and made him mad. When I escaped the encampments he set up, I was only a child and vowed to destroy him for everything he had done, no matter what the cost.

'There have been years of war and fighting, Heather. He has gotten to know my face and name well and wishes me death. That being the reason for the assassins. I lead an uprising of like-minded people against his tyrannous ways, we call ourselves the Alliance. Once we had a great leader named Lux Urofane, who was taken by the Emperor and killed. I have then stepped up as the new leader.

'The longer we let him devour the land and kill and dabble in dark magic, the closer he will be to controlling this world.' Kiel took a breath as if the weight of everyone was on his shoulders. 'Soma's people are all but gone. She has no family, no land and her culture was wiped out. Ollsop was taken as a child and turned into one of the Emperor's slaves, he was lucky to escape with his body and mind intact. LaFare was held prisoner for a long time and he has scars to prove it. What he's been through, I wouldn't wish on any enemy.'

Heather wasn't sure what to say, everything she had seen and heard now made sense.

'You're going to kill the Emperor?' Her voice was soft, yet her question was direct.

'Between LaFare and Ollsop, we have a rough outline of the tower in which the Dark One resides. Within the spires resides deep, dark magic. Years of torment and torture have given him enough power to control all our lands and enslave every one. He has artefacts and spells that are extremely dangerous and outlawed in most the known world. The objects you saw in the back,' Kiel pointed behind them into the rear of the wagon, 'are enough to crumble the tower and everything in it. In two nights' time we are to perform a one off show for the Emperor. We hope his spies have not alerted him to the fact that he is letting the Alliance in the gates. This, Heather, will be his downfall.' A smile crossed Kiel's face.

Heather sat in shock. Ollsop had walked over and climbed into the cabin. He sat on the opposite side of Heather.

'She knows?' Ollsop asked.

'Yes. We should go. Heather can ride up here with you. Travel slowly my friend, and I will see you again at the gates of Cadabra.'

Ollsop nodded and watched Kiel climb down from the cabin and disappear into the crowd leading into the main thoroughfare of Hey Presto!

'But... Scarper and William said the Dark Emperor had a doorway, the only way for me to get home... and you're going to blow it up.' She looked at Ollsop with tears welling in her eyes.

'We've had great discussions about this Heather,' Ollsop said. 'We will see you home before detonating the explosives... I promise.'

Heather looked out over the bustling streets that wound around buildings and bizarre statues. She saw the grand catacombs of Hey Presto! and how all the people here lived free and away from harm and pain. She couldn't imagine living in a fear of a Dark Emperor.

'Okay,' Heather said, wiping her tears away.

'Half way to Cadabra there is a road that leads back to Hokus Pokus. We'll leave the wagons there and travel north until we reach the city. You mentioned a mage called Brim who brought you here. We'll look for him and see if we can get you back that way, if not... the Emperor's castle will be your only chance.'

Heather was lost in her thoughts, she knew Hokus Pokus was not a good place to be, and she had already been chased out of there by Brim and his men.

'How will we get Brim to send me back?' Heather asked.

'Everyone in Hokus Pokus has a price, be it money, information... or other. He brought you here, so he can surely send you home.'

The wagon slowly moved forward, led by the Gazzoo. Heather heard the explosives rock gently in the back and became a little ill at ease.

'There's a good chance the Emperor already knows he has built a doorway and will already be after him.'

'And if he's been,' Heather felt a lump in her throat, 'killed?'

'Then the tower will be your only hope.' The Gazzoo chortled gently as they passed several guards who stared at them intently. 'On the night of the performance,

Heather,' Ollsop said, leaning into her, 'you'll have a small window of time to reach the high point of the Emperor's tower and seek the doorway box. If you don't get to it in time...'

Heather looked at Ollsop, she could see his face had become crestfallen and he was worried for her.

'I understand,' she said. Suddenly Heather felt a knot of anxiety in her chest, the possibility for her getting home was growing closer.

***

After half a day's journey out of the gates of Hey Presto! the roads became wider and Heather started to notice the stalls selling small trinkets and fruit were petering out, until they were gone altogether.

The chatter of bartering and commerce started to slowly subside and the road fell eerily silent. Only the clopping hooves of the Gazzoo, and the gentle snoring of children in the back kept the silence from shaking their nerves.

A long streak of white cloud spread out above them like a smear of cotton wool, behind it a deep blue canvas. Heather could see some stars starting to shine through the daylight. She thought about the stars here, and wondered if they were the same as home. Often she would lay on the grass in from of her caravan with Bounty and look up at the sky, counting the shooting stars.

From behind her, from the cabin, came the sound of movement. The small hatch door opened and LaFare poked his head up.

'The path is coming up.'

Ollsop nodded and tied the reigns to a small burl of wood on the front rail. LaFare climbed up and took the driver's seat. Heather moved nervously to the back. She didn't have any belongings, only the clothes she came here with and the small robe and scarf they had given her for the cold nights. Ollsop walked around the wagon filling his small shoulder bag with bottles, a leather bag of water and sheets of paper. He went to the cupboard and rolled a long piece of bread in paper and took a small sack of meat from the cool box. Heather felt the coolness from the ice circle her feet.

They walked to the back of the cabin as LaFare pulled the wagon to the side of the road. Heather and Ollsop jumped down on the hard ground and walked around to the front. Heather could see a small side path up ahead, on the left. It didn't look like a road she had seen before, it wasn't paved with stone or rock, it was just worn ground.

'Good bye Heather, I hope you get home,' LaFare said, waving to them. 'Safe travels.'

'Safe travels. Stay together and don't let the wagons get too far apart from one another. We'll see you at the Forge Crossing in a day... well,' Ollsop said, 'hopefully only me.'

Heather smiled and waved to LaFare who clicked his tongue making the Gazzoo start trotting again. Heather looked for Kiel, but she hadn't seen him for some time. She even thought Soma would come from the rear wagon to say good bye, but there was no sign of her. The wagons moved slowly past them and soon Heather and Ollsop were left alone on the road, the dust of the wagon's slowly floating around them.

'This way,' Ollsop said, cantering towards the path.

Heather followed. The terrain was rough and overgrown, as if nobody had used this path for a long time. Ollsop suddenly hurried, as if being chased. He rarely looked back.

They ran at a slow pace, Heather's heart pounded in her rib cage. She dared not look around the wooded area as she could already feel eyes watching her. They didn't stop until they reached a small rocky outcrop several minutes later. Ollsop sat on a ledge of stone and caught his breath.

'Sorry, Heather,' he huffed, 'but we had to hurry through the pass. It isn't safe to dawdle.'

'It's okay, Ollsop,' Heather said, seeing his wrinkles bunch up around his eyes.

She wandered over to the edge of the rocky wall and peered over. Hokus Pokus was in view. She had ill feelings about returning there and hoped no one remembered her. Ollsop stood beside her, his scars along his lips were flaming red.

'Ready?' he asked.

Heather nodded.

They made their way down the outcrop. There were several paths intertwining through the stone. Some had carved steps which looked ancient and were covered with lime-green moss. Others were freshly trekked; the grass not yet brown from foot traffic. As they descended, Heather caught eye of a bundle of bones near the bottom. Her stomach lurched into her throat. Her hands started to shake. She pushed her nervousness down, and continued down the labyrinth.

The smells from Hokus Pokus drifted up towards them in great wafts from spices and drying fruit. It also smelled of sweat and the coppery taste of blood. Ollsop had also noted the aroma of burning magic.

They reached the bottom of the ridge and Ollsop pulled a hood over his head. He told Heather to do the same. She tied the scarf around her face so only her eyes could be seen, and pulled the hood over the top of her head. Together they walked towards the large city. Heather hadn't had a chance to take in the view when she was here last. There was a dilapidated brick wall running the circumference of the city, the bricks long ago deteriorated and fallen from their structure. In some areas there were massive holes, possibly put there from a war, or from some great beast. The grass along the outskirts was long and green with tangerine tips and there were strange creatures mulling around, staring and whispering.

'This place is eerie,' Heather said, following the heels of Ollsop.

'If anyone talks to you, don't answer. I'll do the talking,' he said out the corner of his mouth.

There were several entrances to the city of Hokus Pokus. The closest entrance looked like a boulder had been catapulted through a tower and it lay crumbled, on its side. The whole left portion had been walked through over time and created a ramp of brick and stone. It went up, like a tongue and down into the gullet of the city. Ollsop stayed clear of that entrance. Heather glanced behind her and saw two strangers following them. She looked back, unsure if they were after them, or someone else.

They waited at the second gate while a massive armoured wagon squeezed out of the city and onto the road. Along the side were turrets with spears and crossbows. There was a dome on the back end with a wizard crouched down, his hands were holding his head up. His long grey hair spilled over his arms and down his chest. His eyes were snow white and his whole body was shaking.

Ollsop held Heather's arm and pulled her gently back. 'There must have been a very powerful person visiting the city.' Heather looked ahead of the heavily armed wagon and saw three more down the road. 'Why someone with that much magic and armoury to hire would come here, for anything, is a mystery.'

Heather watched the wagon lurch and groan as it scraped along the gate posts and out of the mouth of Hokus Pokus. Ollsop let go of Heather's arm and together they entered the city.

Heather hadn't seen this side of the city when she had been transported from her world. The entrance was as big as any stadium or arena her father's circus had set up in. In the middle of the grand entrance was a large snake carved from stone. Its diamond shaped head was looking up at the sky, its mouth open and a forked tongue slithering into the air. Ollsop stopped when he saw the monstrosity. Heather could hear him mutter under his voice.

'What's wrong?'

'This city is under the watch of the Dark Emperor now, that explains the army.'

They walked towards the giant serpent. Heather could feel a strange vibe emanating from it. It was of sadness and imprisonment. The feeling you would get if you were ever locked in a cell and left to die with no way of getting out. She felt her throat constrict and the feeling of being claustrophobic seized on her mind. She started to choke and she held her chest with her hands, gasping for air. Some of the creatures loitering around the statue started to stare at her through thin veils and strange, anamorphic eye-ware. Ollsop took Heather's hand and pulled her away from it. They bolted down the nearest alley. Heather bent over and dry heaved.

'Heather,' Ollsop cried out. 'What's wrong?'

'That... that... thing; it made me feel like I was trapped in a coffin.'

Ollsop looked over her shoulder at the effigy.

'It has strange powers, Heather. We best keep away from it.'

Heather stood up and wiped her mouth, readjusting her scarf. She felt the dark energy empty from her stomach, but her head was still buzzing. Ollsop lead them to the other end of the alleyway and out into an open arena. On either side of the wide path were bizarre pawn stores and dancing clubs with exotic creatures in the windows wrapped in red silk. Down amongst the lower levels were men with weapons, one wearing an optical contraption that made his eyes glow green. He looked at Heather and Ollsop and nodded.

Ollsop walked briskly away from the stores until he reached an intersection and turned left. He appeared to know exactly where he was going. Heather had a strange feeling in the pit of her stomach and glanced back over her shoulder. The two men she saw at the gates were following them again. She ran forward, clutching Ollsop by his silvery coat. She leant into his ear and whispered.

'I think two people might be following us.'

Ollsop didn't make any indication that he had heard what she said. Instead, he grabbed Heather by her hand and led her further down the street. Along the sidewalk were tall streetlights, taller than any building in Hokus Pokus. There were only a few people milling around this deep into the wretched city. A woman walked passed them, her hands holding a black candle and a small silver emblem of an eye. As she approached them, Heather became scared.

'Get out of this town,' the woman barked, her teeth yellow and green. 'It's a dark town now... not for you folk.'

She hissed at them; it made Heather jump.

'Quickly, this way,' Ollsop said, pulling her along, faster now.

They ducked down beside a small building. Heather pressed her back against the wall and felt the cold stones.

'See if they're still coming,' Ollsop said to Heather, looking around them desperately for somewhere to hide or escape.

Heather stepped to the edge of the wall and glanced around the street. The two men, one wearing a long

crimson coat with small patches sewn all down the front in a haphazard fashion, the other man was hunched over and wrapped in filthy rags and cloth that hung off him in strips, were now talking to the woman who had told them to get out of the city. She was pointing towards them. The man in the red cloak looked over to them, he was holding a staff that had a burl in the middle that looked like an eye. The man in the red coat said something to her and nodded for the other man to follow.

'They're coming,' Heather said frantically.

'This way,' Ollsop said and reached upwards.

Above them was a small balcony made of rusted metal and pieces of wood. Several long bars of iron hung down as a make-shift ladder. Ollsop reached up and swung his other hand to the next. He pushed his feet off the wall and started to climb. Heather looked to the mouth of the alley, the men would be rounding the corner at any second.

'Heather, take my hand,' Ollsop instructed. There was panic in his voice.

Heather reached up and clutched Ollsop's hand. She could feel his strength as he pulled her to the first rung. Heather gripped the iron bar and tried to latch onto the next one, but slipped. She let out a yelp which echoed down the dark alleyway.

'Heather, quickly...' Ollsop pleaded, trying with all his might to pull her up, off the street level.

Heather gripped the bar again, swung her feet onto the wall and used it as leverage to gain a better hand hold. She curled her feet up and Ollsop yanked her to the balcony, just as the two men entered the darkened lane.

'That old witch lied to us,' one of them said.

'No,' said the other. 'I can smell her.'

'What is she?'

The man in the red cloak laid his staff on the ground and closed his eyes.

'She's not from here.'

'Like the other one?'

'Yes.'

Heather and Ollsop were only feet above them. Heather could hear her heart beating in her ears. Ollsop knew it would only be a matter of seconds before they looked up. He searched his surroundings and found a small window that had a grated vent covering it. He unlatched it and it swung inwards. He motioned Heather to climb through. She placed one foot on the railing and stood awkwardly as she pushed her arms and chest through the window. Ollsop pushed her feet and she slipped through the small opening.

'Is she worth anything?' the raggedly dressed man snorted, one bulging eye looking up at his master.

He spat on the ground and looked around the garbage and debris strewn chaotically.

'Worth anything? Not to us... but to the Dark Master she is...'

The man picked his staff up and glanced around the walls and then upwards. The balcony was empty and the small windows lining the upper floors were all closed.

Heather had fallen through the window and into a small room. It was dimly lit by black candles. There was a book shelf to the left, packed with tomes. Ollsop looked around the room until he found the door and opened it an inch and glanced out.

'This is not good Heather,' he said.

'Why, what is it?'

'It appears we've fallen into a dark den.'

'A dark den?' Heather looked around, trying to make sense of what Ollsop was saying.

'It's an illegal establishment for people to practice dark magic.'

A book behind her flew off the shelf and hit Heather in the back. She screeched in pain. Ollsop rushed to her and looked down at the book. It was open in the middle, the images scrawled on the parchment were swirling around like a black vortex. Ollsop closed it and turned it over. Heather rubbed her back, still wincing in pain.

'Who threw that?'

'No one threw it Heather. It's a spell book. One of the curses knows you're not from here and was attracted to you. It knows it can use your power.'

'My power?'

Ollsop turned back to the door.

'We have no time to discuss this Heather. Whatever happens, stay behind me and run as fast as you can.'

Heather's stomach lurched into her mouth as Ollsop kicked the door outwards. It broke off its hinges and fell in three pieces into the hallway. They ran out of the room, Ollsop in the lead. The noise had alerted two guards near the staircase who ran over, wands drawn. Heather saw several doors along the corridor open. All manner of creatures peered out. One creature had no nose and his ears were bellowing with smoke, another had several tentacles wrapped around his neck and his face had gone purple.

The guards wore a thin silky cloth over the top half of their face. It was see-through. Heather could see their skin was charred and twisted. They didn't have lips and their teeth were sharpened to a point. The first guard raised his wand and a giant orange flare shot from it. Ollsop reached back and pressed Heather against the wall. They narrowly dodged its strike. Ollsop's eyes started glowing blue. His right hand burst into cobalt fire. He kneeled down and thumped the ground hard, a blue wave of electricity surged across the ground and sent the guards catapulting into the ceiling. They came crashing down hard, their eyes rolling into the back of their sockets.

Ollsop ran for the stairs, Heather closely behind him. Together they bolted down the staircase, the paint peeling from the banisters and the ancient wood creaking under their feet. Ahead, Ollsop could see a large foyer where a man in a long black coat sat on one of the torn leather couches against one wall. To the right was a long bar, serving drinks. Everyone turned to watch the pair sprinting down the stairs, and then scattered. The bar tenders ducked out of view, all too familiar with dark mages fighting, sometimes even killing each other. The patrons waiting on the couches all disappeared, some through the side door, others evaporated into a cloud of smoke.

'Which way?' Heather gasped, feeling her lungs struggling for air.

As Ollsop looked around desperately trying to find another way out, two large doors ahead of them opened and shut as quickly as a blink of an eye. Heather turned, sweat pouring down her neck and arms. The two men who were chasing them down the alley, were now standing in front of them.

'Give us the girl and you can walk out of here,' one of them said, swinging the staff around as if it was a toy, the burled eye seemed to blink open and shut.

'Leave us,' Ollsop said, his fingertips still burning with blue flames.

The man with rags for clothing looked at Heather, his eyes were deep yellow and he moved his mouth open and shut, as if speaking words that could not be heard by human ears. He lunged forward, arms outreached towards Heather. She screamed and ducked, rolling onto the ground. Ollsop caught the man mid-flight and dragged him to the floor. He wrapped his flaming hand over his face, Heather could hear the man's flesh burning.

The cloaked stranger lifted his staff up high and spoke a curse. A long stream of canary yellow magic shot from the staff's tip and wrapped around Ollsop like a lasso. He was lifted several feet up into the air. The stranger smirked malevolently. Heather knew she had to do something, but she was frozen on the spot with fear. She saw a vase stand near the door, the picture on the vase was of a two headed snake, its mouth open towards the rim. She looked over at Ollsop who was screaming as the pain grew more and more intense. He thrashed about wildly, trying to free himself, but the more he struggled, the tighter the energy rope became.

'If only you'd listen,' the stranger said.

Heather gathered her courage and bolted for the door. She snatched the vase from its stand and turned towards the man holding the staff. The stranger whipped his head around, his facial expression changed from one of perverse pleasure to deep fear as Heather raised the vase upwards and brought it down on his head. It smashed into a hundred shards, sending the man to his knees. Blood ran down his face, but it wasn't red, it was lime-green. He roared with anger, his hand dropping the staff and holding his face. Ollsop dropped to the floor. He shook off the magical hold and ran to Heather, collecting her in his arms and pushing her out the front door. They tumbled down the stairs. Ollsop waved his hand backwards and a small blue ball soared from his palms and slammed the doors shut behind them. The street was dark and a cold wind was snaking through the buildings and houses. Heather slid from Ollsop's arms, her knees still jelly. Ollsop could barely stand, the air flowing in and out of his mouth was laboured. There was a man standing on the other side of the street. He was half cast in shadow. Ollsop eyed him cautiously. The man stepped forward.

'This way,' he said, his hands laying open in front of him.

Heather had seen him before. Shortly before she noticed them being followed she had seen him, he wore a strange eye piece that made his eyes glow green. He had looked them up and down and nodded. Ollsop was hunched over, the beam that held him had squeezed him so tight it almost broke his ribs. He ignored the man and limped away. Heather helped him walk, but wondered how long it would be before both the strange men came back out from the dark den and caught up with them.

'I'm with the light,' the man said.

Ollsop looked at him, the man held out his hands again, showing he had no weapons.

'Please Ollsop, you're hurt,' Heather said.

Ollsop walked towards him as the man motioned them to follow. Heather tried to keep up, but Ollsop was struggling to walk. When she looked up again the man was gone. All around her were windows boarded up and blacked out with paint or paper. The ground was scorched and there appeared to be no other people.

'Ollsop... where are we?'

From behind her a door creaked open, the man stood in the archway. The building was made of small bricks that seeped water. It was built thin and high with an eerie spire adorning at its summit.

'Please hurry, unless you'd like to do battle with Armatige Stooge and Luckworth again.'

'You know them?' Heather said, helping Ollsop through the doorway.

'They are famous around these parts. Bottom feeders; they know a deal when they see one.' He shut the door and the room was cast into complete darkness. Suddenly a light flickered on in the centre of the room, suspended by a small piece of wire from the ceiling.

Heather could see tables and chairs stacked against one wall. She saw a fire place with a large pot. Several bowls and utensils were stacked on one small table. There didn't appear to be much else.

. 'My names Sunn'r. I am a type of interpreter for a very wealthy mage right here in Hokus.'

'Why did you help us,' Ollsop said, leaning back on a chair in the corner. His face had regained its colour.

'Like you, friend,' Sunn'r spoke, looking from Heather to Ollsop, 'I am a friend of the Alliance and wish to see the downfall of the Emperor.'

There was silence for several seconds. Heather could feel a lump in her throat as she waited to see what Ollsop would do.

'How did you…'

'Know?' Sunn'r interjected. 'I have an optical device in which I can see many things. It is part magic, part machine. I could see no darkness in either of you, especially you,' he said looking at Heather. 'Most creatures in this city have some dark magic attached to them. I had also seen your performing group travelling east of here,' he looked at Ollsop again. 'I could see your scars as bright as candle flame… you were once an Incantana? Where you not?'

Sunn'r pushed long, unwashed, brown hair from his face and stared at Ollsop with striking green eyes. He had scars running down his neck which looked no older than six months.

'I was. But no longer affiliate with the darkness. If you say you are a friend of the Alliance and you helped us… then I must pay my gratitude forward to you,' he held out his hand and Sunn'r shook it.

The magic interpreter then turned to Heather and extended his hand. Heather shook it and felt strength. His hands were as dirty as his face and hair, the only clean part on him was around his striking eyes.

'What brings you to Hokus?'

Ollsop licked his dry lips. 'This here is Heather, she is from another place, far from Abara and Cadabra. We are trying to find a man called Brim who has a doorway to her world. It'll be in the shape of a magical sword box or something similar.'

Sunn'r thought for a moment. His eyes scanned the ground, as if searching for the clue amongst the old, rotten floorboards.

'There are several people in Hokus who would have such a thing... none are named Brim.'

'He was a magician,' Heather said. 'Doing magic for money. He had a crowd of people and was surprised that it worked. His poster had *Brim the Dark Mage of Hokus Pokus* written on it.'

'Sounds like the entertainment district of Wormdust. I'll take you there in the morning, but first we sleep. Hokus is a dangerous place to be out at night.'

Sunn'r had lit the fire and the heat filled the room quickly. They slept on the floor of the empty house, using old table cloths for blankets and food sacks for pillows. The old house creaked and moaned through the night, as if alive. A window upstairs rattled in its frame, keeping Heather's attention, from the outside. She could hear whispering outside the house, people scuttling around and moving things. There was a scream far away and it came to their ears softly. Sunn'r had got out of his make-shift cot and walked to the window to investigate, but he soon returned and was snoring again. Heather fell into a dreamless sleep.

She had only felt like she had five minutes' sleep when Ollsop was patting her on the shoulder. When she opened her eyes she was staring straight at him.

'Heather, it's almost dawn. We have to eat and then try to find Brim.'

Heather sat up and blinked the sleep from her eyes. Ollsop left her to wake and walked over to the hearth which had glowing red coals. He fanned them with a piece of wooden board. There was the sound of keys and Heather whipped her head towards the door. Ollsop stood, the wood gripped in his hand. The front door opened and Sunn'r rushed in and shut it behind him. He was holding several parcels of food. He looked at Ollsop and Heather, but didn't speak. He rushed over to the table and put the packages down.

'I believe I was followed,' he said, his eyes darting to the front door.

'By who?' Heather said, getting to her feet.

'I'm not sure, but I managed to lose them a few streets away. They shouldn't find us here.'

He opened one package and pulled out fresh baked bread. He pulled it apart with his bare hands, the smell filled the room. He handed a piece to both Heather and Ollsop.

'We'll get going soon, just in case we're being watched.'

Heather and Ollsop ate the bread quickly and followed Sunn'r back out into the street. Sunn'r locked the door and slid the key into his jacket pocket. He motioned for Heather and Ollsop to cover their face and hands and led them away from the small house they had slept in. Ollsop kept looking over his shoulder; his eyes darted around the empty streets. They got to a large intersection where Sunn'r motioned them into a small sliver of shadow cast from one of the towers behind them.

'We'll make our way to Wormdust and ask around the street vendors if they know of someone called Brim. Be careful who you look at there, they don't take kindly to people prying in their business.'

Ollsop nodded and looked at Heather for her understanding, she nodded and wrapped her scarf around her neck tighter. Sunn'r led the way with Ollsop and Heather walking abreast, behind him. As the sun peered over the distant mountains, the filthy dark roads of Hokus Pokus glowing softly, like candle light. The bricks became washed anew with the sun's rays. The shadows crept away, revealing long, winding streets, all dusted with time and rotted garbage.

Heather saw a man open two large swinging doors and toss another man out. He fell on his face, rolled over and went to sleep. Sunn'r hardly took notice. They climbed a slight incline on the road. Once they reached its summit they could look out over the entire east side of Hokus. Sunn'r turned and pointed.

'There is Wormdust, the furthest and most dangerous of the catacombs.'

Heather looked across the massive clutter of side show alleys and carnival attractions and saw the wall which she had scuttled along like a scampering cockroach, looking for an exit. Past the wall was the grassy tundra in which she had fallen. She remembered it like it was only a few hours ago.

'People are waking, and this city isn't pleasant at the best of times,' Sunn'r said, with a slight grin on his face.

They started the trek towards Wormdust. Already people were starting to bustle around the city, their faces hidden with masks or pieces of clothing, their eyes shifting and darting as if every shadow was their enemy. Large paintings of magicians lined the walls of Wormdust. The paintings towered over ten feet tall and had been hand painted to display the wizards in the middle of battle, wands raised and magical energy pouring from the tips in great splurges of blue and ochre. It made her think of Ollsop's magic that he used against the strangers in the dark den.

Beyond the paintings were side shows of games, most of them throwing daggers at pictures of people Heather did not recognise. The prizes appeared to be small bottles with small glowing moths. Sunn'r ignored the games parlours lining the streets and started to weave in and out of the growing crowd. Heather saw flickering all around her as strings of lights came on, illuminating the darkened stalls. Ollsop placed his hand on Heather's shoulder.

'He's moving faster; we must keep up Heather.'

Together they moved through the crowd, ignoring the dark wonders around them. Ahead of them they could see a juggler standing on a wooden crate. He wore a long coat, the bottoms frayed and torn to shreds. The sleeves were cut off mid-way, around his elbow, to give him more freedom to move. Sunn'r moved to a secluded part of a shop front and stood with his back to the bricks. Ollsop and Heather stood beside him.

'This man here,' he said pulling his goggles from his side bag. He slipped them on and adjusted the dials, 'he has been near intense dark magic... I can see its residue on his hands.'

'He'll know where Brim is?' Heather said, hits of glee in her voice.

'He may,' Sunn'r replied.

He pulled a small round coin from his pocket and slowly merged with the crowd. He stood in front of the juggler. The man flipped four balls through the air, his eyes moving with them, watching each one with effortless precision. His nose was burned red and his eyes were watery blue. He had long dreaded hair tied back and there were small tribal tattoos up his neck and along his chin.

'Nice magic, friend,' Sunn'r said to him flipping the coin into his busking tray.

'Ah!' the juggler said, smiling. 'No magic here, just skill.'

'We're looking for Brim, a dark mage.'

The juggler's hands paused and a ball dropped to the ground. He caught the others and looked down.

'Show's over,' he grunted and jumped from his box and started walking away.

Sunn'r rushed at him and seized him by the arm.

'We just want to talk.'

The juggler looked at him through the corners of his eyes. Heather shifted her weight from left to right nervously. Ollsop stepped forward, as if showing the man he really didn't have a choice.

'Brim's dead.'

Heather looked at Ollsop, tears welled up in her eyes. Sunn'r stepped closer to the man.

'Tell me more. How did he die? Where are his belongings?'

The juggler tried to pull his arm away from Sunn'r, but he held it tight.

'Let go of me, or I'll...'

'You'll what?' inside Sunn'r's goggles, the dark magic flared. 'If you move I'll get my friend here... trained by the Meniphesto Incantana, to tear your hands off.'

He looked at Ollsop and saw the scars along his lips.

'Brim was beheaded two nights ago. Looked like Knights of the Dark Order. They came from the tower of the Emperor... wasn't hard to tell, their steeds were as black as night, with eyes as red as fire.'

'Where is his head?' Sunn'r asked.

Heather looked at Ollsop.

'Don't worry Heather,' Ollsop whispered in her ear, 'he may be lying. If not, we may be able to track the doorway. It could still be here,' he thought, knowing perfectly well the Knights would have taken it with them.

'Come, I'll show you.'

Sunn'r was half a step behind the juggler with Ollsop and Heather behind them. They moved through the bustling streets, now in full morning trade and headed towards the wall.

In the far corner of Wormdust there weren't as many traders, as the people of Hokus Pokus didn't like being cornered. The shadows were longer and the conversations were drowned out by the wall. The stalls here were mostly shut and there were mage's sleeping off the previous night's transformations or concoctions. Heather watched a figure limp out of the dark crevasses of the shadows. He had the distinguished features of a wolf, then, right before Heather's eyes, he turned back into a man in a matter of seconds. He twitched and groaned and his eyes blinked open. He stood up, wiped the dirt from his arms and legs and wandered into the bustle of the city.

'Look,' the juggler said, pointing to a giant crater in the wall.

'Before I look,' Sunn'r said, 'If this is a trick, or you try and run, I'll find you.'

'I know who you are Sunn'r D'Angelo,' the juggler grunted in his face. 'Employee of Lucero the Crimson.'

Sunn'r seemed to relax now knowing the juggler knew who he was. He walked to the hole and climbed on top of the crumbled brick. He looked down and waited a few seconds. He returned with a sullen look on his face and pulled his goggles on top of his head. He looked at Ollsop, his facial expression not changing in the slightest.

'He tells the truth.'

Heather ran to the wall, tears streaming down her face and looked down. Far below was the body of Brim, his head and body detached from one another. Giant birds that looked like vultures with long red tails were pecking at his carcass. Ollsop went to her and she collapsed in his arms.

Sunn'r grabbed the juggler and threw him against the hard brick wall that ringed the city. The wind was knocked out of his lungs and he grunted. He tried to struggle for freedom but Sunn'r's grip was too tight.

'I know you're the Alliance,' the juggler spat, his cheek pressed against the brickwork. 'I can smell it on you. You're fighting a battle you can't possibly win.' His laughter was both malevolent and childish.

All around them people started to stare.

'Tell me where Brim's belongings went,' Sunn'r snarled.

'There's a field, outside of Bunker's Gate... you'll find them in there.'

Sunn'r let his grip release and the juggler turned to face him. He raised one fist and saw Ollsop heading towards him. He lowered it again, tossing a hood over his face. He spat on the ground near Sunn'r and wandered into the crowd, disappearing within seconds.

Heather felt her heart burning. Ollsop gripped her shoulders and stared at her with watery green eyes.

'Heather, listen. All is not lost. There is still a chance. Where there is hope, there is a way.'

Heather wiped her eyes. She felt like breaking down in great sobs. She could feel her state of mind melting away as the idea of never seeing her father or the circus ever again was becoming all too real. Ollsop took her hand and they returned to Sunn'r's side.

'I can take you as far as Bunker's Gate but then I must leave you. I've been summoned by my employer and I must return.'

Ollsop put his hand on Sunn'r's shoulder. 'You've done more than enough for us friend, more than we can repay.'

Sunn'r leant closer. 'All I ask in return is you rid this place of the Dark Emperor. The darkness grows with every passing day. Soon I will not be able to stay in this city without being killed for my magic. Do what you can and rise up.'

Ollsop nodded and followed Sunn'r out of Wormdust.

ADMIT ONE
COME ONE, COME ALL
THE GREATEST PERFORMANCE IN THE WORLD
CHAPTER 18
TO FORGE CROSSING
No. IOIOI987

Wormdust faded like rolling thunder clouds. The streets gave way to trodden ground. The dirt was black and the air was hot like an open stove that emanated up from the gravel and stone. Heather rolled her sleeves up, but kept her hood on. They had been walking for only an hour when she noticed the scenery changing. Ahead were large iron gates. They had been manufactured with precision and care. The metal used was blackened around the base, but had a sharp silver glare as it towered over the other buildings. Each column was no thicker than a finger. It soared into the air and appeared to pierce the clouds above.

Heather's eyes were on the very peaks of the gate when she felt a hard thump on her left shoulder. She took her eyes off the sky to see she had walked into a very large man wearing thick, grey armour. His shoulders were as round as hub caps and his face was hidden by an arcane helmet. It had a slit across the eyes where small black pupils stared out. There were polished metal spikes across the top of his head and down each side, and smaller ones running along his chin line. His armour looked like scales from some medieval creature. Heather felt the heat bouncing off the armour.

'Touch me again and you'll be next in the pit, girl!' the man snarled.

Heather looked around and saw Ollsop and Sunn'r several meters ahead of her, staring despairingly through the gate. She ran to them as Sunn'r placed his goggles back over his eyes. Micro mechanisms whizzed around in his eye piece and small lights flashed on the sides. His mouth opened to speak, but he closed them again. Heather turned away from Sunn'r and looked beyond the gate, there was a massive field. The grass along the forecourt had all been burnt to cinder and it was smoking wildly, the dirt had turned to soot and the rocks had crumbled to powder. In the middle of the field, great billowing streams of smoke poured from an open pit. Heather pushed her way through the crowd and stood at the cusp of the hole, staring in. She had never seen anything so big in all her life. The pit was as big as ten circus tents, and just as deep. The edge slowly receded in until it reached the middle where red hot lava was sitting like a stagnant pond.

'What is this?' Ollsop asked, almost too scared to ask the question.

Sunn'r looked at him. Soot fell from the sky like rain.

'This is where they bring the magic the Emperor wants to dispose of...'

'Why haven't I heard of this?' Ollsop said, gloomily.

'It is only new... and the residents here aren't too keen on letting the world know the Emperor has control of Hokus.'

'There!' Heather shouted and ran past two more guards who tried to grab her as she ducked under their massive arms.

'Heather, no!' Ollsop shouted, running after her.

Heather bolted past two armoured pit-dwellers, their armour burnt from the heat and glowing red. One by one they were tossing artefacts and books into the salacious pit. Some items burst into flames before they hit the liquid fire. A large, tangerine face burst from one book and screamed so loudly Heather's ears rung. It twisted and turned and evaporated into a thin dust that was carried away with the wind. The pit-dwellers didn't seem to care about the crowd lulling around watching them as they continued their laborious work, pulling items from large wooden carts and out of trunks and troves.

Heather's feet burnt wildly. She skipped and hopped across the ash and melting rocks, ducking as strange candle holders and book cases were tossed over her head. She looked at the artefacts closely, then she eyed something in the far end of the pit. It was Brim's magical box. It lay in a small crater near the edge. She tried to get to it, but the heat was overwhelming and she felt her hair start to singe. Ollsop came behind her and grabbed her.

'Heather, no! You can't go any further, you'll get burnt.'

He pulled her back. Heather struggled in his arms. Heather watched as the flames covering the door-way box licked the air and started to eat away at the wood. It was crumbling before her very eyes. It broke in two, falling in amongst other items and turned to ash and soot. Heather stood, ignoring the heat that was melting the soles of her shoes. Her heart hung heavy and no tears could come from her eyes, the heat was evaporating them.

'Get out of here!' a blackened pit-dweller chortled in their direction.

Ollsop pulled Heather back to Bunker's Gate were Sunn'r stood, his face crestfallen.

'I'm sorry I have failed you,' Sunn'r said, eyeing the gathering crowd.

'It was not your fault, Sunn'r. The Emperor knew about the box. If Heather had not escaped, she would have met the same fate as Brim, surely.'

'Come,' Sunn'r said, getting agitated as the spectators starting gathering around Heather. 'We must leave. We've drawn far too much attention to ourselves.'

Ollsop wrapped his arms around Heather and could feel the burnt fabric of her shawl and head scarf. Her body throbbed as she cried. Ollsop dragged her through the crowd and back onto the path leading out of Wormdust.

'We must get to the path that leads to Forge Crossing,' Ollsop said, noticing the crowd whispering to each other and pointing in their direction.

'Forge Crossing? The only way there is through Angeldust Pass.'

'Will you take us there? I will ask no more of you,' Ollsop commanded.

'Of course, this way.'

Sunn'r wrapped his long coat around himself and took his goggles from his head and placed them inside his jacket. Heather looked at Ollsop and could see fear in his eyes, they were unnerving and still reflected the redness of the pit.

Sunn'r led them down long, cracked and hardened stairs. They appeared to be heading underground. They soon reached a platform and then another, smaller series of stairs. They rushed quickly, their surroundings become darker and darker. Soon they entered a long corridor where several large tunnels opened like sewer drains. Sunn'r went to the far left. Ollsop and Heather followed, apprehensively. They travelled north in near blackness.

People lay against the walls and shivered from whatever magic they had inappropriately used. Trash lined the walls and was scattered across the floors. A small man with his arms stretched outwards approached Sunn'r who pushed him away. The man screamed and merged back into the shadows. Heather was scared, she could also hear the echoing footsteps of someone following them.

'Why were you after that magic box?' one called, his voice more curious than malevolent.

Ollsop didn't turn around to answer.

The tunnel reached a darkened fork and Sunn'r didn't hesitate in which way to travel.

Ollsop caught up to him and asked, 'Why are we travelling in such darkness? I prefer the open streets where we can blend in!'

'You want to get to Forge Crossing without being hunted down? Then this is the only way. It may be dark and it may be dangerous, but it's nothing compared to what would be waiting for you in the pockets between Wormdust and Brimstonia, where Angeldust Pass is.'

'There are three men following us,' Heather said quietly. 'We *are* being hunted.'

'I know,' Sunn'r said. 'As soon as we get through this bend and out the other side. There is one more tunnel. There, I will kill them.'

Ollsop clutched Heather's hand tightly and held her close to him. Ahead of them the tunnel darkened. There was a pin prick of light at the other end. Heather could see small fires scattered against the walls, there were lanterns and cooking utensils hanging from make-shift hooks. As they approached, the fire's went out and the lanterns extinguished. The clatter of footsteps behind them ceased. Heather stood in completed blackness. The small halo of light at the end of the tunnel was now gone. She could hear Ollsop's breathing becoming erratic and she could feel his grip tighten.

'Sunn'r?' Ollsop said.

'We're surrounded,' Sunn'r's voice whispered in the dark. He seemed metres away from them.

'What's happening?' Heather said, trying to keep her courage in her words.

'They know you're not from here Heather. Anything from other planes will reap a fine reward from the Emperor... especially ones looking for a gateway.'

Ollsop closed his eyes, there was no difference in the darkness. He raised his old, wrinkled hand into the sky and a blue flame erupted from his fingertips. The tunnel ignited in a brilliant cobalt glow. Sunn'r was to their right, his goggles on his face, his coat flapping back behind him. They were surrounded by twisted creatures. All their fingers were bent and curled backwards. Their eyes were blackened pearls, reflecting the blue light. Their legs were long and slender, and whatever garments they possessed hung from them in shreds.

'Whoever was following us has alerted these creatures,' Sunn'r spoke, distain dripping off every word.

Ollsop opened his eyes, his pupils had dilated and his lips moved without words. Long tentacles of magical energy soared from his fingers and struck the tunnel creatures around their necks and torsos. They gagged and hissed wildly. Sunn'r pulled a blade from his belt as four creatures jumped at him and dragged him to the ground. Heather screamed as she felt cold, deathly hands wrap around her arms and legs and drag her to the floor. She kicked and flailed her arms violently. She found the creatures weren't that strong and she could break their grip with hardly any strength. There were so many around her though, she lost sight of Ollsop and Sunn'r in a matter of moments.

'Ollsop!' she screamed.

'Heather, hit them in the eyes!' he yelled, his voice struggling through the leathery arms and legs.

Heather raised her fists up high and slammed her knuckles into the closest creature's face. She felt its eyes on her skin like rotten plums. It shrieked and howled, its hands clutching its face as it fell backwards. Heather managed to get to her feet. One by one, as the creatures approached her, she slammed her palm, flat, against their faces, but there were too many. Sunn'r swung his blade from right to left, carving the tunnel dwellers across their abdomen and chest. As soon as they bled, they retreated back into whatever hole they had crawled out of.

She kicked and fought the creatures, knocking them to the ground and stomping on them. Soon, Heather could see the speck of light at the end of the tunnel again, hope filled her chest like warm honey. Her hands were covered in blood and liquid from their eyes and mouths. When she broke free of the remaining creatures, she ran to Ollsop, his hands blazing in blue flame. He pushed spheres of magic out from the palm of his hands, the creatures flew against the wall and slumped in a heap of dead flesh. He turned and saw Heather, her face cast in a sapphire hue.

'More will come,' Ollsop stated, nodding to the end of the tunnel. 'We have to run and not look back. Sunn'r!'

'I'm right behind you!' he yelped, digging the knife into a creature's skull.

Heather bolted towards the light, Ollsop struggling beside her. Heather tripped and fell; righting herself, she kept going. She couldn't see anything on the ground or the walls. Long hands reached out of the darkness and tugged at her clothes and skin. Their fingers felt dry and coarse and it made her spine tingle with revulsion. She could hear Ollsop behind her, he was keeping up with her fast pace.

Slowly the light became bigger and bigger and Heather could see the land beyond the exit. She heard something that sounded like a bundle of fire wood falling to the ground. She turned around and could not see the flaming hands of Ollsop any longer.

'Ollsop?' she cried out.

'Keeping running, don't stop!' called a voice in the dark.

Heather turned and could see several silhouetted figures standing in the exit way. Their arms were reached outwards from their body, their legs akimbo. Heather gritted her teeth and ran at them, too afraid to stop. Suddenly Sunn'r was beside her. His speed was incredible and soon he was past Heather. He ran for the first creature and cut its head clean off with his blade. It bounced on the ground and out into the light where it sizzled like a piece of meat on a hotplate. Heather felt like she might puke, but held it back. A second creature wrapped its arms around her, squeezing as tightly as it could. Heather yelped in fright and kicked around wildly. Her left heel connected with the creature's knee and it buckled, letting go of her immediately. She ran out into the sun. It was welcoming and relief washed over her body. She stood hunched over, dry heaving and trying to catch her breath. She looked up and Sunn'r was several seconds behind her, but she couldn't see Ollsop.

'Where is he?' she screamed.

'He was right...' just as Sunn'r spoke several limbs flew out of the darkness and into the light. They turned to ash in a matter of seconds. Heather and Sunn'r waited, watching the darkness. Sunn'r was about to run back in when two feet appeared. Ollsop was steadily walking out to the tunnel, seemingly without a care in the world.

Heather ran to him and wrapped her arms around him.

'I thought they had got you,' his long beard and weathered skin felt warm in her embrace.

Ollsop walked over to Sunn'r and grabbed him around the throat. Heather couldn't believe her eyes, she ran to them and tried to pull Ollsop away.

'What's wrong with you! Get off him!' she bellowed.

'You could have got us killed!' Ollsop screamed, shaking Sunn'r with all his might.

'I knew... you... could get... through,' Sunn'r said, trying to push the old man off him. 'But... you could thank... me.'

'Thank you?' Ollsop said.

Sunn'r took one hand off Ollsop and pointed behind him. Ollsop let his grip go and Sunn'r fell to the dusty ground.

'We're here?'

'Yes,' Sunn'r said, spitting onto the ground. 'Angeldust Pass... and down that trail is Forge Crossing.'

'It was a short cut,' Heather said, under her breath.

'A short cut that almost got us killed.'

'I beg your forgiveness, old friend,' Sunn'r said, turning to Ollsop. 'But I have been through the tunnels of Hokus Pokus many a time, and have yet to lose a limb or friend. The creatures in there are golems of wasted magic, they've grown out of pure waste that is washed away or tossed out by weaker mages than yourself. They are hardly powerful and only really crave the dark. I knew we would make it and I knew you would be angry.'

Ollsop waited a few seconds and saw the sincerity in his eyes. He opened his fist up and they shook hands.

'I'm not as nimble, nor powerful as I once was and this girl here, we've grown quite attached to her and want to get her home. I must beg your pardon as we must be on our way. Our carriages wait for us and I'm afraid they won't wait long.'

Sunn'r nodded, as if he understood the deeper meaning behind what Ollsop was saying.

'It's been a pleasure, friend.' They shook hands again. 'And to you, our prayers are with you and your journey ahead.' He shook Heather's hand and headed towards the throng of bystanders awaiting their turn to get back into Hokus Pokus.

Heather looked around and saw a clear cut path through a wildly dense patch of forest. There were people carrying their belongings and travelling the path, escaping from the horrid city behind them. Ollsop put his hood over his face, as did Heather and they joined the nameless travellers, and headed towards Forge Crossing.

The road was hard to walk due to the congestion and uneven ground. People walked in packs to keep safe, barely looking up from the road and never talking to anyone they weren't with.

Heather didn't say anything to Ollsop as they followed the path for nearly an hour. Heather's mind was still reeling from finding the gateway box burned to cinders. She looked at her hands and they were still covered in ash and blisters. She wanted to cry. She wanted to sit down with her head in her hands and give up, but she knew she had one more chance. She lifted her head up and saw that Ollsop had stopped.

'What is it?' she asked.

Ahead of them the path separated into three different roads. Several feet before the intersection was a tall wooden pole. It had been carved without skill and looked haggard and roughly scraped with a blade or saw. The first sign pointed to the far left – *Cadabra*. Heather looked at it. It was written in neatly scrawled writing, etched into the wood by someone with care. It stood out from the other signs, someone had taken care when preparing it. Heather felt a dark, ominous feeling, pulsating from the sign. The next sign, which was around the side of the pole read – *Wandlore*.

'Every fibre in my being wishes we were headed for Wandlore, Heather,' Ollsop said.

Just the word made Heather's heart glow. 'What is Wandlore?'

'It's a city like no other. Filled with intelligent magic, rich and transcendental. The city centre is older than the woods here. Evil and darkness does not reside there and if they were to find out what we were trying to do, we may have had to face the Wizard High Court.'

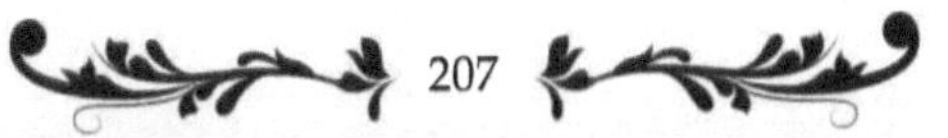

Heather looked away from the sign, there was no use in thinking about it. She had already resigned to the fact that she was headed for imminent danger.

She looked at the last sign and saw the familiar words – *Hey Presto!* The exclamation mark was carved like a lightning bolt and the dot underneath dripped like it had been thrown onto the sign. She turned away from the large sign as others gathered around it.

Ollsop had found a small heap of flat stones near the mouth of the path that lead to Cadabra. He rested his tired bones, looking weary.

'The end of one journey and the beginning of another,' he said to Heather.

He stood up and they walked alone down the path. The journey was void of noise and the trees surrounding them didn't whisper or move. The air was still, as if it was holding its breath, waiting for the travellers to move on. Heather didn't want to speak, so she just followed Ollsop.

It took less time than Heather expected before they were off the path and looking at another wide road. Ollsop looked worried. He turned to his right and looked down the long thoroughfare. It dipped, as if going into a crater. There was no one there. He looked left, the path was straight for miles and there wasn't a soul to be seen.

'What is it?' Heather said, moving her auburn hair from her eyes. She was glad to be away from the dark, dreary road that was now behind them.

'They're meant to be here,' Ollsop replied, looking left once again.

'This is Forge Crossing?'

'Yes,' Ollsop answered, he pointed across the roadway. 'There used to be a path that way,' Heather could see the trees were smaller, and there were no boulders or stones. 'But in recent years the Emperor had it closed off. It was a direct line straight to the domain of Cadabra. Once, you

could see the tip of his morbid tower from here, but no more.'

'Why did he close it off?'

Ollsop took a leather sack from his belt and drank from it. He handed it to Heather. The water was warm, but still tasted better than anything she had tasted back home.

'There's now only one way in, and one way out of Cadabra. Some who go in... do not come out.'

'But he allows your circus... I mean, your travelling show to enter the grounds?'

'He has annual festivals for his people, and we are but one of many entertainers booked.' Ollsop suddenly whipped his head to the right.

A soft clip-clop was coming down the road. Heather stood on her tippy toes to see. A breeze rustled the trees and brought with it the smell of mint and lime. Heather felt it on her face and smiled as the travelling wagons came over the small incline.

'They made it,' Ollsop said with a smile.

They waited by the side of the road till the wagons reached them. The first carriage was driven by LaFare. His muscular arms gripped the reigns tightly.

'Aren't we glad to see you Ollsop! The road has been harsh to say the least and we were attacked twice. As for you Heather. I'd like to say it's not good to see you too. I'm sorry you didn't find what you were after.'

'Where's Kiel?' Heather asked as Soma jumped down from the second wagon.

She walked over to Ollsop without saying a word and hugged him for several minutes. She touched his face, her eggplant coloured skin was dark amongst the shadows of the woods, but her yellow eyes glowed intensely.

'This would not have been the same without you.'

Ollsop smiled. Soma turned to Heather.

'From here on in, we are silent as the dead. And we especially don't speak Kiel's name. Understand?'

Heather nodded. Soma marched back to the carriage. LaFare waved them onto his wagon and Heather leaped aboard, sitting up front. LaFare smiled and whipped the reigns. The Gazzoo pulling the wagon coughed and spat up a large ball of dried grass and started moving slowly.

***

The roads leading up to Cadabra snaked through darkened woodlands and deep, bubbling mangroves. The once beautifully laid cobblestones of Abara were now replaced with hard stone, blackened by ash and time. The trees that grew on either side of the road were twisted, as if by some invisible hand to ward off intruders or animal life. Their roots grew from the ground like vicious hands of a witch, made with demented magic. The soil was black and grew no grass, only weeds sprouted in abundance.

Earlier on in the day LaFare had switched places with Ollsop so he could rest. Heather had moved from the front carriage, and was now riding in the back with LaFare and two others. She tried to rest too, but her anxiousness kept her awake. Everyone in the rear cabin looked sullen and nervous. She didn't want to talk to them about their mission as she could see true fear in their faces and movements. When the cart cracked and popped over a pothole, they would jump and look about nervously.

'Damn it, Ollsop,' LaFare shouted from the rear, 'We're sitting on enough dynamite to make a crater, please be careful.'

Ollsop either did not hear, or ignored his requests. The cart jittered and moved awkwardly through the winding path. Occasionally they would stop and make a fire and cook a small animal that Heather could only describe as a cross between a rabbit and a rat. Ollsop called it a Sinllot.

He would often go into the woods and set traps and within an hour they would have two or three. They had long tails that were fluffy with dark red hair. Their paws were long for digging warrens and their eyes were almost always cross-eyed. LaFare or Soma would skin them and hang their hide over one of the tent poles to dry and sun bake. Heather never knew why there were keeping them.

They ate a stew made from two Sinllot's and moved again. They spoke very little as they approached the lands of Cadabra. Heather lay back against the wagon and tried to sleep, which came late in the afternoon. She didn't know how long she had been out for before she heard a commotion and stirred awake. The wagon had stopped and there were guards all around them. Ollsop was near the back of her carriage, talking to one of the armed men with yellow teeth and a long white beard.

'...we have an appointment, check your books Sir! The Great Lord is awaiting our arrival! This has been booked for months!'

The bearded guard looked at him with narrowed eyes.

'Stay here. If you move, I'll have you killed.'

He turned and headed for a small barricade hidden between the burnt trees and mounds of ancient dirt, kicked up from some large animal Heather hoped to never encounter. Several guards stood around the wagons, sniffing and checking under everything they could reach. One demanded they take the tent down and unwind it. LaFare leapt from the back of the wagon and started to walk over to the guard that had given the request.

'You take another step, young blood, and I'll take your head off and feed it to my Scavenger Montlope!' A blade came at LaFare's throat and stopped a mere millimetre from his skin. The guard holding the long blade was missing his right eye. He didn't bother hiding it, instead there was a fleshy crater with overripe boils hanging from the socket.

'It will take us most the day to unwrap it and rewrap it. If you want the Emperor to be annoyed at our tardiness, then we will do it, but it will be your head he will feed to the Montlope, not mine.'

Heather and the rest of the performers watched on with baited breath. LaFare wiped his sweating hands on his thin, white shirt that hung loosely off his chiselled frame. The one-eyed guard gnashed his teeth and pushed the blade deeper into LaFare's skin. He could feel it's cold steel.

'Take it down and unwrap it... now.'

LaFare caught the guard's eye and they held their glare for some time. LaFare looked away and nodded his head to the second wagon. Two men jumped down and started pulling the tent off the roof of the carriage. It was a job meant for five or six men, but two could do it if it had to be done.

The lead guard that had been talking to Ollsop when Heather woke, marched over to the disturbance. His armour was dark, wine red with small nicks from sword fighting along the chest and abdomen. On his shoulder he wore several medallions, one had a picture of a green hand with a red cross through it. Heather thought it reminded her of Kiel's hand, and thought that they made have been part of the war fought by the Dark Magician that had killed Soma and Kiel's people.

'The Dark One is pleased that you have arrived,' the lead guard snorted, resting one hand on a long sword attached to his right hip. 'You are to go in the gates and meet with a representative and he will take you to set up.'

Heather felt a huge weight suddenly lift off her shoulders, she found herself breathing again, unknowingly, she had been holding her breath. LaFare turned to climb the wagon when the guard stepped forward and placed one hand on his chest.

'Not so fast, young blood,' he said, his face leaning into LaFare's. 'First we search the wagons, then you can proceed.'

Heather felt the familiar anchor catch in her throat again.

'Search them!' the guard called out, waving his hand in the air.

A rush of guards, all wearing crimson armour and holding swords started climbing over the wagons. One pulled Ollsop by his shirt sleeve and tossed him from the cabin. Heather leaned back as another reached in towards her.

'Don't touch me!' she screamed.

The guard grinned manically, reaching for her leg. Heather kicked out at him. His rough skinned hand wrapped around her foot and dragged her towards the edge of the wagon. This close, Heather could smell the guard's sweat and stench. It was as if they never bathed, or changed their armour. The pungent aroma almost made her gag. The guards lifted her up with ease and walked over to the side of the path and dumped her down amongst some weeds. Small beetles scurried away from her.

The guards tore through the wagon, tossing out the poles and lights and the performer's clothing. The seats were thrown and a few broke when they fell to the hard ground. Ollsop and Soma were marched over to Heather and told to sit. The guard looked at Ollsop's scarred face and stared. Ollsop looked away, waving his hand at him, as if shooing a fly. The guard suddenly looked dazed and returned to ransacking the carriages.

All of a sudden, one of the guards was at the end of the wagon that held the explosives. He ran his thick fingers along the lining of the roof, feeling for hidden compartments or weapons. He tapped the wooden walls and listen for hollowed echoes. He ran his hand along the flooring. Heather saw Soma murmur uncomfortably. Ollsop looked on, his eyes wide with trepidation. The guard rapped his large knuckles on the floor. A solid, timber sound echoed back. He moved his hand and knocked again, this time it came back empty and without depth. The guard hit the wood again, and listened. It was different from the last time. Soma reached into her thin vest and rested her hand on a blade handle. Heather suddenly got very nervous. They were outnumbered, and the gates to Cadabra was only a short distance away.

'I've got something here!'

Ollsop turned to Soma, who rose to her feet and pulled her blade from its sheath.

COME ONE, COME ALL
THE GREATEST PERFORMANCE IN THE WORLD
ADMIT ONE
CHAPTER 19
MENIPHESTO OF THE DARK ONE
No. 101010987

The guard turned his head and saw another smaller soldier pulling a long yellow cloth from a wooden chest at the rear of the wagon. The guard Soma had been watching marched towards the rear carriage, ignoring the hollowed sound he heard and yanked the cloth from the soldier's hand. He held the two corners and flicked it outwards. The cloth unwound and rolled to the guard's knee. It was a flag with a red skull in the middle. The guard instantly dropped it and spat on it. He lifted his huge booted foot up and stomped the flag into the ground, crushing into the dust and mud. The other guards saw the flag and reached for their weapons.

Ollsop looked over to Soma whose knuckles had turned white from gripping her knife.

'Skull of the Alliance!' the guard grumbled, eyeing each person in the carriage.

Ollsop gingerly paced over, his head bowed down. The other guards were about to attack him.

'It's part of our act Sire,' he pleaded, not making eye contact. 'We mock the frivolous Alliance. We believe the Emperor will take humour in this. It's a new special act, prepared only for your Highness, no one has ever seen it before.'

The guard looked doubtful.

'Show me this act before I throw you all in prison,' he said, resting his hands on his sword, the foul stench emanating from his arm pits wafted in the breeze over to where Heather and the others were standing.

Ollsop stared up at the guard whose shadow crossed over his face. He could tell the guard had darkness in his soul and would not hesitate to attack them with an instant.

Ollsop took his cloak and threw it over his head. Suddenly all the guards rushed towards him, thinking he was about to perform some sort of magic ritual. With their blades drawn they descended on him, then, with a flare of fire shot from somewhere under the hood, Ollsop appeared. His face was covered in green make up, shoddy looking and pasted on thick. He had red swirls drawn on his face.

'He looks like...' Heather squinted, 'Kiel?'

Ollsop started hobbling around, tripping over the guards and mumbling frantically about killing the Emperor. The guards all doubled over with laughter. The head guard laughed so hard, clear liquid came out of his nose. Ollsop twitched like he was having a seizure and fell onto the ground, his hood back over his face. The Cadabra guards held their stomachs as they cried with joy, wiping tears from their eyes. Ollsop got up off the ground, the makeup gone with only a few dollops around his ears.

'Pack your things,' the red bearded soldier said, his teeth still rattling with laughter, 'and get inside. His Lord will enjoy that. The Alliance are a joke! *Hahaha*, nothing but a bunch of war slaves!'

Soma felt her blood run cold, every instinct in her body wanted to morph into the werebeast and tear these cruel soldiers asunder. LaFare glanced over to her, to make sure she was calm. She locked eyes with him and felt her heart beat steadily again. They repacked the wagons and climbed back aboard. Heather was still shaken from the encounter. As the carriages rolled away from the guard towers and towards the large gates of Cadabra, she crawled through the wagon and into the driver's seat where Ollsop was sitting.

'How did you do that? I mean, is it a real performance? Mocking yourselves?'

Ollsop looked at her and smiled broadly.

'No Heather, that was what I call thinking fast on your feet! I feared we were about to be found out, so I had no other option,' he laughed to himself, something rare from Ollsop, of which Heather had never seen before.

'The worst is not over yet, Heather.' Ollsop nodded his head towards the front of the wagon. Heather looked over and saw the gates to Cadabra. Wrought iron gates like spears sprung up from the ground, their tips pointed and rusted. Loitering around the outside were deviants of all kinds: merchants trying to sell illegal herbs and potions, story tellers whispering to small crowds about the power of the Dark Emperor and warlocks selling black market spells from their coat pockets. Some were scarred along their fingers and hands, some on their faces. Heather tried not to look at them. She gazed upwards and saw the Emperor's tower. It looked like a witch's bony finger sticking out from the twisted remains of smouldering ash. It curved around and upwards like a cork screw. A flock of dark red and green birds flew around its peak, not daring to land on the structure. Two guards yanked the rusted gate open and it creaked loudly. The screeching inside Heather's ears made her clap her hands over them. The wagon rattled and bumped over the small hump at the entrance. After the third carriage was inside, she heard the gates shut behind her with a sickening clunk. For a moment she was too afraid to look over her shoulder, afraid she would see no way out.

The grounds of Cadabra were dry dirt leading up to the first of several adobe huts. They were painted with white streaks, zig-zagging across the roofs and walls. Words were written in a language Heather could not decipher.

'Magic detectors,' Ollsop leaned over and whispered.

The Gazzoo trudged past the hut and kicked wildly, rearing up on its hind legs. Ollsop steadied it and clicked his tongue. The beast shuffled, shaking its legs as if it were drunk. It stumbled past the huts and snorted wildly, liquid dripping from its nose. A man dashed from the makeshift kiosk, one leg was gone and in its place a wooden stump with a rickety, buckled wheel. He saw the Gazzoo being sick on the dirt and backed away instantly.

'What is going on here?' he questioned. He had a tightly pinched nose with several burn marks under his left eye. They were intricately placed by some torturous person, and it had never healed.

'We are the travelling performers. We are to meet someone to take us to the location so we may set up.' Ollsop stayed astride the wagon, knowing perfectly well he had set the detectors off, but the one-legged man had not questioned them about their magic.

Through narrowed eyes the man glared down the line of wagons, seeing the tent and performers sitting on top, staring nervously at the surrounding buildings and cloaked commuters.

'Yes, yes,' he snarled, one hand coming up to his burns and picking them, he was missing two fingers from his right hand. 'I see, I see. Come forward out of the thoroughfare and wait, someone will be along shortly.'

LaFare climbed down off the second carriage and helped direct the third wagon so they were all side by side. The wheel-legged man disappeared back in the hut. Heather looked at the Gazzoo who had appeared to have recovered from its punch-drunk seizure.

'What happened to it?' She asked.

Ollsop leaned forward and patted the rear of its back. He hummed to it gently.

'The Gazzooates are excellent magic absorbers. Anything trying to detect and eradicate magic will know that this creature is highly charged. Although,' Ollsop went on, 'they can do nothing with it, they are an awesome deterrent.' Ollsop winked.

Heather knew that if the wheel-legged man knew Ollsop was a magical being, he would have pulled him aside for questioning, and that would have wasted precious time. LaFare had wandered over to their wagon and tightened the stirrups on the Gazzoo.

'Here comes our guide,' he said, catching something out the corner of his eye.

Heather and Ollsop looked over. A man, no bigger than LaFare was making his way through the darkness of a giant tunnel that led through a dilapidated building and into the side of a small rock formation. The man had long spring loaded contraptions on his legs. His feet were strapped into large iron boots, their silver buckles shining dimly in the afternoon sun. Under the boots were large springs that crunched and creaked with ever step the man took. The springs lifted the large robotic feet high into the air and slammed them down hard on the dirt. Dust clouds puffed up around his metal clawed feet every time he stepped. He stood erect with his hands on his hips. Heather had to strain her neck to look up at him. His walking mechanism was far more advanced than the wooden, clonking legs and arms of the Meniphesto Incantana. The mechanised man stood and peered down at them with a stony stare.

'I am Elder Cane. Bring your transport and follow me through the paths. Don't approach anyone and don't let anyone approach you. These are dangerous grounds if you are not familiar.' His voice was gravely and deep. Something in his tone told Heather he was a serious man, and if crossed, would not hesitate to kill.

The man nodded and turned his springed feet around and stomped back off towards the tunnel. Ollsop cracked the reigns against the wooden splashguard and the Gazzoo slowly started moving again. The other wagons followed, their Gazzoos still recovering from absorbing the magic detectors.

The convoy slowly made their way off the dirt track and onto the stone paved roads of Cadabra. Creatures of all types milled around, dealing their magic and hiding from Elder Cane as he towered passed them. The wagon's wheels splintered and moaned on the road, but no one was paying much attention as they watched the surrounding inhabitants come out of the shadows to see the travellers make their way through the city.

A serpent lay across a small fountain where the road forked into three ways. It was thick as a tree root and as long as the gates of Cadabra. It was dusty red in colour, each scale slightly changing hue as it uncoiled itself and arched its head up towards the wagon. It's one eye blinked and Heather could see a rounded diamond instead of a pupil. She pushed herself back towards the door of the wagon, ready to jump in the back. The serpent relented and lay back down across the edge of the small pond and continued bathing in the dying afternoon sun. Several cloaked figures came out of a store and stared in starry-eyed amazement at the wagons. The first one bowed his head when he saw Ollsop. The old Incantana looked over at the bowing figure and ignored him. The cloaked men started to follow the head wagon. Heather looked over to them and saw they weren't walking, as the shuffle of their long, black cloaks would have indicated. Instead, they floated, seeming gliding along the ground as if they had no feet at all.

'Take heed traitor,' the hooded figure mumbled, gliding closer to Ollsop. 'We know you're a Meniphesto of the Dark One. A much as you remove your vow of silence, you can never undo the black heart.'

Ollsop glanced at him through squinted eyes. He stopped the wagon and the surrounding creatures all stared. Ollsop raised one hand, dark blue electric waves coursed from his fingertips. Heather felt the static send her hair up into the air. An arrow, seemingly shot from nowhere, whispered through the air and struck the cloaked man through the shoulder. He gasped in horror and stumbled backwards. Heather stood up on the carriage seating, not knowing if to run or not. A noise came from ahead of them and Heather and Ollsop turned to see Elder Cane holding an archaic bow. His right hand was still cocked, with two fingers straightened, as if he had kept his pose until his target was dead. The cloaked figure pulled the arrow from his shoulder, dark green blood spurted onto his cloak and cobbled walkway.

'Suffer me!' the figure grumbled, gaining his footing awkwardly.

'Follow,' Elder Cane demanded the entourage, placing his bow back over his shoulder and into its holster.

The troupe passed thin buildings made of blackened wood, still smouldering. Their occupants looked out through thin slits in the woodwork. Heather could feel a chill seething off the ground as they rolled closer to the Emperor's tower. They turned into a long street and went towards the tunnel, Heather looked down into the abyss and wondered where it led. The wagons were far too big to fit down it. The roads ahead went east, west and north. They kept on the straight path until they came to running water. Elder Cane stopped at the tip of a bridge. It looked as ancient as the iron gate, but made of old wood which was buckled and warped from the weather. It looked like it had been designed by some twisted architect to defy gravity and understanding.

'I cannot cross here. Go ahead, I will meet you on the other side.'

Elder Cane turned back towards the rushing rapids of the river and squatted down low. Heather thought he was about to unbalance and topple over backwards onto the Gazzoo. With an almighty leap, the mechanical feet sprung into the air and rocketed up towards the dark clouds, disappearing for a moment. Heather watched his arc as he soared like a giant metal frog and landed on the other side of the water. There, Elder Cane turned and motioned them forward with his hand. He then walked towards the bizarre, darkened landscape of Cadabra. Over the bridge and past small patches of dark land were rolling hills of houses and buildings. Chimneys bellowed smoke and there were lights shimmering like small pin pricks from the windows. Heather was stunned at how far back Cadabra went, it was clearly twice as big as Hey Presto!

Ollsop clicked his tongue at the Gazzoo and it started its nervous journey towards the bridge. They halted just before the tip and looked out over the aged timber. No pieces were cracked or splintered, yet they looked as old as time itself. Heather noticed the running water of the stream underneath it and tried to see where it was going. It was rushing so fast it made her eyes blur. The sound coming off the small waves was a soft, pounding hush. It snaked around the small encampments of buildings, all their windows boarded up. Scorch marks were sprayed up the doors, as if a fire had taken over this land not long ago. Dead trees, with nothing but their ashy stumps, scattered the fields beyond the bridge. The Gazzoo bucked gently, just as it had done walking though the magic detectors. Ollsop steadied it with his reigns and the gentle animal began the walk over the bridge. Its hooves hit heavy on the bridge, sending echoing clops against the running water.

Heather had just noticed she was holding her breath. The bridge arched up in the middle, with long, dark red boards running horizontally over to the other side. The railings were made of thick beams, elegantly carved and apparently unaffected by the fire. Heather looked over the edge of the bridge and saw the murky green water. It had a distinctive smell of decaying waste and something that was similar to vinegar. She felt Ollsop's hand on her arm. He pulled her back from the edge of the cart.

'You fall in there and the liquid with eat your flesh off in seconds.'

Heather swallowed loudly and moved closer to the middle of the bench seat. As the wagon shuffled and swayed over the peak of the bridge, Heather could see over the burning tree stumps, laying ahead of them was a large vacant block of land surrounded by blackened trees. It appeared to be a small town centre as the houses petered out behind it. To the right was the twisted tower of the Dark Emperor looming over all the residents that lived in Cadabra. Around the vacant area was a makeshift wall made of cobblestones. At the entrance was a compass carved of dark grey stone. It looked like a medieval statue or shrine to their macabre master. Along its dial it had different carved creatures, none that Heather could recognise.

'What's that?' she asked Ollsop, pointing towards the centre as they got closer.

The cart took its last turn off the bridge and then they could hear the second cart coming over. It's soft clops getting louder and louder.

'That's the Emperor's magic-vane. He'll use it to find magic. I believe it hasn't worked for some time. When I was...' Ollsop's head bowed down and his voice dropped,

'...in his employ, he would stare at it for hours, sometimes days. This was before most of these buildings were even built. It showed him the path to find and harness magic. He could find it in creatures and rare minerals, or even places like Hokus Pokus or Abara. Even your world, Heather. If it carries magic, he will want it. Now he must use the gate ways to retrieve the magic. A more dangerous route, but an effective one, nonetheless.'

Heather thought of Mr Harlow.

Maybe this is how he found the sword box and got Mr Harlow's magic. She thought about the magician being here and could see him fitting in very well. *Some of his clothes are even the same as those in Abara.*

Standing dead still, like a statue made of granite, Elder Cane waited for the wagons to make it across the bridge. To the mechanical giant's right was a tall building. It was so thin three people wouldn't have been able to stand inside it side by side. It was painted dark, cobalt blue. The paint had started to peel and the window glass was cracked and caked with soot.

'This here is the ticket box,' Elder Cane said, hardly moving a muscle. 'A Representative will be along shortly to go through the proceedings, then men from the farm and mill will be along to help set up.'

The second wagon had just pulled up beside Ollsop and Heather. LaFare had caught the last sentence.

'Help set up? We don't need help to set up. We do this almost nightly, we have it down to a fine art.'

Elder Cane's eyes twitched. 'In due respect, you are in our land, performing for our Lord, it will be by our rules.'

LaFare didn't speak again. Elder Cane turned towards the tower and started his great, lengthy steps towards the twisted archway that was the entrance to the tower grounds. Heather slid off the seat of the wagon, her bum was numb from all the bumps and humps on the way. She stretched and heard her bones pop and crack. Strange creatures mulled around the centre, they looked like giant insects with bulging yellow eyes. Their wings were transparent and flattered frantically. Heather saw a group of people walk out of a house that was leaning so far to the side that if Cadabra abided by the same gravitational rules as Earth, it would have fallen over years ago. The men were wearing long purple robes with rope tied around their waists. Their faces were covered by a long hood that hid their heads entirely. They hummed gently and Heather froze with fear, they were humming the same tune as Amol who Soma had killed only nights before. She walked around the back of the wagon and saw LaFare and Soma embracing. They broke apart when Heather saw them.

'Are they dangerous?' Heather said, nodding her head to the robed men.

'More than likely,' Soma said, taking a ruck sack from the back of the wagon. 'They're bodyguards of the Emperor. They're just scoping us out, making sure we're not up to anything we're not supposed to be.'

LaFare stood with his hand in his pockets, his trousers were filthy and worn around the hem. He was almost always barefoot and Heather had never seen him without his grease stained vest.

'We don't have anything to worry about Heather. They do.'

Just as LaFare spoke, an ear splitting scream echoed from the tower and the entire band of performers looked up. Hashnay, a juggler wiped her eyes as a tear formed in the corner.

'I'm scared,' she told Soma, who kept her glare at the deformed building rising up from the ground like a macabre tree root.

Suddenly, from the cluster of houses all leaning one way or another came a long centipede creature. Ollsop saw it first and told all the performers to gather around the rear of the wagon. It was longer than all three wagons in a line. It had hundreds upon hundreds of feet, each with three wicked talons. Its skin looked spongy and rippled along its back like a wave of congealed fat. The creature's ribs were pocked with small craters, all cracked like age old rocks or mud that had been left to dry in the sun. Heather was mesmerised by the way it moved. It was like watching a snake slither across the top of water. The creature reared the front of its body up and Heather could see it had a humanoid face. It had small, black eyes, sunken deep into its skull. Its mouth was thin, slitting its face like a knife wound. When it opened its mouth to talk, Heather could see small pin-teeth and a wicked, green tongue.

'Ahh,' it said, breathing out lime green smoke, 'the performers... Your Highness welcomes you and apologises for not greeting you in person, but he has... other matters to attend to.' The enormous centipede coughed and beat its chest with one of its feet. A puff of smoke drifted from its nostrils.

Ollsop stepped towards it. Heather could see he was nervous.

'I would not expect the Great Lord to meet us in person, but we are humble servants and wish to only entertain the Dark One,' Ollsop bowed.

Heather could see Soma moving uneasily. LaFare took her hand and whispered something in her ear that Heather could not hear.

'To the right of me is where you are able to perform. The Emperor will be attending just after sunset.' Heather wondered how anyone could tell when sun set was here, as it was overcast and grey.

'So be it,' Ollsop said, bowing again.

LaFare stepped forward. 'Here?' he said, pointing to the burning grounds that must have been a forest of trees once, but now only the stumps remain, 'How can be set up our tent here?'

The slug looked at the blackened stumps. They looked like gothic tombstones sticking out from the ground. The representative hissed loudly and spat a thin stream of phlegm from its throat. It travelled across the air and hit one of the stumps. Suddenly, it started bubbling and iron-grey smoke ribboned into the air. The stump melted before their eyes and all that was left was a mushy pile of gunk.

'Tear them out of the ground if you must, but this is the only lot where the Emperor has nominated, and this is where you will perform your show.'

With that, the slug slithered around and headed back towards where it had come. LaFare kicked the ground in anger and marched to the rear of the last wagon and told the men to start pulling the stumps out and unfold the foundations for the tent. The men, four in all, eased out of the wagon and looked around the environment with nervous eyes. They wandered through the burning remains of the woodland and started pulling out the stumps with their bare hands.

Heather walked over to Ollsop. 'Is there anything I can do?'

'So we don't arouse suspicion, we should all help set up the tent. I can feel eyes watching us.'

'Is it evil?' Soma said through gritted teeth.

'I don't think so,' Ollsop replied. 'I would have felt his darkness in my soul.'

Heather glared up at the tower and wondered how she was going to get inside the tower and find the Emperor's chamber where the door-way box was.

'So,' she said turning to Soma and Ollsop. 'What's the plan?'

'For you, Heather,' Soma said, almost looking annoyed. 'You leave everything to us. We've practised this over and over and have everything in place. We'll set the explosives around the base of the tower and when Ollsop takes the stage for the grand finale... well, let's just say by then you should have found your way home.'

Heather looked at her. The door-way box could be anywhere in that elongated castle.

'How long do I have to find it?'

'Once the show begins? Two hours.'

Heather felt her heart beat faster. If it was the only way home, then she had no choice but to find it.

ADMIT ONE
COME ONE, COME ALL
THE GREATEST PERFORMANCE IN THE WORLD
CHAPTER 20
THE ARRIVAL
No. IOIOI987

Heather peered through the curtain veil and watched as the hordes of hideous creatures that inhabited Cadabra lined up to buy a ticket for the show. There were creatures with long tails, much like a scorpion's, and creatures that were huge and hairy with one great big yellow eye right in the middle of their forehead. Many of the townspeople wore robes to hide disfigured faces. The line went from the ticket building around the city centre and down along the archway of the tower. Heather could see two armed guards at the archway. They were standing breathlessly still, their long spears by their side. She closed the curtain and turned to see Ollsop and Soma sitting on small wooden stalls applying their makeup.

'Big crowd tonight,' she said, with uneasiness in her voice.

Soma ran a long, black brush along her left eyelid. 'It should be; we've been planning this for a year's worth of full moons.'

Suddenly the main entrance curtain peeled open and a strange cloaked figure rushed in. Soma was on her feet in a second, her hand on her concealed blade. The figure backed away and pulled the hood back.

'Kiel,' Heather whispered.

'Sorry for my late arrival. It was harder than expected to get in through the gates.'

'Being the Emperor's number one most sought after person, I would think so,' Ollsop said, not turning away from his small, hand-held mirror.

'Is everything in place?' Kiel asked, looking around the room suspiciously.

'We have three teams: Hashnay and two others, LaFare and myself, and Ollsop and you.'

Kiel nodded, 'Good.'

'This is really going to happen then,' Heather said, looking up at Kiel's canary yellow eyes.

'It has come down to this Heather. Years of planning and strategising. Do you know your place? What you must do?'

Heather nodded. 'I know the gateway door is in the Emperor's chambers... but I have no idea where his chamber is.'

Kiel took her hand and led her to the curtain. One long finger peeled back the veil and they both looked up at the tower.

'There, you see it? The top cone, it's painted white. See, through the clouds?'

Heather could see the summit of the twisted, cyclonic-shaped building.

'I see it.'

'He resides there. A large room filled with many magical artefacts. You'll find it in there.'

'How will I know what it looks like?'

Kiel placed his hands on her shoulders and looked her deep in the eyes. 'I'm sorry Heather, I don't know what it looks like. But I believe you'll know when you see it.'

LaFare came bounding into the room, his head whipped around as he saw Kiel and they shook hands and hugged briefly.

'He has arrived.'

Ollsop stood up, as if still possessed to stand in front of dark royalty.

'Already?' Soma snapped and marched to the curtain.

The crowd lining up for the performance all parted at the archway and got down on one knee. Even the monsters that Heather had only seen in nightmares, that didn't have knees, slithered down to the ground. A great, big, raven-black horse with large, curled horns came from the under the archway. Its legs were covered in long, thick woolly hair. The horse's hooves were as large as dinner plates, and when it stomped, the ground shook. Its body was strapped with a leather harness dotted with sharp studs. It stopped briefly and snorted large plumes of hot air from its enlarged nostrils. No one in the crowd looked the beast in the eyes.

It yanked its head forward and Heather could see it pulling a large carriage. It looked like a hearse with cryptic circular writing engraved along the sides. The panels were lacquered with perfection and shone with an elegance that Heather had not seen since arriving in Cadabra. The side door had stained glass window that had a motif of two wizards fighting in hand to hand combat. The yellows and reds and blues of the glass glowed brilliantly, as if shone from behind with a powerful light. The carriage itself was round and sat on springs that ran across the axels to the wheels. It was no bigger than the wagons used by the travelling performers. Behind the Emperor's transport were several long, black snakes. Their eyes all gleaming like red, gypsy rubies. Heather felt the familiar knot in her stomach again.

The beast pulled up in front of the entrance to the tent and five men rushed out and lay a lime green carpet in front of the stained glass door. Heather felt the knot turn to sickness, as if she was going to vomit. They all watched on in stunned amazement as one of the officials opened the door to the carriage and stood back, his eyes averted, as if waiting to be slapped across the face, or blasted with immense light. A single leather boot appeared. There was dead silence as the hundreds gathered all held their breaths. The next boot hit the ground and squirmed, as if smudging out a flame. The Emperor climbed from the wagon with grace and stood on the carpet, looking up at the big tent in front of him. He wasn't tall, as Heather had guessed he would be, but rather short. His dark brown hair was cut back, but still hung slightly over his forehead and ears. His nose was stubbish and his hands rested casually by his side. He wore a suit of black and grey with a white flower in his breast pocket.

'I can't believe that's him,' Heather said, being the first one to break the silence.

'I would cut his throat this instant if I thought I could get close enough,' Soma said through gritted teeth.

The Emperor walked with a slight shuffle. He headed towards the tent door and produced a ticket from his pocket and gave it to the ticket collector. They took it with stunned silence, tore it in half and handed the stub back. The Emperor then turned back to the crowd, grinned and disappeared inside.

'It's time,' LaFare announced. 'I will get dressed and tell the announcer to start the proceedings. Once everyone's settled inside the tent, we'll get the charges ready.' He left the room quickly. As he went, Heather could see his hands shaking.

Soma turned to Heather. 'Good luck to you Heather. May your journey into your world be safe.' She stretched her arms out and took Heather's hand pulling Heather into her. Soma's skin was cold to touch, but smooth.

Heather was lost trying to define her feelings. She felt equally scared and overwhelmed with happiness. Soma looked at her and Heather could feel a spark of friendship. She was going to miss Soma Rowmoon, she thought to herself. Soma didn't say anymore. She let Heather go from her grasp and smiled. She strolled over to Kiel, acting as if it was the last time she would ever see him. She hugged him for a long time. Heather could tell she was crying, even though her head was turned away. After a minute she let him go. Ollsop stood up and fastened a large belt around his waist. He hugged Soma and she left the room without saying another word.

'Your courage is an inspiration, Heather,' Ollsop said, holding her by one hand. 'It was a pleasure to have met you... a kindred spirit from another realm. I wish you the best in your journey.' He lent forward and kissed her on the cheek. 'If you are to get into trouble before the explosives go off, do not hesitate to return here. There will surely be another way home.' He gave her a smile and headed for the doorway. Before he left he glanced over his shoulder and looked at Heather one last time. Heather could see his scars under his makeup. A tear rolled down her cheek and she wiped it away quickly. She stood in the room with Kiel who was standing at the curtain slit, looking out at the Emperor's carriage.

'Something's not right,' he said, and turned to Heather.

'You're just nervous,' she told him, looking up at his deep yellow eyes.

His mouth opened to say something, but he closed it again. He lifted one dark green hand up and ran it through her hair. His hand coursed around her ear and he held her chin in the cuff of his palm. He tilted her head up to meet his gaze and saw twin tears roll down her face.

'It is time for you to go home, Heather,' he told her, his face leaning down to her and he kissed her. There was silence for some time. For Heather it felt like a millennium. She blinked her tears away and watched as Kiel wrapped a scarf around his face and hid his hands in his robes.

'Thank you, Kiel,' she said, a small part of her now wanting to stay and continue the journey with the performing travellers, to watch the tower crumble and to witness this world have its land and people back. But, Heather knew she couldn't stay, her father would already be sick with worry. She turned towards the door. Like a wisp of smoke, Kiel was gone.

***

Heather had changed out of her Abara clothing and folded them gently on the table where Ollsop had done his makeup. She tipped out the bag that held her clothes from when she arrived. She got dressed and slid her sneakers on, that familiarity of home hit her suddenly and she could see her father in her mind's eye. She could see Bounty and her own circus tent. She could see Guntha the muscle man and Mr Harlow with his broad cape, his top hat and his deck of cards. She could also see Nancy, his daughter. The feeling to get inside the tower and find the sword box was at the forefront of her mind. She went to the slit in the curtain and saw the last of the crowd buying their tickets and going inside the tent.

The dull grey skies were now replaced by darkness. Small lanterns burst to life, as if controlled by some magical switch. The leaning houses and stores around the tower gate had flickered to life with small fiery lights. Each bulb glowed red or dark orange. Heather stepped out of the change room and into the streets of Cadabra. She looked up at the ill-formed tower and started running towards the archway.

The grounds of the castle tower were abandoned. A gust of wind swirled around the front staircase that led up to the mouth of the building. Small dust devils swirled and evaporated. Heather slid along the wall and waited to see if anyone was around; after a moment, she sprinted to the stairs and ran up two at a time. Her heart was pounding in her chest. She could feel the cold stone under

236

her shoes. As she got closer to the top she could see the grand doorway.

Two huge wooden doors stood open, as if inviting her in. They looked nearly ten metres high and carved from the richest, darkest trees in the forest. The hinges were as big as Heather's arm and fashioned from metal forged by a dark blacksmith. The intricate designs were small and precise. Heather went to the corner, near the left door and stood with her back against the tower itself. She could feel its foreboding presence seep into her skin. The door handle was a black goats head with a large ring in its mouth. The ring was the size of a hula hoop Heather used to own as a child. Small skulls were carved into the metalwork. She tried not to look at them.

She walked along the open door and glanced inside. It was a long hallway with flickering candles stationed every few feet. The flames were nothing but a lick of fire, and hardly lit the ground. She looked back at the tent and heard the soft music of the show starting. She took a deep breath and turned back to the open maw of the entrance. She stepped inside and the doors slammed shut behind her.

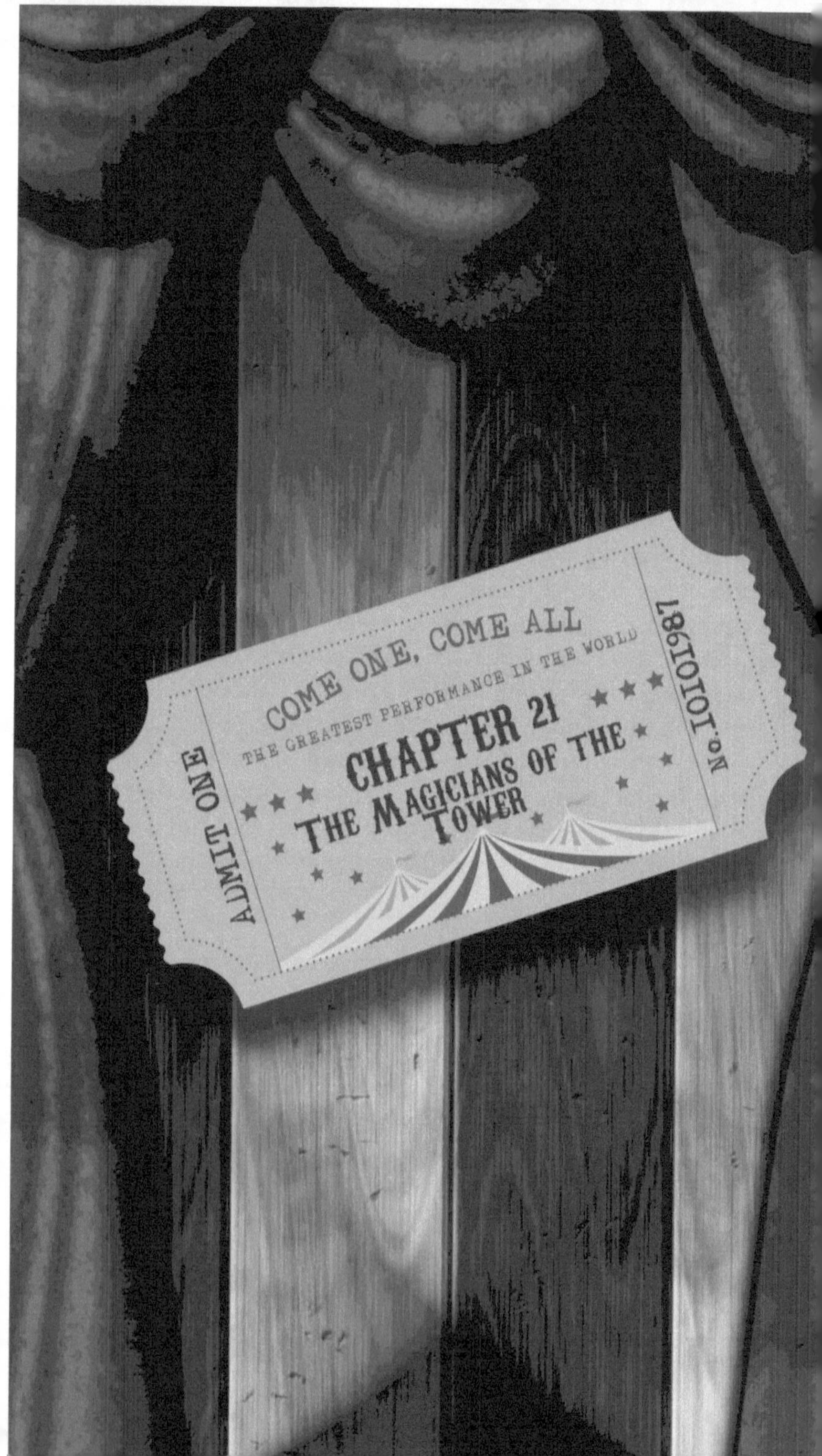

COME ONE, COME ALL
THE GREATEST PERFORMANCE IN THE WORLD
CHAPTER 21
THE MAGICIANS OF THE TOWER
ADMIT ONE
No. 1010101987

A moment of panic tickled its way up Heather's arms and down her legs. She ran back to the door and pounded on the hard wood with her fists. It didn't budge. She turned around slowly. All she could see was the faint glow of the lanterns lingering in the air, as if held by ghosts. She turned back to the door and felt around for a handle or pull ring. She found a small handle. The metal was cold and made her fingers numb to touch it. She pulled on it but the doors were shut tight.

'Maybe it's just a safety precaution,' Heather told herself. 'Everyone's at the show. I would lock the doors around here too.'

She slowly stepped away from the entrance and looked down the long hallway. One nervous step at a time, she headed down the corridor. Around her she could hear water dripping on the cold cobblestones. The flames flickered and one went out with a sharp hiss. Heather jumped nervously. Towards the end of the hallway she could see a circular room. She walked slowly, cautious not to make a noise. A large, round rug lay on the floor. It looked ancient and was made by someone with an uncanny eye for detail. The patterns were so intricate, Heather thought no human could ever had made it. The design swirled around the outside like a vast ocean of reds and blues, then, towards the middle the pattern became more square and the colours started to run into each other until the final picture in the middle was a face. Heather stopped in her tracks and started down at it. The face was white; she had seen it before. It was the Dark Emperor.

For a moment she felt hypnotised and pulled her eyes away from the picture. looking around the room, she saw two staircases, one on her right and one of her left. They spiralled up into the next level, disappearing through darkened archways. Heather went to her left and saw the walls of this room were made of bricks bigger than her head. Along the sides hung massive picture frames. She stopped, one foot pausing on the first step and looked at the painting. It was a man, tall and slender leaning on a large wooden crate. Heather leant forward, her head casting a long shadow across the painting. She recognised that crate.

'The sword box,' she said to herself. Her soft voice echoed around the room.

Heather took her foot off the step and went to the next picture. It was of a very robust man. His shirt buttons were straining to hold each side of his shirt together. He was standing in front of what appeared to be a massive fish tank. Bolted to the bottom of the frame was a gold plaque.

'Baron Von Munstrum,' Heather read out at a whisper. 'Magician of the People.'

She ran to the next picture. This frame was huge, it went up into the ceiling and almost touched the next level. A man, with dark skin was climbing a rope that was apparently not attached to anything. He wore no shirt, but had a white wrap around his head and he was reaching upwards with his thin hand to the very top knot. Heather's eyes scanned down to the bottom where she found the rope disappeared into a cane basket. She had seen this sort of magician on TV. Her head swirled around the room and she saw all the paintings were of magicians through different ages. Some appeared to be from her world. From somewhere outside she heard the *bang!* and *pop!* of small fireworks. Her brain was suddenly jarred with the memory of time and she looked up at the marble staircase in front of her and began to climb, two steps at a time. The banister was cold to touch as were the steps.

By the time she reached the next level, her heart was pounding in her chest so hard she thought it would tear straight through her rib cage. The level opened up into a catacomb of different rooms. Heather stood in grim silence as she scanned the doors to her left, then her right. There must have been nearly fifty paths to pick from. Several hallways branched off, with more and more hallways branching off again. *How could this place contain so many rooms?* She thought.

To her right she could see a long window with a mosaic design of what appeared to be a wand with silver and blue fire emanating from the tip. On either side of the window was a dark red curtain, pulled back in the middle by a golden rope. Light flared in through the stained glass window. The light appeared to be coming from outside, but Heather knew perfectly well Cadabra was a dark city with hardly any natural light. The window made psychedelic patterns of light across the ground and Heather found herself walking towards it, mesmerised by its colour and movement. As she neared the light that shone across the dark marble floor, she heard two voices arguing and spun around in a panic. There was someone coming from one of the other rooms. The strange, soft voices could have come from any one of the rooms around her. The noise echoed and bounced across the walls and ceiling. Suddenly footsteps pounded the hallways and Heather knew she had only moments before she was spotted. She looked to the window and ran towards it. Her shoes were soft and barely made a sound. She skidded to a halt and wrapped one of the red curtains around her thin frame. Her chest was heaving in and out, but she had to slow it down or whoever was coming, would be able to hear her.

'The Dark Lord's reign is nearly upon this world. When will we move our army, and stop this foolishness with entertainment?' said a voice. 'I'm not entirely convinced the Dark Lord has all his wits about him.'

'Shut your mouth!' someone snapped, their voice was low and gravelly. 'If the wrong person was to hear you speak of the Emperor like that, he would toss you from the spire of this tower.'

'Forgive me, I am just eager to move my men out and destroy anything that gets in our way,' the first voice said.

Heather found a small slit through the curtain and peered out with her left eye. She could see one massive soldier, dressed head to foot in dark, grey metal armour, similar to the armour worn by the guards near the gate, but this soldier's armour was clean, as if he had just polished it recently. He had a greying beard and long fingers. His knuckles were all bunched together like grapes. He had long crow's feet spreading out from each corner of his eyes, and he walked with a slight limp. The other man, who's head only came up to the soldiers' underarms, was wrapped in a robe of chocolate brown. A light blue rope was tied around his waist and he held his hands together over his stomach.

'If you don't show your face in that tent, the Dark Master will have you torn limb from limb.'

The robed man swallowed loudly. He shook his bald head.

'I'm the magic adviser to the Dark Lord, but he does not listen to me. Maybe you can? These are times of great concern. My witches have seen many visions of Abara Cadabra where the Dark One has fallen. These are pressing matters for us all.'

The solider stopped dead in his tracks, one foot on the step leading down to the ground level.

'Pressing matters,' He lifted his foot and stepped towards the monk. 'You want to travel between worlds stealing magic? Your near sightedness will cause our very own world to be stolen from right under our eyes. Your witches are as blind as you! And twice as stupid! There are so many doors open now they don't know which world they are looking at.' The solider stepped closer to the monk and prodded him with a long, wrinkled finger.

The monk stepped back and bowed. 'I am only doing as instructed.'

The solider stared him up and down and twisted his face up in disgrace. He turned on his heels and marched down the staircase. Heather could only hear one set of footsteps echo off in the distance. The wine red curtain wrapped around her body was starting to itch, but she didn't know where the monk had gone. Her left eye scanned the area, which she could see, but couldn't find the magic advisor anywhere. She was about to step out from her hiding spot when she heard his voice.

'I know you're there,' the advisor said.

Heather closed her eyes, fearing her time was now at an end. She was frozen by utter fear.

'Oh Holy Spirit of Houd...' the advisor paused mid-sentence.

Heather's eyes were squeezed shut so tight tears were pushed out the sides. The advisor turned and ran to the banister. He sniffed loudly three times and growled like a cornered, wild animal.

'An outsider has gotten in! Guards!' the man bellowed.

Heather had to do something fast, the advisor would alert the people outside and they would arrest her, or worse. She darted out from the curtain. The bald man had his back to her, but it would only be a matter of seconds before he smelled her and turned around. She looked for something, anything to use as a weapon. The golden rope holding the curtains back were tired to a massive hook bolted to the old brick wall. Heather ran to it and unhooked the rope, it was heavy in her hands and was the softest material she had ever felt. It was like silk, but the touch was similar to running water. She raised it above her head, the knot dangling at her back. She moved at him quickly, but as she did, the advisor turned, his mouth open to call out another alert.

'Who are you?' The magic adviser went cross- eyed as Heather brought the rope down on his head. The knot hit the monk hard on the side of the temple and he fell to the ground like a sack of stones.

'Sorry,' Heather whispered and dropped the rope. She ran to the next set of doors and opened the first one. There was a staircase going up, without hesitation she bolted for them. Her thighs burned and her hands were sore and achy from swinging the rope, but she was determined to find the gate-way box before Ollsop and the others set the charges. Once she reached the next level, the stairs opened up to a large room that was lined with more framed pictures. Heather barely looked at them, as she saw a door at the very end. It was dark red with golden images carved into the wood.

'I must be close,' she whispered, knowing she was getting higher and higher into the castle tower. Her footsteps echoed loudly throughout the empty room. As she reached the door she saw it had two metal bars that rested across it on four iron hooks.

'Why would they put the lock on the outside when they're trying to keep people out?' Heather wondered to herself. She lifted the first bar up, it was heavy and clattered on the ground loudly. She lifted the second bar off and let it fall to the ground, atop of the other. She gripped the heavy handle and pulled it towards herself. The door opened widely and she slid through as the weight of it closed behind her.

ADMIT ONE
COME ONE, COME ALL
THE GREATEST PERFORMANCE IN THE WORLD
CHAPTER 22
THIS IS THE HOUSE OF
DARK MAGIC
No. IOIOI987

Heather stood in opened mouthed shock.

'This can't be...' she said, staring at the room she was in.

The floor was wooden and looked like someone had serrated the ground repeatedly with a knife. The dents and dings in the timber were deep and gouged open. It looked like scars, shining morbidly in the light from small lanterns. Several feet in front of Heather was a podium, similar to the plaque on the fountain where the circus was set up. She walked over to it, careful to scan the room for anyone nearby. The podium was made of white granite, carved with explicit detail. It was covered in engraved eyes and mouths. Hundreds upon hundreds of them. One of the eyes blinked and Heather yelped in horror, leaping backwards. She took a moment to catch her breath and looked again, the eye didn't move. She felt her throat tighten up. She told herself that she didn't see it move, and that it was all in her head. Upon the pedestal was a large book. It was open and as Heather scanned the contents, she could see that it was almost full of people's names and comments, almost like a guest book at a wedding. Heather read the first line;

'*I come here seeking... Healing power, in order to save my sick children... my name is... Greenwitch Pallah.*'

Heather read the next line;

'*I come here seeking... Wealth and Fame, in order to spread my name throughout the land... my name is... Wedrat Blinko.*'

Heather looked over to the middle of the room. The wood was faded and several layers had been tarnished off.

'It's a book of... needs,' Heather whispered. 'People wanting something from the Dark Master.' She looked back down and ran her finger across from where Greenwitch Pallah had written. In a curved, twitchy script was the word – *denied*. She ran her finger across where Wedrat Blinko had written – *denied*. Heather looked down the last column, all the results from the people's pleas were denied.

'He is evil,' she said. 'He does nothing to help anyone.'

She walked around the podium and stared around the quiet room. The first thing Heather noticed were there was no stairs. She looked around frantically, there were numerous open doors and broken pieces of wood from the floor scattered around randomly, but no stairs. She walked to the middle of the room and felt the small area she was standing in was more sunken than the surrounding floorboards. She felt like she was in the middle of a washing machine, as if it was about to turn very quickly.

'But how do I get up to the next level?' She suddenly felt her eyes being pulled upwards. She craned her neck back and saw the tower spiralling up and up into a cone of twisted darkness and mortar. Every hundred feet or so were small platforms, they were randomly placed until the very top. Heather could see the dim tip of the tower if she squinted. There was a small opening, no bigger than a manhole for a sewer drain.

'You've gotten far, little one,' said a voice.

Heather whipped her head around and saw Elder Cane with his mechanical legs strapped to his feet. The springs creaked like a rusted gate.

'How you got this far into the Dark Chambers, surprises me. Even with everyone at the performance...' Elder Cane stopped in mid thought. 'It was a lie. Wasn't it? Yes, how stupid could I have been.' His voice was mechanical, much like his robotic feet. Elder Cane stepped one step closer, the massive springs where the Achilles heel were, whined with power.

'I'm not from here,' Heather pleaded. 'I need to get home.'

'Liar!' Elder Cane shouted, spit flew from his mouth. 'You've brought your gang of thieves into this castle to steal our magic. You've come here to *kill* the Dark Master.'

'No! That wasn't me...' her voice softened on the last few words.

'It wasn't you? Then who?' Elder Cane glanced over his shoulder at the door where the podium and book stood, as if to see some mass army coming up the stairs to support the small girl in front of him. Suddenly, his eyes flashed with rage and he gritted his teeth.

'Those travelling performers! How dare they! This is the house of Dark Magic! This is the tower of Cadabra!' His voice boomed throughout the circular room. He took another step, this time it made the wood under him creak and moan. He took another step and then started to run. He was sprinting straight for Heather.

Heather let out a scream and bolted. There were several archways circling the room. None of them had doors. She ran into the closest one. The wood planks under her feet rattled and bounced as the spring loaded feet of Elder Cane pounded after her. Heather snuck a peek over her shoulder and saw his ghastly eyes bearing down on her. She looked back and tripped on a splintered shard of wood sticking up from the floorboards and rolled across the ground and into the room. She crawled on her hands and knees to the far wall and slammed her back against it. She could see Elder Cane's boots; they were as high as the door was. He bent down and peered in through the archway, his knees bent and his back at a right angle.

'Come out, come out, little one,' he mocked. 'You can't stay in there forever.'

Heather felt her heart beating in her chest. It felt like it was trying to bounce right out of her ribcage. She pulled her hair back and tied it in a ponytail. Looking around the room, she saw it was some sort of repair workshop. There were spare springs on the wall, bolts and screws and metal frames. Two pairs of large mechanical boots, half built, lay unused on the workers' bench.

The wall she was leaning on had several pictures nailed into the brick. Heather turned her head to see. They were the blue prints for the spring boots. As the pictures progressed, she could see how they were going to be made into a full suit of armour. She stood up, momentarily forgetting about the man outside the door. The very last picture was the most horrific. Elder Cane was dressed in a full techno-metal outfit. His hands were ablaze with blue magical fire. His eyes burned red, flames licking into the sky. Below the picture were the words; *Amount: 3000*.

'Three thousand suits,' Heather said, looking over to the rows upon rows of half built mechanical suits.

'That's right girl,' Elder Cane barked, his voice hoarse. 'With these suits all of Abara and Cadabra will be the Dark Master's. There will be no stopping him.'

Heather spun her head towards the archway. She could feel her palms sweating and her blood running cold. Elder Cane had gone. All she could see was the splintered wooden platform outside the workshop. She turned and looked around for another door, or window, anything. But there were only four walls and the archway. She ran over to the bench and looked for something to use. She had to get into the towers top, but how? Then it all fell into place. *That's how they get up!* Her mind reeled. She looked at the spring boots one at a time. None of them were fully completed in their construction. She took down the last pair and sat on the floor by the rear wall, facing the archway. The mechanical boots felt strangely light in her hands. The springs were new and had a thin blue wrap around them. The elongated, metal feet stuck up into the air like rabbit's legs. Heather didn't know how to work them, but they were her only hope of getting up into the tower and away from Elder Cane. She slipped her right foot into the boot and without warning the clasps tightened and fastened themselves around her ankle and shin. In a panic, she tried to get it off, but it was strapped to her foot securely. Through the doorway came a noise, Heather looked up to see one of Elder Cane's boots being tossed across the launching platform.

'If you won't come out, girly, I'll come in after you! The Dark Lord will be more than pleased that I caught you trying to enter his chamber!'

The second boot was tossed through the air and landed with an abrupt thud, near the centre of the wooden stage. Heather felt the fear rise up from her stomach and into her chest. Her hands started to shake as she slipped the robotic boot onto her left foot, the clasps fastened by themselves and she tried to stand. Suddenly, a silhouette stood in the archway. It was Elder Cane, his legs were thin and bowed, as if he spent too long in the mechanical shoes and they had warped his muscles and bones. Heather gasped when she saw he was holding a blade.

'You have no idea what you're doing in those war shoes. Now, come quietly or else.' He lifted his left hand outwards and the dagger gleamed diligently.

Heather tried to stand again, but the boots wobbled and were too big for her small frame.

'Leave me alone!' she shouted. 'All I want to do is get back home!' She felt the familiar trickle of tears merge in the corner of her eyes. Elder Cane stepped towards her, his legs shifting awkwardly and his stride almost whimsical. He raised his knife up high. Heather's face blushed with adrenaline. She couldn't stand, or get out of the boots in time to run, then she had an idea – quickly she spun her backside around and placed the bottoms of the boots on the wall that she had her back to. She felt the springs surge with energy, then she kicked off. As if the shoes were reacting to her very thoughts, they pounded the wall so hard it left twin foot prints pushed into the mortar. Elder Cane's eyes peeled open with surprise as Heather shot towards him, knocking him off his feet and sending him hurtling through the air. Heather hit the ground, scraping skin from her shoulder and rolling several times before coming to a halt near the middle of the arena. She moaned in agony and felt her shoulder, there was blood.

Elder Cane sat up and shook his head, 'Stupid girl!' he screamed. 'You don't know how to work the war shoes!' He looked around desperately for his dagger and saw it a few feet away. He got to his feet and hobbled over to it, clearly hurt from being knocked over. Heather scrambled onto her knees and looked up towards the spiralling dome. She was almost in the middle. She dragged one leg around in a circular motion, resting the heel on the ground and pushed her body upwards. As if the shoes knew what was happening, they pushed gently and lifted her up onto both feet. Heather waved her arms around thinking she would fall to the ground, but the boots were so heavy they kept her upright.

'Don't you dare!' yelled Elder Cane, snatching his blade from the ground and turning to her, his teeth gnashing together.

Heather looked over to him, he started to bolt towards her again, this time his eyes were narrowed and saliva dripped from between his gritted teeth. She felt blood run down her shoulder and looked back up at the open ceiling.

She knelt down, squatting, and felt the springs sing wildly. Elder Cane launched himself towards her, his knife slashing the air. Heather leapt upwards, feeling the boots take her orders and release their full energy. Elder Cane's swing had connected the blade with the bottom of her boot and bent the tip slightly. He lost balance and fell to the ground in a puff of splinters and dust.

The ground disappeared below her as Heather was catapulted upwards like a dart, soaring through the air. Heather closed her eyes for an instant and felt the world vanish below her. She opened them just in time to see two platforms pass her, then she noticed she was only about half way up the tower. Suddenly, gravity began to take hold and she slowed. Then, her body suddenly felt heavy and she started to fall back towards the arena. The sudden rush down made her stomach fly up into her throat. She tried to look down, to see were Elder Cane was, but the ground was coming up so fast it was a blur. She straightened her legs and prepared herself for the impact of hitting the ground. The flooring rushed towards her in great big splashes of beige and grey, then, Heather felt her feet hit the ground. It was the softest landing she had ever felt. Her mind had expected her body to be a crumpled mess on the floor. The springs absorbed all of the impact, making her feel like she was landing on a mattress full of feathers. She looked around for Elder Cane and saw him whimpering, holding his knife between his teeth as he was putting his war shoes back on.

Heather lent down and placed her arms upright, as if diving into a pool, and sprung back in the air, this time determined to land on one of the platforms before Elder Cane could get close to her. She tore through the air, feeling the air on her face again. Everything around her was a haze of colours. As the trajectory started to slow, she saw a platform to her right and tried to lean her weight in that direction. The springs in the feet reacted to the shift in balance and let out a puff of air from below the spring belts. Heather felt herself soar towards the platform, but she was going to fall short of landing on it. She reached out, her shoulder aching. The blood that had dripped down her arm had started to dry. Her fingertips gripped the edge of the wooden platform just before she started to fall. The war shoes made her swing wildly, but they didn't appear to be too heavy. Suddenly she could hear the whirling noise of another pair of war shoes somewhere below her.

She hung, dangling, a hundred meters up from the floor. The whole tower spun around her and made her dizzy. She looked over her shoulders to see Elder Cane soaring up towards her. Heather quickly tried to swing her leg up on to the platform, but didn't make it. She swung again and the tip of the boot barely managed to grip the tip of the platform. Elder Cane flew up beside Heather just as she moved her foot, slicing the air with his blade. Heather ducked her head and tried to clutch something on the platform, but there was nothing to grasp. All she could see was dust and pieces of shaved metal, and the wall of the tower. She chanced a look over her shoulder and Elder Cane had started his descent back to the ground. In one more leap he would be able to get to her with his knife.

'I'm coming for you, child,' he grunted as he dropped like a stone back to the bottom platform.

Heather swung her other leg up and rolled onto the small stage. She looked up; in one good leap she could reach the top. But what was up there? How could she get into the Dark Emperor's room? She stood on shaky legs and heard from below her the clicking of Elder Cane's springs shooting up from the ground. She didn't have time to aim, or balance herself. She just leapt. The boots rocketed, spearing her high and fast through the thinning cone of the tower. Elder Cane was only a short way behind her. His leap was powerful, having the war shoes on for so long made him a master of his craft.

He soared faster and faster, approaching Heather at an alarming speed. His fingertips scratched the bottom of Heather's boots, then he managed to grab hold of them. Heather screamed in horror as Elder Cane began climbing up her body as they propelled upwards. His extra weight was slowing her rise and she would never reach the top now. She kicked out at him, hitting the knife right on target, but he kept hold of it.

'Let me go!' she cried out.

'I will cut those boots off you and let you fall to your death before I let you enter the Dark One's chamber!'

They reached the peak of their flight, Heather could see a small dark opening in the ceiling. Then they started to fall. They were headed straight for one of the platforms on the right. Heather braced herself for impact, but Elder Cane was too focused on carving the shoes off her feet. They hit the landing platform hard, knocking the wind out of them both. Heather rolled to her side, grasping her stomach and wheezing in a fit of panic. Elder Cane flopped on his back and fell from the small ledge, his eyes glazed over in shock. Heather could hear him fall. His knife fell from his hands and speared downwards onto the leaping pad. Air filled Heather's lungs once again and she took several large breaths to get back to normal. She looked over to her arm and the blood trickling down from her shoulder. She was in so much agony she thought she would pass out. But she was so close. She gained her composure and balanced herself on the podium. She looked up at the small hole in the ceiling and leapt one last time.

ADMIT ONE
COME ONE, COME ALL
THE GREATEST PERFORMANCE IN THE WORLD
CHAPTER 23
THE EMPEROR'S ROOM
No.10101987

Heather saw the dark hole coming towards her. As she sped closer, she could see that it wasn't a hole at all, but a hazy wormhole of spinning magic. She thought she might hit the ceiling and break her neck. Fear struck her brain and she was momentarily paralysed. She closed her eyes and thought of her bed, back in her father's caravan; the warm sheets, all her old programs from the shows and her friend Bounty. As she flew into the wormhole, it felt like stringy spider webs tugging at her skin, then came a soft caress of what she could only describe as fine silk. Suddenly the softness became rougher. It was like landing in a pool of raw sugar. Then, with a disturbing plop, she fell onto something hard. She lay motionless for several seconds before opening her eyes. For a few moments everything was hazy. She blinked and saw that she was looking up at a wooden ceiling. The beams ran from the corners of this octagonal room to the middle.

'I must be in the Emperor's room,' she whispered to herself, sitting up.

Her feet ached and her back was still spasming. She checked her shoulder, the wound was still freshly open and bleeding. She unhinged the war shoes and pulled them off. She stood up, her feet were rickety, her calf muscles ached like mad and she could feel her shin bones moaning from the jumps. She felt very short without the shoes on.

The hole she had come through was now just a red rug. There was no sign of the entrance at all. She tapped the rug with her big toe, thinking it may ripple or that there may be a trap door, but there was nothing. Just a woven rug.

She looked around the room. It was large and spacious. On the left hand side was a massive book case with ancient tomes and small glass displays with various objects and paraphernalia in them. Her eyes scanned around and saw an archway into a small room. She could see the walls were lined with candles and a long rope that went up to the ceiling and was attached to a massive iron bell.

In the room was a bed, not much bigger than her bed back home. Past the bed was a desk. Heather's mouth dropped open at its splendour. The desk was carved of fine, dark red wood. The burls along the top looked like giant eyes of a serpent. Half burnt candles rested along the edge, their wax dripped down like white lava. An ink well sat on the right hand side, its handle the spine of a dragon, its body, curved with intricate detail. Sticking from the ink well like a flag was a quill. Its feather was fine and long, dark green with spots of purple. Then, as the spine of the quill curved, the feather became bright yellow and then finally cobalt blue. In front of the desk was a massive leather chair with its back to her.

She looked around to her right, taking in the full scope of the Dark Emperor's quarters. There was a giant tank, too big for fish, but big enough for a human. The glass was stained green, with patchy black moss housing the corners. On the wall hung a white coat adorned with weathered silver buckles; they no longer shone. The coat was dirty and Heather could smell its rank, unwashed odour from where she stood. The floor appeared to be littered with balls of crumbled paper and broken pieces of wood. She walked over to one and picked it up. It was a wand that had been snapped in half. She put it down. Then something caught her eye. There was a large wooden box sitting against the cold brick wall, hiding in the shadows. The front had twin opening doors, the handles gold and the key was sticking out of the lock with ruby-red lace tied to the end. Heather walked over to it, it looked exactly the same as Mr Harlow's sword box. The one that brought her here. To the right of the box was a stand that held an emerald coloured cushion. On the cushion was a smaller box, no bigger than a shoe box. There was a gold lock on the front with a key sticking out of it. She reached out and touched it, it hummed brilliantly in her hand.

William and Scarper said the gate way box would take me back, she thought, looking between the two boxes.

'If you're looking to get home, Heather. I would look inside the one on the right.'

Heather froze. Her feet suddenly had the prickly feeling of pins and needles. Her mouth gaped open and she turned her head, ever so slowly, over to the desk. The voice was coming from the chair. She watched as it turned around. A small man was sitting with one leg crossed over the other. His hands in a pyramid in front of his chest. His face was sallow and white, with sunken cheeks and a small chin. A long, curled moustache rested under his nostrils. His eyebrows arched in the middle, giving him a sinister look. He stood up, straightened his suit and bowed gracefully.

'You are Heather Cassidy aren't you?' the man asked.

Heather fumbled backwards, trying to figure out a way out of the room, but there were no doors, only windows, and they were extremely high up. She would never reach them without the war shoes.

'Who are you?' Heather shouted, her voice quivering with terror.

'I'm the one they call Emperor. Or the Dark One. Or the Dark Magician. Or the King of Cadabra. It all depends on who you talk to really.'

Heather felt her mouth dry up, 'But you're... you're supposed to be... down...' She couldn't get the words out.

'At the performance?'

Heather nodded, 'Yes.'

The Emperor strolled over to the massive wooden cabinet and picked up a golden compass. The dials spun erratically. He placed it carefully on the desk, as if it was made of egg shell. He looked down at it, marvelling at its workmanship. 'I'm afraid not, Heather. I've known about the Alliance coming for some time.' He turned back towards her. 'There isn't much left in these lands that I don't know about.'

'All I want is to get home,' Heather demanded.

'Home? That's easier said than done, Heather.' The Emperor looked down towards the ground one last time before switching his gaze back to Heather.

'You're not the first from your world here, did you know that?'

Heather didn't respond, she just tried to keep her distance from him.

'A little girl, by the name of...' he pushed his thick black hair back from his eyes and thought for a moment, 'Nancy Harlow.'

Heather gasped, 'Mr Harlow's daughter!' she yelped involuntary, then slammed a hand over her mouth.

'That's right. She had a grand proposal for me. One that I obviously couldn't refuse.'

'And what was that?' Heather said, finding her voice.

'You see Heather,' the Emperor paced around the room with his hands behind his back, not looking at her, 'she came here through the sword box also. She didn't want her father to do magic anymore. She was sick of moving from city to city, country to country, living out of a wagon... or what you call a caravan.'

As he stepped around the room, Heather kept on the opposite side of him, not taking her eyes off him.

'She blamed his magic on her mother leaving. I invited her to stay here but after a while here she grew tired of this place and wanted to go home once again. In order for me to do that, I needed something to add to my collection. Something special from your world.'

Against the wall was a small collection of wands and short swords. They all gleamed with fresh polish, but one. The Emperor stood in front of it, with his back turned to Heather.

'You see, Heather, I'm a collector of Magic. In all its forms. I have wands that once belonged to Merlin. I have trinkets and objects from all over this world and many others that are pulsing with fine magic. But what magic is greater than a daughter's love of her father?' He turned quickly. It was a split second, and he was facing Heather with the short sword in his hand. The blade was darkened red.

Heather glanced quickly at the sword box, then back at the Emperor. He was holding the sword up in front of his face and examining it.

'She...' Heather started, looking at the small man in the suit, his moustache twitching as he stared down the blade, 'traded her father's magic to get home.' It dawned on Heather like a large curtain being pulled off her eyes. 'And that's why he can't do magic anymore!'

The Emperor stopped looking at the sword and let his hand fall to his side. 'Very good Heather. You're quick like she was and eager to give up her father's magic for passage home.'

'How do I get it back!' Heather said defensively.

The Emperor raised his sword and pointed to the small podium next to the sword box. 'The answer is in there.'

Heather snuck a look over to it, 'Why would you just tell me? Nothing has been this easy so far.'

'Go look, Heather,' the Emperor said. 'If you can figure it out, you can have the magic back.'

Heather rushed over to the podium, stopping only inches away from it. The box was clearly wood, without any detail whatsoever. She turned the key and the lock instantly turned to dust. She looked over to the Dark Magician, thinking that this would be a trick and he would come after her when her back was turned.

'Its contents will free Mr Harlow. If that is worth a sneak peek, then the choice is entirely yours...'

Heather turned, knowing she would hear his steps coming behind her, if he did approach. She touched the wood top and opened it up. Her ears went fuzzy and everything around her turned to white static. Inside, the box was empty. All that there was, was a mirror on the inside of the lid. She placed her hand inside it and felt around. She could feel her heart beat in her ears and became unsteady on her feet. She was about to turn around and face the dark magician when she caught her own reflection in the mirror, it wasn't her, it was Nancy Harlow.

Heather blinked and saw Nancy looking back at her, but she was younger. The room behind Nancy was this room, but laid out differently. She blinked again and stared into Nancy's eyes. Like a film running on a slow reel, Heather could see Nancy as a smaller child, helping her father set up the magic tricks, helping him perform and laughing together. The Cassidy Travelling Circus was packed to the rafters, with people cheering for Mr Harlow. Nancy climbed into the sword box and her father performed magic around her. Once inside, Mr Harlow slowly slid swords through the slits, one by one. The crowd was cheering. Mr Harlow slid the last one in and then came a howl of pain. He yanked the sword out quickly and the end was covered in blood. He ran around to the door and pulled them open. His daughter lay at the bottom of the sword box, holding her side. She had been cut. Mr Harlow let out a guttural, animal cry and dropped to his knees, cradling his daughter in his arms as hundreds of people looked on. The image scrambled and Heather could see Nancy talking with the Emperor.

'His magic,' she said to him, rubbing her stitches under her shirt, 'for a ticket home.'

The Emperor nodded. Heather leant backward, her eyes became fuzzy and she shook her head, returning to the room.

'Touching, isn't it.'

Heather had broken from her trance, looking down she could now only see her own reflection. She spun around and saw the Emperor suddenly lunged towards her, the short sword was held to one side, ready to slice. His teeth gritted together. Heather quickly ducked. The sword split the cushion in half behind her. Snow white feathers rained all around them and the purple cloth lay in half at the Emperor's feet. Heather scrambled away from him, desperately trying to get to the magic box, but the evil magician stood between them.

'Belief is the key to magic, Heather. When her father accidently hurt her during one of the performances, her trust and belief in him died. So, can you really blame her for getting rid of his magic?' he said, staring at the sword as he pulled the white feathers from the blade.

Heather slowly stepped backwards to the other side of the room. She knew she didn't have long and her hands started to shake.

'If you believe what you are seeing, then it's magic,' the Emperor continued. 'If you make the audience believe what your doing is real, then that is how magic is created.'

He slashed the floor with the sword and sparks shot up in great yellow embers.

'But since you don't have magic, and your father is just a ringleader, then I'm afraid you have nothing to trade to get home. And since breaking into my tower is a crime, not to mention trying to kill me... I'm afraid you'll have to die here.' The Emperor's grin turned to a malevolent grimace and he darted towards Heather with the sword raised over his head.

***

As Ollsop performed, Soma became increasingly anxious.

'It's okay, once the acrobats go on, we'll have time,' LaFare told her, placing his hand on her shoulder.

Soma looked down at her feet; his skin was warm on hers. She peered through the curtain once more and saw Ollsop bowing and throwing confetti into the crowd. The audience screamed and hollered. Ollsop picked up his coat from the ground and made his way off stage. Sweat was pouring down his face and his eyes looked weary and forlorn.

'I think there's something wrong,' he said, peeling his costume off as he stepped through the curtain.

'What?' Soma spat, her nervous getting the better of her.

'It's the Dark One, he's...' LaFare held Soma's hand as she looked like she was about to jump at Ollsop and rip the words from his mouth. 'he's... enjoying it.'

Soma looked at the curtain, as if she could see through it. 'What do you mean?'

'I saw him smile and clap.'

'So?' Soma peeled away from LaFare and snatched a crowbar from under the makeshift bed.

'He's vile and evil. I've never seen him so much as smirk.' Ollsop slipped on a black robe and hood. He picked up a belt from the wooden crate and latched it around his waist.

'You've seen him before?' LaFare said, helping Soma tear the crate lid off.

'Even when he punished the Incantana, he didn't crack a smile.'

LaFare stopped what he was doing, he looked over to Ollsop and saw the scars across his lips.

'Here,' Soma said, gently unloading the dynamite from the crate and handing them to LaFare.

LaFare took them and stacked them into three brown sacks. Once LaFare and Soma had changed, they looked through the curtain and saw the acrobats twirling and twisting in the air. The entire audience looked on in awe.

'Okay,' Soma said, pulling a scarf up over her nose and mouth. 'It's time.'

They snuck out the small tent they had been using to get ready and into the coolness of early night. They hid amongst the shadows along the tent until they reached the edge of the grounds. Soma lead the way, scampering between dead trees and tombstones until she was close to the wall that surrounded the tower. LaFare followed her, turning his back against the cold wall and crouching down. Ollsop followed, the fire inside him starting to burn stronger and stronger. His scars throbbed with ancient memories of being beaten and nearly killed by the Dark Magician. He looked in his bag and felt a strange peace flush over his mind.

'This way, Ollsop. Hurry up,' Soma barked, eager to get out of sight from wandering guards.

The trio made their way along the wall until they reached a small gate. The archway was made of small bricks and on each pillar was a concrete goblin holding one hand out. In its palm was a small lantern which glowed softly, but not enough to light the ground under them. LaFare pushed his way in front and peered around the corner. One guard stood stock upright, in his right hand he held a long spear. His helmet was bronze in colour and hid his eyes in a dark abyss of shadow. Soma took one of the explosives out of the bag and attached it to the wall, she pushed a small black piece of metal into the soft body of the dynamite. LaFare looked at her, feeling more nervous now than courageous. He turned back, reached into his trousers and pulled out two throwing knives. He breathed out to steady himself and spun around the corner, rolled across the ground and threw them with perfect accuracy. The two blades cut through the air in a blink of an eye. The first one impaled the guard through the throat and he let out a gurgle of surprise, before falling back against the wall. The second blade had hit the wooden door behind him. Soma ran through the archway, an explosive and detonator in her right hand. She slammed it onto the door.

'This is attached to a support beam that holds up this side of the tower, now let's get around the other side –'

Suddenly there was a rush of movement and LaFare stumbled backwards. The guard had gotten up, blood rushing out of his throat and down his shiny armour. He had thrust his spear several meters and it had slid through LaFare's skin like a hot knife through butter. LaFare gasped and looked at the guard with wide eyed shock.

'No!' Soma cried out, dropping her bag of explosives and running over to LaFare.

The guard, now gushing blood from his neck wound, pulled a long sword from his hip sheath and darted towards them. From out of the darkness came a cloaked figure with glowing green hands. A sword appeared, covered in mist. It cut the guard down in two swift slashes. The guard hit the ground, dead. Ollsop, who had been behind Soma, roared with anger and both his hands burst into tangerine flames. Soma held LaFare who was already cold in her hands. The figure removed its head gear.

'Kiel!' Soma cried out. 'Help him, he's been hurt!'

Ollsop and Kiel ran to LaFare who was cradled in Soma's arms. He had specks of blood on his lips and Soma could hear his lungs struggling to keep air.

'Go on...' he murmured.

'I'm not leaving you,' Soma said, pushing his hair back.

Ollsop looked up at Kiel. Their eyes met and both knew what the other was thinking. The long spear had run deep into his stomach, severing several large veins. LaFare coughed and winced in pain.

'Go! Go!' LaFare jolted, he pushed Soma away. 'Drag me to the edge and come back for me. Bury me in Havenloft field, next to my people. Now, you must... destroy this tower... or all this planning will be... for... nothing.'

Ollsop and Kiel picked him up and wrapped his wound. LaFare rested against the wall of the tower in the darkness, his eyes closed and his mind unconscious. Soma looked over her shoulder as they ran into the dark tunnel that led to the front of the tower. The main entrance was empty. Ollsop ran up the stairs, not bothering to look around for any more guards that may have been checking the perimeters. Soma wiped tears away from her eyes with the back of her hand and reached in her bag for the next explosive. She planted it on either side of the door. Kiel went in through the main entrance and stood inside the

Emperor's tower. He looked through the darkness and felt an imminent fear.

'Quickly, Kiel!' Ollsop shouted, giving him a nudge. 'We need to get out of here as soon as possible!'

Kiel looked up and thought about Heather, had they given her enough time?

Soma ran past him and into the main foyer where the large pictures of magicians and wizards hung from the walls. She ran to every structural beam and planted the explosive. Ollsop ran up the stairs and did the next level. Kiel had one left, he grabbed it out of his bag and bolted up the stairs.

'Where are you going?' Soma called, heading for the front door.

'I've got to do one last thing.' Kiel turned and disappeared from view.

As he entered the next level, Kiel noticed his hands shaking. He felt his blood run cold and rush through his veins and muscles like electricity. He walked around the banister until he spotted the stained glass portrait of the wand. He stood in front of it for some time, hearing Ollsop and Soma call out for him.

'You made us build this for you. My people moulded this glass with their bare hands before you slaughtered them, and then you used it for dark magic. By destroying this, I take back everything we have ever done for you... and free my people,' Kiel placed the explosive right in the middle of the glass.

He ran his fingers over the fine workmanship and closed his eyes.

'You will not own the last remnants of my people.'

Soma ran up the stairs and saw him standing in front of the magnificent glass-piece.

'Kiel, we have to go.' He nodded and turned away. Together they ran back down stairs to Ollsop who was hiding by the front door.

'Everything set?' he asked.

'Yes, now let's get out of here. It's going to be chaos!'

The trio ran outside and along the wall until they reached LaFare. He looked extremely pale, but he was still breathing. Kiel picked LaFare up from the ground and wrapped his limp arms around his broad shoulders.

'Come friend,' he said softly. 'We must move quickly.'

Soma pulled a small metal bar from her waist pocket. It was the same as the one's she had planted in the dynamite, except this one had a red tip.

'Ollsop,' she said, looking at him with large eyes.

Ollsop lifted his hand and closed his eyes. He spoke an incantation under his breath. The words appeared from his mouth in blue text, floating serenely through the air. Soma watched as the words approached the small wick and the red tip turned green with a small spark of emerald fire. Somewhere within the tower the first explosive went off, the ground shook and the wall vibrated, dropping lose bricks. The candles in the lamps went out and Ollsop and Soma jolted in fright.

'Let's go, now!' Kiel said, helping LaFare to his feet.

They scurried off into the darkness as the second and third explosives went off. The front steps and door blew off the tower in a shower of mortar and debris. Huge fireballs enveloped the sky, raining down charcoal pieces of wood. The detonation was so loud it could be heard all the way to Hey Presto!

As each device was set off, the next one went in succession, filling the sky with fiery comets and shaking the tower from side to side. Soon the sky was filled with black smoke.

ADMIT ONE
COME ONE, COME ALL
THE GREATEST PERFORMANCE IN THE WORLD
CHAPTER 24
ALLA-KAZAM
No. IOIOI987

Heather dodged the Emperor's attack, swerving to her right and running over to the window. The tower shook violently and she could see a mushroom cloud of dark red and yellow lift into the sky.

'No!' the Emperor cried out, falling to his knees and holding his face in his long slender fingers.

Heather looked out the window and down to the ground. She could see great licks of fire coming from the bottom of the tower. Another explosion rocked the flooring and Heather toppled over. The Emperor managed to get to his feet, he picked his sword up and sliced the air, as if practising.

'You will pay dearly for this, child!' his voice quivered. His eyes stared with murderous rage. 'You dare distract me! You will pay with your life!' The Emperor screamed and sprinted forward, his blade coming down hard towards Heather's chest.

Heather tried to move, but the tower shuddered from the blasts and she lost her balance. For a moment she saw small black circles in her vision. She looked to her right and saw the edge of the sword cut deep into her collar bone. It had opened up a large wound. Blood gushed out as she turned and clumsily moved away from mad magician. Her shirt was ripped and a piece of fabric was hanging off her like a rag. The Emperor stood as if proud of his attack. Blood dripped from his sword onto the ground in large dollops of crimson. Heather felt woozy but tried to keep standing.

'Just let me go home. You don't need to do this,' Heather pleaded as another explosion went off. This time the tower lurched sideways.

The Emperor fell backwards, but held onto the wall to stop himself hitting the ground.

'I do need to do this, Heather. I could have ruled this world, and it would have only been the beginning. I could have crossed realms, into your world and made it my own. This tower is about to fall with all my collection inside it. This is a life time of work that you and your friends have destroyed in a matter of minutes. For that? I want your head.'

He charged her again, slicing the sword from left to right. Heather moved quickly, dodging the first throng of attacks. The sword sliced over her head and she ducked and wove around it. The third swing cut her pant-leg, but not enough to draw blood. The Emperor screeched as he darted the sword towards her head. It impaled into one of the candles, carving it into two and imbedding in the brick. Heather ran around him, pushing him as she went. The Emperor moaned with frustration, trying to pull the sword from the wall. She looked around frantically, she couldn't outrun him for much longer. Her collar bone and shoulder were throbbing with intense pain. Then she saw the sword box in the darkness. All she had to do was get inside it, she didn't have time to figure out how to get back to her world, she just needed to get out of the tower and away from the Emperor. She would either be beheaded or crushed to death.

The tower creaked and moaned on its crumbling foundations. Another explosion went off and the tower appeared to jolt downwards, towards the ground. The Dark Emperor spun around, yanking the sword free. He shook it wildly and cursed it. He raised it over his head and ran for Heather, baring his teeth. Heather knew she wouldn't make it to the sword box in time, so she ran to her left, hearing the magician's footsteps pounding close behind her. She glanced over her shoulder and saw the sword slicing downwards and she moved quickly, almost running into a tall wooden bookcase. It missed her arm by mere millimetres. The Emperor slid sideways and crashed into the bookcase. Tomes, large and small, toppled down, covering his head and shoulders. He slumped to the ground. Heather saw her chance, she bolted across the room, feeling her feet tire and her shoulder pulse in sheer agony. She made it to the sword box and opened it. It was exactly the same as Mr Harlow's. She climbed inside and shut the doors. Suddenly, everything was very dark but the few strands of light coming through the slits for the swords to go into.

'Oh dear, dear me,' the Emperor said, pushing the books off him. 'You've made it into the box and have no idea how to get home,' he snarled, searching for his sword amongst the rubble. He plucked it out of the fray of pages and held it high. The light caught it and Heather could see it through the slit, it looked sharper than it had before.

As if he had all the time in the world, the Emperor strolled over to the sword box and stood in front of it, sword in hand. Another explosion rocked the tower and it started to crumble, the rear wall cracked and the ceiling started to fall in. Heather could feel the floor starting to give way as the tower fell. She searched the box for anything that would indicate how it would work, then, she looked up at the door and saw a small plaque. It read: *Alla-Kazam.*

The Emperor stood beside the box and lifted his sword up, 'So long Heather Cassidy. Looks like Mr Harlow will never get his magic back!' With that, he placed the tip of the sword into the slit and placed both hands behind the handle.

Heather sat, bleeding and half unconscious, watching as the sword tip entered the slit, it was pointed right at her. Heather closed her eyes and read the word out loud, 'Alla-Kazam!'

With a forceful shove, the Emperor pushed the sword into the box as hard as he could. It slid all the way through the centre and out the other side. The tip of the sword was dripping with blood. He smiled malevolently. The windows in his quarters blew out as fire sprung up through the wooden floor. The bricks toppled down as the roof started to collapse. The whole tower swerved and started to fall. The Emperor ignored all that was happening around him. The floor gave way and he stood on two single pieces of wooden plank. Below him a fiery pit was engulfing everything that fell into it. The Emperor swung the doors open to survey his kill.

'No!' he screamed, as the tower lurched one last time, swallowing the floor and all its contents. The Emperor lost his footing, the sword flew from his hands and he toppled backwards, his arms swaying as he fell into the fiery abyss.

COME ONE, COME ALL
THE GREATEST PERFORMANCE IN THE WORLD
ADMIT ONE
CHAPTER 25
ONLY SKIN DEEP
No. 1010107

Nancy stood tapping her foot on the ground.

'So?'

Bounty pointed to the sword box, his fused fingers shook nervously.

'She was in there! We were trying to help...' Suddenly the sword box doors shut with a loud thud. Both Nancy and Bounty jumped backwards.

'W-w-what's happening?' Nancy said, stepping further back as the sword box shook and rattled.

There was a strange smell that wafted from the box, followed by gentle weeping. Bounty looked at Nancy, who didn't return his glare. He walked over to the box and placed his fleshy claw on the handle.

'Wait,' Nancy said, clutching him by his shoulder. 'Don't open it.'

Bounty didn't take his eyes off the sword box. 'Why?'

'You don't know who it could be.'

Bounty ignored her and peeled the doors open. Heather slumped out onto the ground. Nancy let out a gasp of shock. There was blood coming from her shoulder, a large gash near her collar bone and now a cut on her cheek.

'Heather!' Bounty yelped, rushing to her.

Heather looked up. 'Bounty,' she said with struggled breath. 'I'm back... I made it back...'

'Back?' Bounty questioned, 'Where have you been?'

Nancy pushed her way past Bounty and bent down to Heather.

'You're bleeding. We need to get you out of here, before my father comes in and sees what you've done.'

Bounty and Nancy helped Heather to her feet and took her outside. Nancy went back into her caravan and cleaned the blood off the floor and re-shut the sword box. She looked at it strangely and went back outside. Bounty had taken Heather over to a large tree where there were containers stacked up high and sat her out of view. Nancy ran over, looking over to the tent and could see the lights flash and strobe, it was her father's final act, she knew they didn't have long.

'Bounty, go get a wet cloth, some straps and antiseptic.'

Bounty didn't argue, he ran towards the medical area in the main caravan that carried the tent and animals. Nancy waited until he was out of ear shot.

'What happened?' she asked.

Heather looked up at her. 'The Dark Emperor did this.'

Nancy fell back, as if push by an invisible hand. She gained her composure. Her eyes were wide and fearful.

'The Dark Emperor?'

'I know what you did, Nancy,' Heather said, watching as Bounty rummaged through the caravan a few feet away.

'I don't know what you're talking about!' Nancy snapped, standing up and folding her arms.

'Nancy... don't,' Heather said, wincing at the pain in her collar bone.

Bounty returned with a dripping wet cloth and handed it to Nancy. She took it and kneeled down to Heather and wiped the blood from her shoulder.

'It won't need stitches, just a gauze.'

'How do you know?' Bounty said, peering over her shoulder.

'Trust me, I've stitched my dad up plenty of times. It's not that deep.'

Nancy took two strips of bandage and wrapped Heather's shoulder. She did the same to her collar bone.

The cut was long and bled profusely, but it was only skin deep. From the tent came a round of applause, followed by some shouts of dissatisfaction and booing. Heather heard someone yell out, 'I want my money back!' then suddenly, Mr Harlow kicked the curtain door wide open and marched out.

'Your dad,' Heather shouted, pointing towards the tent. 'He's coming!'

'Stay here,' Nancy ordered and rushed over to the caravan.

Mr Harlow walked off the rear platform and down the stairs. He swung his cape off and snatched his top hat from his head. He marched through the darkness until he reached the line of caravans. Heather tried not to make any noise as he approached where they were hiding. If he saw her the way she was, he would ask what happened to her. Bounty bent down and wrapped his arms around Heather and picked her up. She closed her eyes from the pain and they slowly walked through the darkness, making their way through a line of trees and away from where Mr Harlow was walking. Nancy had rushed into the caravan, tidying the floor and anything else her father might think was suspicious. She had just reached the door and opened it, her father was standing there, his face had a look of utter defeat.

'Nancy?' he said in bewilderment.

'Dad... Did you manage to get the rabbit out of the hat?' Her smile was forced and she nervously looked over her shoulder. She could see the sword box, the door had reopened and was swinging gently. A shiver went up her spine.

'No, Nancy. I didn't...' He looked crestfallen. He turned and sat on the front step of the caravan, resting his head in his hands. 'I don't think I'll ever be able to do magic again, Nance. Maybe we should quit the circus. I'll start a magic shop or something? Selling books on how do to magic. We won't have to travel around so much. Would you like that?'

Mr Harlow looked up at his daughter with eyes that were full of regret and worry. Nancy took her father's hand, it was cold.

'Magic will come back to you Dad,' she pleaded. She looked over to where Heather and Bounty were, but they were gone.

'I don't know Nancy... I don't think it will.'

***

Bounty took Heather to her caravan. He gently laid her on the step and opened the door. Inside, he placed her on the small table. She slumped forward, with her eyes closed, moaning.

'What happened to you? You just disappeared!' Bounty said, his eyes looking through the window to see if anyone was coming.

'I – I – I went somewhere, Bounty... Somewhere...'

Bounty looked confused. He sat opposite Heather and looked at her.

'Where? I mean, I opened that wooden box and you were gone. Then you came back covered in cuts and you're bleeding.'

There was commotion outside and Bounty shot to his feet.

'Someone's coming,' he gasped, his heart pounded in his throat.

The door swung open and Heather's father stood there sweating in his ringleader outfit.

'Heather!' he cried out, 'There you are, Mr Goodwill needs a hand feeding the dogs...' He stepped up into the van and saw the bloodied bandage around Heather's arm. 'What happened to you? Why are you bleeding?'

Bounty felt his heart skip a beat. His palms started to sweat. He felt his knees turn to jelly and he sat down, his eyes lazily moved over to Heather's. Heather took a deep breath.

'I fell over the dog cage... stupid really. I was pushing the dogs through for the next performance and... yeah, I just tripped. It's okay, Nancy looked at it. It doesn't need stitches.' She felt guilty lying to her father, but she knew she couldn't tell him the truth about the other world she had been to. No one would believe her, besides Nancy.

'Tripped?' he repeated, thundering up the stairs into the caravan. He placed his fingers gently on her arm, turning it around to look at the bandage. 'Are you sure you're okay? These are pretty nasty wounds Heather; we may need to take you to a hospital.'

'No, it's fine. I'm fine dad, just fine. The bleeding will stop in a minute. I just needed to sit down.'

'Okay, then,' he said worried. He glared at Bounty, as if he had something to do with it. 'I'm off to the showers. Very good show that was!' he announced. 'Pity about... anyway. Never mind about that.' He went through the small, cramped caravan and snatched his towel from his bunk bed and headed towards the bathroom.

Bounty waited until he was out of earshot and leant over to Heather. 'What are you going to do?'

'Do? What do you mean?' She stood up and walked gingerly to her own bed, she felt like she hadn't slept for weeks.

'About... where you've been? Your dad will need to know.'

'I'll tell him one day, Bounty. Just not today. I need rest. I'll see you tomorrow okay?'

Bounty nodded and headed towards the door; he felt bad about leaving her alone, but he knew it was what she wanted. Heather climbed into her bed and was engulfed

by the feeling of being home and comfortable once again. The sheets were soft and smelled good - she almost cried. She lay looking at the ceiling thinking about Abara and Cadabra. She thought about Kiel, Soma and Ollsop and hoped they achieved what they had planned. She blinked once and fell asleep, and slept through the night without waking or dreaming.

ADMIT ONE
COME ONE, COME ALL
THE GREATEST PERFORMANCE IN THE WORLD
CHAPTER 26
THE MAGNIFICENT
MR. HARLOW
No. IOIOI987

Nancy woke when the sun peered through her curtains. She climbed out of bed and made coffee, only enough for herself. She was still mad at her father. The cold morning had made the windows foggy. Drips of mildew streaked down the windowpanes, giving her a columned view of the outside world. She saw her father's cape and top hat hanging on the coat rack by the door. Along the side wall were pictures of her father. He looked so young. In one black and white, framed photo he had just pulled a sheet off an elephant. His grin was from ear to ear. There was a banner behind him, large and bold, that read: *The Magnificent Mr Harlow*.

The crowd was gathered around the elephant, everyone looked amazed and in awe of his performance. She looked at the bedroom door where her father was sleeping. She felt her scar under her shirt and the initial feeling of remorse grew in her throat, then came a strange realisation. He had hurt her, and she had in turn, hurt him. She stood, leaving her steaming coffee and went outside. She scrambled across the wet grass. No one was awake yet except Guntha who was doing push ups in front of his caravan. Nancy ignored him and approached Heather's caravan slowly. She went up to the side window and tapped gently.

'Heather,' Nancy whispered and rapped her knuckles on the window again.

Heather wiped the sleep from her eyes and sat up. Her collar bone ached and her arm had bled a little during the night. She looked to the window and saw someone standing there. She pushed it open keeping her eyes shut from the bright morning sun.

'Nance?'

'Heather, I need to talk to you.' She looked up through the window. Heather's hair was pushed to one side and she still looked sick from the blood loss.

'Now?'

'Meet me in the arena in five minutes.' With that Nancy walked off towards the tent.

Heather climbed out of bed and slipped on her pyjama bottoms. She brushed her teeth and went into their small kitchen. She unwrapped her gauze and looked at the wound. It was healing well, the redness and swelling had gone down a lot. She checked her wound in the reflection of the microwave and grimaced at the sight. It was healing like the other cut, but it was much bigger and would leave a lasting scar. She was just about to slip her fluffy shoes on when her father came through the hallway.

'Who was at the window? I heard banging.' He was wearing his silk boxer shorts and a filthy singlet with *World's Greatest Circus Ringleader* scrawled across it. Heather had given it to him when she was five, it barely fit him anymore.

'Um,' Heather said, racking her brain for another lie, but thought she had lied to her father enough already. 'It was Nancy.'

Her father poured a cup of coffee and stirred in three large spoonful's of sugar.

'Really?' he turned to her, his eyebrows pushing together. 'What did she want?'

'She wants to talk.'

Rollo paused with the mug of muddy liquid halfway to his lips. 'Really? To... talk? To you? Are you guys friends now?'

Heather went to the door. 'I wouldn't say that. I'll be back soon to cook some eggs okay?' Her father nodded and sat down at the table to watch the news.

Heather strolled through the caravans until she reached the tent. She climbed up the stairs and went through the red curtain. Under the tent, the air was humid and thick. The circular performance arena was bare but for the occasional peanut shell or empty soda can. The grandstand was vacant. Nancy stood near the centre pole, which was painted with red and yellow stripes, rising up and up into the tent peak.

'You know Heather, when my father chose the circus over my mother, I was very angry at him.'

Heather stood at the edge of the platform looking at Nancy with her back to her.

'Nancy...'

'No Heather, I already know. You don't have to say it. You don't have your mother either, but my father *chose* this over her and I can never forgive him.' Nancy turned to Heather. 'What did you think of... the other world Heather? Did you like it?'

Heather sat on the small plastic stool used for the dog performances. 'I liked... some parts. Other parts, like being chased by people who wanted to kill me... not so much.'

'When I went there, I didn't want to leave. I wanted to get out of the circus so badly I would have given anything to get away. But after a while, Heather, I wanted to come home. All I could think about was dad's stupid magic tricks and all the people who come out to see him.'

Heather sat and listened; she didn't want to speak until Nancy had finished saying what she wanted to say.

'I exchanged dad's magic to get home,' Nancy started to cry, the tears fell down her face. 'I don't know how to get his magic back. I can't get it back Heather.'

Heather stood and walked over to Nancy and put one hand on her arm.

'I saw the Emperor, Nancy. I saw what you did and I saw how he kept your fathers magic. I know how to get it back.'

Nancy's eyes lit up, her mouth opened, then shut again. 'You know how to get it back? How?'

Heather looked around the tent, it still amazed her at the size of it.

'Tonight is the last night here and all the town's coming out to see the grand finale.'

Nancy looked perplexed. 'So? What do you want me to do?'

'I've got an idea, but it'll involve something you haven't done for a long time.'

Nancy looked at Heather and felt she could trust her. She had never cried in front of anyone before, not even her father when her mother left, or when her father cut her doing his magic trick. She nodded her agreement and they stood in the silent tent, staring up at the sky through the tent hole.

***

The crowd had gathered early and lined up down the street. Everyone was talking about Mr Harlow and if he could perform magic or not. Some people even brought their rotten fruit to throw at him if he didn't.

Bounty's father, the Lizard Man, was strolling around the winding crowd, breathing fire and sliding swords down his throat. Some townsfolk cheered, while others had to look away, the very sight making them feel sick. Heather looked through the fence and saw the brothers that had come to the previous show. The younger one in the wheelchair held a deck of cards. *He must have been practising card tricks,* she thought. She looked back towards the caravans and saw Mr Harlow pacing nervously. She hoped her plan had worked.

'Heather!' came a strained voice.

Heather turned to see Bounty running towards her. 'Nancy sent me to get you; she's by the animal pens.' He was short of breath and breathing loudly.

'Okay, thanks Bounty.'

'Why does she want to see you? Hey, wait... Are you guys friends now?' he asked, his hands on his knees as he caught his breath.

'I'm not sure. Not like you and me Bounty. Oh, and remember to come get me just after Mr Harlow goes on.'

Bounty smiled and nodded and headed back to his caravan to help his mother get ready for the show.

Heather ran along the fence and up the rear stairs. The dogs were all dressed in their tutus, eager to go on stage to perform. She slid her fingers through the bars and let them lick her fingertips. She looked over to see Nancy pacing back and forth and nervously biting her fingernails. Looking up she saw Heather and waved her over. Heather went passed the rear opening and saw all the town's people piling in and finding their seats. The arena was cast in a dull blue glow.

'Heather,' Nancy said, clutching her shoulder and pulling her into the dark corner by the stage. 'I-I-I know what you want me to do... I think. But, I can't...' Her scar twinged.

Heather placed both her hands on Nancy's shoulder and looked her in the eyes.

'You have to perform the sword box trick with your father, Nancy. It's the only way he will get his magic back,' Heather's voice was stern.

Nancy's eyes flickered and darted around the arena nervously. 'Are you sure? Are you sure that its gonna work? How do you know?'

Heather let her hands fall to her side. Her wounds still ached.

'The Emperor told me that belief is the key to magic. Once you stopped believing in your father, he stopped believing also.'

Nancy stopped jittering and looked at her. Her hand went to her scar under her ribcage and she felt the raised flesh.

'Okay, Heather. I'll do it.'

With all the town attending the final show, Ringmaster Rollo was a little nervous. He stood at the velvet curtains with his cane in one hand and his huge top hat in the other. His red and yellow suit was ironed to perfection. Reaching over, he pressed a button on the tape recorder and a drum roll echoed through the speakers. The crowd sat in apprehensive excitement. The curtain was yanked open and Ringmaster Rollo marched through to the centre of the arena to the largest applause he had ever witnessed.

Bounty helped push a large wood crate with wheels up the rear ramp and position it for the Freak Show where his mother was the main attraction. He looked through a split in the fabric and saw the clowns juggling and throwing cream pies at one another. He looked at his watch and saw it was only a half hour before Mr Harlow went on. He pushed the crate to the entrance and ran back down the ramp, looking over to Mr Harlow's caravan where he could see him through the window. He didn't look well. He was pacing back and forth, shaking his head and occasionally slapping his hand down on the bench top.

'Bounty! Bounty! Over here!'

Bounty turned and saw Heather hiding behind a tree by the side of the caravans. He ran over to her.

'Sorry I'm late. Mum needed- '

'You're not late. Relax.'

'So, what are we doing? We're not breaking into Mr Harlow's quarters again are we?' Bounty whined. 'I don't want you to disappear again.'

'No, nothing like that. We have to wait until Mr Harlow leaves for the stage and get Nancy to open the door.'

Bounty looked around the tree trunk to the window.

'What exactly are we going to…'

'*Ssshhhh*, here he comes.' Heather pulled Bounty out of view as Mr Harlow opened the van door and stepped down onto the grass.

He paused for a moment, took a deep breath and looked up at the circus tent. He could hear the audience cheering the clowns and then the dog performers. He shook his head again and started the long walk to the tent. His head hung low. Heather ran to the edge of the caravan and spied Mr Harlow heading towards the tent.

'Okay, Bounty, come on.'

Together they ran to the door and knocked loudly. It was flung open in an instant and Nancy stood there in her old performance suit that she hadn't worn since the accident. Heather was almost knocked backwards with shock.

'He didn't see you wearing that? Did he?'

'No, I had it on under my clothes. Come in. This box is heavy.'

Bounty and Heather piled into the caravan and stood in front of the sword box. Bounty walked up to it, using his human crab claws, he tried to lift it. His face went red and veins popped on his neck.

'It's *real* heavy.'

'How're we going to get it to the tent in time?' Nancy said, trying to lift it on the other side. 'It barely fits through that door. We haven't had it out of the caravan since…'

Bounty suddenly started jumping up and down. 'I think I know how!'

He ran to the door and out into the grassy knoll. There wasn't anyone around, everyone was up watching the performance. He bolted to the tent and up the ramp where the large crate with wheels was. His mother was sitting on it combing her beard. She had just come off stage from doing her show.

'Mum! Get off! Get off! I need that.' He scrambled over to the wooden wagon and started yanking it down with ramp with his mother still on it.

'Bounty!' she cried out, leaping off it.

'Sorry! I'll explain later,' he yelped over his shoulder.

Bounty dragged the wagon across the grass. It was hard to pull as the grass was wet and snagged in the wheels. Finally, he reached the caravan and Heather and Nancy stood in the doorway.

'Genius, Bounty,' Heather screamed. 'All we have to do is get it to the door and drag it back to the tent.'

Bounty positioned the wagon right by the front steps, as he was about to enter the caravan he heard Ringmaster Rollo announcing Mr Harlow to the crowd.

'He's going on!' he squealed.

'Okay, don't panic. We have some time, just not much,' Heather said, jerking Bounty inside.

The three of them pushed the sword box away from the wall. Bounty heaved it by the side and managed to turn it slightly towards the door. Heather and Nancy got behind it and pushed as much as they could. Heather felt her wounds pull and it sent bolts of pain up her arm and neck. Nancy didn't like being this close to the box again. She felt anxious. Bounty went around the rear where the two girls were and helped push. The box moved a few feet. He lent on it and caught his breath. His muscles ached.

'Come on,' Nancy said, her chest heaving in and out. 'We don't have long.'

Heather and Bounty pushed their feet against the wall and pressed as hard as they could. The box moved to the doorway in two more pushes. Nancy went around the front and angled it through the doorway.

'Okay, now be careful...' Nancy instructed as Bounty and Heather pushed with their shoulders.

The box slid from the door way and rolled down the stairs in three loud thuds. It landed crooked on the wagon. Nancy thought it was going to slide off and onto the grass where they would never be able to pick it up again. Heather and Bounty came running down the steps.

'Nancy, are you okay?' Bounty said, going around the front of the sword box.

'Yeah, I'm fine. Get the swords from the rack, Bounty.'

Bounty turned and ran back inside, snatching the swords and throwing them inside the box.

'Now, let's get this to the stage.'

Bounty grabbed the handle and pulled as Heather and Nancy pushed from behind. It was a little easier to drag through the wet grass with two people pushing, although the wet blades of grass still got caught in the wheels. Finally, they reached the stage. Bounty looked at the ramp and sighed loudly. From inside the tent came a round of boos and hisses. Ringmaster Rollo announced the final act.

'Quickly!' Heather yelped.

Together they pushed the sword box up the ramp. The weight was too much for them and it slid back down, almost running over Bounty's toes.

'Again,' Nancy commanded.

They tried again, but the box was made from old redwood, and it was too much for their small arms.

'We're never gonna get this up there...' Bounty said, crying defeat.

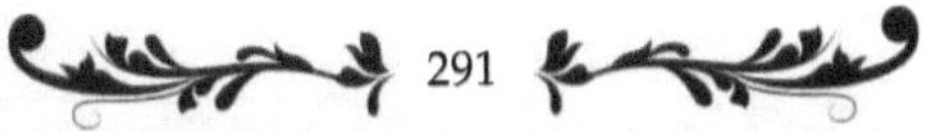

Suddenly a huge hand slapped the rear of the box and it moved as if it was made of matchwood. Heather, Nancy and Bounty looked up and saw Guntha the Muscle Man. He grinned widely.

'Need a hand?'

Together they pushed and the wagon rolled up the ramp with ease and onto the first platform. Heather could see the lights streaming out through the slit in the curtain. Her father was standing to the side holding the microphone and shaking his head. Heather ran over to him.

'Heather? What are you doing here? Aren't you supposed to be helping feed the dogs?'

'Dad, I know you're not going to want to do this, but I need to ask you for the microphone.'

Rollo looked at his daughter, then the microphone, then back to his daughter.

'Why?' Rollo averted his gaze to Nancy and Bounty standing behind her, then to the sword box. His eyes widened. 'Oh...'

Heather took the microphone just as Mr Harlow failed at yet another card trick.

'Dad, dim the lights,' Heather asked. Her father obeyed, unsure what was about to unfold.

'Ladies and Gentlemen...' Heather spoke into the microphone, her voice echoed throughout the tent, loud and grainy. 'It is now time for the most spectacular event in magical history!'

The crowd looked around as lights flickered and splashed yellows and reds along the ground and ceiling. Mr Harlow stood back, also looking around, wondering what was happening.

'This magical trick has not been performed for over a year! And tonight is the grand return of the Sword Box!'

Bounty and Guntha push the sword box through the curtains and onto the stage. Mr Harlow blinked twice and shook his head.

'No, no, no, no,' he waved his hands in front of him, his top hat sliding off his head and falling onto the floor.

Nancy walked out in her uniform. Bounty and Guntha smiled as they exited the stage.

'Please welcome Mr Harlow's daughter... The Magnificent Nancy!'

The crowd erupted in a round of applause, they got to their feet, excited to see the new magical trick with the magician and his daughter.

'Nancy... what are you doing?' Mr Harlow asked.

'Don't worry dad,' she said, looking up to her father. 'I'm okay. I believe in you.'

Mr Harlow felt his fingertips prickle. A feeling of warmth travelled through his heart and into his chest and arms, then down into his legs.

'Are you... sure?'

Nancy nodded. She looked to the audience and bowed. She waved her arms in the air, as if casting a spell and walked around the sword box. She opened its doors and took out the swords and placed them on top. Mr Harlow didn't want to take his eyes off his daughter, it had been too long since she performed magic with him.

Heather watched from the side with her father beside her.

'I don't know how you did this Heather, but thank you.' Heather smiled and wrapped her arms around her father.

Mr Harlow walked to the sword box and placed his hands in the body of it, indicating it was empty. The crowd stared on, their eyes peeled open. He moved to the right of the box, pulling a sword from its sheath. He ran one finger along the blade and shook it. A small droplet of blood beaded on his finger. The audience shook their heads. He turned to his daughter and bowed. Nancy bowed back and climbed inside the sword box. Mr Harlow walked around to the front.

'Are you sure about this, Nancy?' her father asked.

'Yes, Dad. I know you can do it. I trust you.'

Mr Harlow smiled and shut the doors. Inside, Nancy could see the small plaque that read *Hey Presto!* She got into position. Mr Harlow held the sword up high, the lights gleamed off it. He swung it around and slid the tip into the first slot. The audience held their breath. With a twitch and a shove, the sword entered the box. The crowd gasped. Some even looked away. Mr Harlow waited for a second, there was no noise from inside the box. He gently took the next sword, held it up so the town's people could see it and slid it in the next hole. Heather and Rollo watched from the side. Bounty had covered his eyes after the first sword went in. Mr Harlow entered the third and fourth sword. Now the sword box looked like a pin cushion. There was no way that a person could fit in that box and not be skewered by a blade. The final sword; Mr Harlow held it up and placed the tip on the top of the box. Everyone in the room was dead quiet. He let it go and the sword fell straight down the middle. Someone in the audience yelped.

Mr Harlow stood and looked at the box, he could feel the tension in the air. A strange memory of what happened last time entered his mind. When he had pulled the swords out, his daughter was hurt, and he had done it, and ever since then he had lost his magic.

He swallowed and gripped the first sword, pushing the thought out of his mind. He yanked it out and tossed it to the floor. It rattled and slid off to the side. He pulled the next one out, quickly, then the next. The swords lay in a heap of steel, sparkling in the single light above them. He reached up and gripped the final sword and slid it out, throwing it in the pile. He quickly stepped to the front of the box and turned the handle. The crowd lent forward in trepidation. They were holding their breath, waiting to see what was about to happen. The doors fell open and out sprung Nancy. She stood with a huge smile on her face and not a scratch on her. She bowed graciously. Mr Harlow choked back tears. The crowd stood up and clapped so hard it shook the tent poles. Heather, Rollo, Bounty and Guntha all applauded wildly. Nancy waved her hands towards her father, giving him the spot light and the audience responded with an even louder round of applause. Tears poured from Nancy's eyes; she was so happy for herself that she had finally faced her fears and also for her father.

'You did it, Heather,' Rollo said, slapping his daughter on the back. 'I don't know how you did it, but you did!'

Heather smiled and ran onto the stage to help Guntha and Bounty wheel the sword box off. Nancy was just about to leave when she saw her father's top hat laying on the ground in the dark. She ran over to it and picked it up, dusting off the dirt. She handed it to her father.

'Do the rabbit trick dad,' she said.

The crowd started to chant for Mr Harlow. Rollo grabbed the microphone and tapped it gently. The audience sat back down.

'Mr Harlow will now perform his last trick of the night... Pulling a rabbit out of his hat!'

The drum roll cracked through the speakers. Mr Harlow looked into his hat, there was nothing but an inky black abyss staring back at him. He lifted it up and showed the entire crowd. He walked over to the boy in the wheelchair.

'Hello, can you please inspect my top hat and let the audience know if you find anything?'

The young boy took the hat and put his hand inside it. He felt around and handed it back.

'It's empty,' he yelled out.

Mr Harlow stepped back into the spot light and reached into his jacket pocket. He pulled out a wand. It was raven black with pearl white tips. He waved it in a circular motion and tapped the hat. He placed it back in his jacket and reached into the hat. Bounty looked through his fingers, his curiosity beating his nervousness. Mr Harlow felt around, then, as the entire town and circus family looked on, he pulled a snow white rabbit from his hat.

COME ONE, COME ALL
THE GREATEST PERFORMANCE IN THE WORLD
ADMIT ONE
CHAPTER 27
JUST MAGIC
No. 1010101987

Mr Harlow stood in his caravan. The room was empty and still. He stared at the sword box for several seconds before slowly stepping towards it and opening the doors. Over the past year, he couldn't even bring himself to look at it – now he was touching it. Inside was dark. The wood grain reflected the light and looked like winding rivers. He was about to shut the door when he noticed the plaque on the back of the door. He kneeled down and read it, in his mind. He turned and looked at the front door, as if expecting someone to appear. He looked back to the plaque. Slowly he ran his finger across it and spoke the words out loud. The box didn't move or make a sound. Mr Harlow smiled and closed the doors once more.

Outside, the circus tent had been deflated and was being rolled up. The ropes were wrapped around it and pulled tight. It took several people to slide it onto the main truck. Bounty was kneeling on the front bonnet, cleaning the windscreen with vinegar and several torn lengths of newspaper.

'Bounty, my lad,' said Goodwill. 'Make sure the grease and bird droppings are completely off. I need to see through it clearly when I drive.'

'Yes, Mr Goodwill,' Bounty said, rolling his eyes. He wasn't sure why he had to clean the windscreens. It wasn't even his car.

Beside him Guntha was packing his weights into his van. They weighed a lot when stacked on top of each other so he had to put some in the front of the van, and some in the back. Stepping back and looking at the van, it appeared to be leaning to one side. He walked around the front of the van and kicked the tires. The bolts didn't budge. Heather saw the confused look on the Muscle Man's face. She was talking to Carol and wondered over.

'Everyone good here, Guntha?'

'This van, Heather. I don't think it's gonna last much longer. The tires are getting old and the spark plugs need replacing.'

Heather saw Mr Harlow leave his caravan. He had a strange, gentle smile on his face. He joined his daughter who was chatting to Mr Lockjaw. Heather leant into Guntha.

'When word spreads that Mr Harlow has his magic back, people will flock from all over the country side to get a glimpse of how magnificent he is.'

Guntha smiled. 'Then new spark plugs?'

Heather nodded.

Guntha rubbed his tired eyes. He considered climbing in the back of the van with his dumbbells and heavy weights and having a nap before he started the long drive to the next town, but he was too excited about the next performances. He looked up from the rear of his truck and saw the others gathering around Rollo's caravan. Rollo was trying to straighten a map out. He had his glasses on top of his head and a red pen in his mouth. He twisted the map around, then around again. Then he flipped it over and mumbled something under his breath. He tried one last time and tore it nearly in half. Out of frustration he threw it onto the ground and kicked it.

The Bearded Lady who was leaning on the car next to him, wearing a long dress and dark sunglasses, was drinking lemon soda through a straw and had her other arm around her son, Bounty.

'Where to next, Rollo?' she laughed as Rollo handed Heather the scrunched up map.

'Well,' he started. 'I was thinking about heading east. There's this small town called Fountain. It's not too far, with a population of about two hundred. We could do a few shows there and then keep moving.'

The Lizard Man emerged from the engine bay of his truck, his face smeared in oil and grit.

'Sounds good, Rollo. As long as old Betsy here doesn't have to travel too far, we should be good.'

Heather saw Mr Harlow and Nancy by their van and ran over to them. They were laughing.

'How's everything?' she asked.

'Oh, Heather,' Mr Harlow said. 'I can't thank you enough. You gave me my daughter back, and my magic. How can I ever thank you?'

Heather felt shy. 'You don't need to, Mr Harlow. Nancy did it all. Just perform your magic every night for people who come out to the circus.'

'It's a deal,' Mr Harlow said, wrapping his arms around his daughter.

Heather turned to head back to the car as the other vehicles started to form a convoy and leave the town of Weavers Peak.

'Just tell me one thing,' Heather asked, turning to see Mr Harlow and Nancy climbing aboard their vehicle.

'Anything,' Mr Harlow replied.

'How did you pull that rabbit out of your hat?'

Nancy smiled and looked up to her father.

'Magic, Heather. Just magic.'

The circus rolled out of the grassy oval and onto the main road. The brothers were on the side footpath waving them good bye. Heather waved back and watched as they disappeared in the rear vision mirror. She turned to her father and smiled. There was a certain magical feeling in the air that she hadn't felt in a long time.

ADMIT ONE
COME ONE, COME ALL
THE GREATEST PERFORMANCE IN THE WORLD
EPILOGUE
10 YEARS LATER
No. IOIOI987

The dilapidated mansion sat on an apple acreage an hour's drive from the nearest town. It was well hidden behind an overgrown wall of hedgerows. The trees that struggled to grow through them were covered in a thick film of moss. Vines tangled around every branch, burnt brown from the sun and beaten by the winds. The road that lead down from the main road had barely been used in the last few years because the previous owner was the only one that had used it.

Sitting on the front steps, Heather sipped barely warm tea and watched the squirrels fight over the nuts that had fallen on the gravel driveway. She stared out at the solitude of the rolling land before her and waited. She checked her watch and stood up. White paint was splattered on her shirt and there was a smudge under her right eye. She sipped her tea and grimaced, tossing it into the garden.

Inside the house there was a drop-sheet against the left side wall. Two ladders stood with a plank of wood held between them. A bucket of paint rested on the ground with the brush still in it. Heather stood up and stared at the wall.

'Another two coats and you should look like new.' She checked her watch again and looked towards the door.

In the kitchen she filled a kettle. The metal tap shook and clunked as the water spurted out in spits and dribbles. She turned the stove dial and a blue flame ignited.

'Well, at least one thing is working.' She placed the kettle on the flame and looked out the kitchen window.

The backyard was last on the list of renovations. Nestled between two large trees, was the barn. Its massive wooden door was locked with a chain and dead bolt. It was painted blue, but was now aged and was starting to peel. She stared at the barn as if it was calling to her. Suddenly she heard the sounds of crackling gravel and she smiled. She took the kettle off the stove and turned off the hotplate. She wanted to run through the house, her excitement flittered in her belly. She crossed the threshold in three steps and stood in the doorway. A rickety old truck was driving up from the front gate, its occupant looked lost and almost grief stricken. The man behind the steering wheel saw Heather in the door way and waved. With a puff of smoke from the exhaust, he pulled up to the right and got out. Heather walked down the front steps, eager to see him.

'Heather,' he calls out. He held his arms open, his fingers fused into claws.

'Bounty, it's been too long.'

They hugged tight and leant back so they can see each other.

'Look at you,' Heather said, almost in tears.

The young boy she once knew was now a man. His jaw, a defined line running down to a corkscrew chin was brushed with stubble. His hair was cut short, unlike the scraggly mess it used to be. His eyes were piercing blue and shoulders wide and muscular. Heather wiped away a tear.

'You look great... and the house, wow!' Bounty kept hold of her hand and he looked up at the mansion before him.

The windows were boarded up and the balcony had crumbled away leaving only jarring pieces of steel and concrete.

'You know, I almost didn't find this place. I got lost twice.'

'Well, you're here now. Come on inside, I'll make coffee.'

Bounty followed Heather through the house as she showed him the renovations she had done in the last few months.

'You've done this all yourself?'

'Yeah,' she said nonchalantly, as they strolled through the hall and into the kitchen. The blue flame ignited again and the kettle was placed back on the stove top.

'That's really impressive. And your dad?' Bounty said, leaning on the bench top, his t-shirt half tucked into his leather belt, half hanging out.

'Still in Paris training the circuses over there. He's been there a year and loves it.'

'Will he come back here? I mean, to this house?'

'Yeah,' Heather said, pulling two mugs down from the pantry cupboard which was otherwise bare except a few cans of spaghetti and several packs of old noodles. 'When he gets sick of it I told him there's a room here for him, plus the truck and the tent are here.'

She motioned with her head out the window to the barn. Bounty stepped forward and bent down to see the barn in full view.

'It's here?'

'Sure is. I drove it here from our last show in Cooper's Crossing. Broke down five times and I was stranded on the side of the road for two days until someone came to help.'

Bounty shook his head. 'Always amazing Heather. Always very independent.'

'I guess that's how my mother was?'

Heather shovelled two heaped teaspoons of coffee in each mug and filled them with boiling water. The aroma filled the kitchen instantly.

'What about you Bounty? I haven't heard much from you in a few years.'

'As you know, dad passed away.' Heather nodded slowly, the stinging reminder made her heart sink. 'And mum moved back to Venezuela, but she comes back every year for the kids.'

Heather paused, her coffee cup touching the tip of her lip, 'Kids?'

Bounty smiled. 'You didn't know? I have two kids, Heather. A boy and a girl.'

Heather slapped him across his arm. 'You didn't tell me that!'

'Sorry,' he laughed. 'I thought you knew?'

'No! My god Bounty, look at you all *adult*. That's great.' She paused, a question niggling at her mind, 'Do they...'

'Have claws?' Bounty said, holding up one hand. Four fingers fused together to make, what resembles a claw. The thumb also misshapen with a slightly pointed end. Bounty looked down at his coffee. 'Unfortunately only one does... my girl, Rosie.'

There was a strange silence for a second, then Bounty looked up. 'She's okay with it. In fact, she's one of the most popular girls in school. She wants to be a doctor.'

'So cute,' Heather said.

'You know Heather, since you have the tent here... I was wondering...'

'You want to see it, don't you?'

'For old times' sake.' Bounty smiled, putting his empty mug in the sink.

Heather looked at the barn out the corner of her eyes. There was a sickening feeling in her chest, one of apprehension and fear. Her hand went up to the scar on

her shoulder and she felt anxious to the point of crying. The Dark Emperor and his tower had never really left Heather, not entirely.

'Okay,' she said and led the way outside.

The air was warm and filled with the smell of flowers in bloom. The grass crackled underfoot. There was birdsong and the gentle hush of trees swaying in the wind.

As they approached the barn door, Heather started digging in her pocket for the key. She noticed Bounty was a little behind her, his denim jeans smudged with grease and his shoes worn and old.

'What's wrong?' she asked.

'You know, you did tell me what happened once,' he said, his voice quiet, barely audible over the birds. 'But not... everything.'

Heather held the key in her hand, not quite ready to turn the lock.

'I know you were hurt, and you were gone longer than it appeared from this world.'

Heather looked at her feet, then back up at Bounty. 'When Mr Harlow left the circus, he went to Russia and performed over there for several years. You know he's missing, don't you?'

'Yes,' Bounty said, a sadness in his voice that hung heavy. 'It was on the news. Nancy went there for three months to try and find him.'

'Neither of them have been seen for over two years.'

'Nancy's gone too? I didn't know.'

'Before he left the circus, he gave me...' Heather paused, then turned the lock and pulled the large doors open, '...everything of his.'

Before them, covered in a plastic sheet was the circus bus. Its wheels were flat and cobwebs hung from the side mirrors to the door, on the hubs and underneath it, attaching it to the ground like a silky net. Dust covered the windows and piled up along the frames, an inch thick. The corners of the bumper and rims were ginger with rust. In the rear, barely visible in the dark, was the van. On the roof, the circus tent poles were bound together with tape, the stick long gone and starting to peel away.

Bounty stood in amazement as a flood of memories came back to him. Different emotions brewed in his mind, some sad, but mostly fun times, growing up on the road, seeing his parents perform and the crowd cheering.

'Heather, I didn't know all his stuff was here, or I wouldn't have asked to see it.'

'It's okay Bounty. I have to face my fears from time to time. And it's definitely time I moved on.'

Bounty walked up to the bus and ran his finger along the side, leaving a long clear streak. He looked at the tip of his finger and started to laugh. He wiped it on his pants.

'It's like a life time ago we were running up and down the bus, trying to hide from old Mr Lockjaw.'

'Sometimes I wake up in the middle of the night from a nightmare and I feel like coming out here and just sitting in the van. It's like I need to smell the tent, or the old stale ropes. It's weird.'

'Nah,' Bounty said, moving to the back of the bus. 'It's not weird. I feel the same, that's why I asked to see it.'

Heather walked to the control panel and flipped a switch. Two fluorescent lights flickered to life. Moths, as large as small rodents took flight, disturbed from their warm den.

'You ever thought about bringing your kids and wife out here to show them how you grew up?'

There was no answer. Heather looked down the side of the bus, long shadows crisscrossed the ground.

'Bounty?' She walked softly along the cold metal side of the bus. Towards the end was a jumble of boxes, several caravans and trucks.

'Bounty? Are you back here?'

Something hit the ground hard and rolled towards Heather. She shrieked and pounced backwards, her heart beating out of her chest. A pigeon took flight and flapped its filthy wings up into the ceiling, in its mouth a small field mouse.

From the shadows emerged Bounty, in his hands an oil sheet.

'Heather, don't come back here, okay?' Heather looked at him, his eyes showed a deep sorrow, an emotion buried deep that he couldn't help but display on his face. 'You don't want to see this. Let's go back inside. I'll have another cup of coffee.'

'You found it... didn't you?'

Bounty kneaded the sheet with his fleshy claws nervously. He placed it on the car bonnet beside him.

'I found Mr Harlow's caravan and all his stuff... I found the sword box.'

Heather's stomach dropped and her fingers started to shake.

'Heather, are you okay?' Bounty rushed to her, his hands felt welcoming on her skin.

He looked her in the eyes and she seemed a thousand miles away. He shook her gently.

'Heather!'

As if snapped out of a trance, she shook her head from side to side. The great cities of Abara and Cadabra swiftly disappearing from her mind's eye like vapour.

'Bounty,' she said. 'I want to see it.'

Bounty looked at her, his eyes large and fragile. 'No, Heather. Let's go back inside.'

'I need to see it.' She pushed passed him and wandered down a small clearing that he had made.

Deep in the dark recesses of the barn was Mr Harlow's caravan. Its door slightly ajar from where Bounty had

opened it and looked inside. She waited at the door, scanning the inside.

'Heather,' Bounty pleaded, but it was too late.

As she stepped inside more memories came back to her, sharp and electrified. Mr Harlow's magic show, his rabbit that he pulled out of his hat, the card tricks; they were so fresh in her mind it was as if they happened yesterday. Along the walls were the photos Mr Harlow kept in frames from where he travelled around the world and met famous people. They were all crooked and covered in dust and cobwebs. When her father Rollo had brought the caravan here for storage, Heather hadn't looked inside it, the memory of what had happened was too strange to confront, but now, it seemed it was time.

She walked through the cramped space, boxes piled up against one wall. There, in the corner was the sword box. She stood and stared at it, not feeling nostalgic or fearful, but calm. Her hands had stopped shaking. Bounty stepped up into the caravan and waited in the doorway, he could see her approach the box and put a hand on it.

'What are you thinking?'

Heather shrugged. 'I don't know.'

She hooked one finger around the handle and gently tugged. The door popped open with a creak. The smell of mould and age wafted out and up her nostrils. There was the smell of burnt magic and the rich aroma of the Dark Emperor's chambers. She closed it. She turned to run, but Bounty was right behind her and she collapsed into his arms. Bounty helped her to her feet, moving her long hair away from her eyes. They walked slowly back through the barn, not saying a word. He held her for several minutes at the doorway before shutting the large doors behind them.

Long spikes of tangerine light shone through the maple trees, igniting the silver stones across the drive way.

Heather and Bounty sat at the dining room table, one half had been sanded down to its light coloured wood, the other half had fresh varnish.

'If you wanted, you could stay over. Leave in the morning. The roads leading back to town are hard to navigate in the dark. If you get lost in the day light you have no chance at night.'

Bounty laughed, 'You know…'

'I know you have a wife and kids to get back to, but if you get lost out here, you might spend the night with the wild deer and frogs.' Heather smiled. She had missed company once her father had left and there wasn't any reception out here for the TV.

'We divorced last year, she has the kids with her now. I'm due to pick them up tomorrow evening. So,' he looked at her and could see her loneliness, he could also feel that she was shaken by seeing the sword box again, 'I'd love to stay the night.'

Heather cooked a light supper consisting of some canned stew and some bread she had made the previous morning. They ate by candle light and talked about the old days of the circus. The darkness outside grew blacker and blacker, the air was pinch-cold until it frosted the window glass and came up through the floorboards.

'Do you remember when Guntha dropped his weights on his toe during his show? He yelped like a little girl,' Bounty said, slapping his thigh and laughing hysterically.

'I do remember,' Heather replied, bent forwards, laughing so loud she snorted, which made them both laugh more.

'People thought it was part of the show. Poor Guntha.'

'Yeah, he had to go to hospital and couldn't walk properly for nearly a month.'

Bounty took a sip of wine. 'Yeah, your dad was pissed. Guntha was a big draw card back then.'

Heather nodded, pouring herself more wine.

They talked to the small hours of the morning until Bounty started to nod off in his chair. Heather got up and made a make-shift bed for him on the couch. She gave him an extra blanket to protect himself from the chill coming through the many cracks and fissures of the house. Bounty got up from his chair, yawned loudly and stumbled over to the couch. He slid his shoes and shirt off and lay down.

'It's good seeing you Heather,' he said, his eyes already closed.

'You too, Bounty. I'll see you in the morning, we can have bacon and eggs.'

Bounty smiled and licked his lips, his head gently rolling to one side and he started to snore.

Heather made her way up stairs and climbed into bed. The sheets felt cold on her skin, but the wine had made her feel drowsy and she fell asleep almost immediately.

Bounty rolled to his side. The couch wasn't very comfortable and a long, hard, plank of wood has strategically placed in the middle. He pulled the blanket up to his chin and wondered how long he had been asleep for. The house was completely dark except for the soft, haunting light of the moon coming through the windows. He knuckle-rubbed his nose and tried to get back to sleep, but wherever he moved to, it would be equally uncomfortable. He closed his eyes for several seconds and then reopened them. He saw a dark shadow cross the hall archway and gasped in horror. He sat up in his bed, his heart beating fast in his chest.

'What was that?' he whispered to himself.

He heard the back door open and shut without care. The door rattling gently against its metal frame. Bounty got out of bed and walked over the cans of paint and strewn-out drop sheets and brushes and looked out the window. He could see Heather walking across the grass and over to the barn.

'Heather!' he called out.

Quickly, he ran through the kitchen and out the back door. The grass was so cold it stung his feet. The air pushed into his lungs and made them feel as if they were restricting.

'Heather!' he called out again, but he could not see her.

He looked along the grass lawn that led to the barn. The door was open and the chain lay on the ground. He ran through the darkness, careful not to trip on any unearthed tree roots or fallen branches. He got to the door and saw the barn light was on.

'Where are you Heather?' There was no answer, only the gentle creak of a door opening. Bounty knew instantly what she was doing and ran as fast as he could to Mr Harlow's caravan.

The door was open. He pounded up the metal stairs and went inside, from across the room he saw Heather climb into the sword box and shut the door.

'No!' he screamed and bolted towards the sword box.

There was a flash of light from inside the chamber. Bounty covered his eyes. The white light burnt bright and florescent for two seconds, and then died away. He swung the sword box doors wide open. He stumbled backwards, his hand brushing through his hair.

'No... Heather,' his voice broken and dejected.

The sword box was empty.

THE END

ACKNOWLEDGEMENTS

I would like to thank everyone who supported me over the years. Anyone who bought a book or asked about it - thank you.

Thank you to all my family and friends for their endless support.

Thanks to Sabrina for her amazing effort and editing my work.

To Clash the cat and anyone who liked my author page and came out to the conventions to talk books.

www.ingramcontent.com/pod-product-compliance
Lightning Source LLC
Chambersburg PA
CBHW031215120726
47905CB00002B/346